TEMPEST

ALISON RHYMES

Editors: Zainab M. at the blue couch edits
Proofreading: Proof Before You Publish
Cover Design: Ben | Pilcrow
Cover Photo by: Ren Saliba
Formatting: Sunshine Tucker

A NOTE FROM ALISON RHYMES

Any trigger or content warnings for Tempest, or any of my other titles, can be found on my website: alisonrhymes.com

The pain of our youth
Never leaves but always fades
Don't let it break you

ODETTE

Sixty-nine. A semiprime made up of exactly two prime numbers. An odious number. A dirty one if one's mind tends to dwell in gutters.

A large number in some ways. I wouldn't want to eat sixty-nine meatballs in a single sitting, for example. The idea of sixty-nine people at my house for a dinner party induces anxiety.

Yet it is a small number in so many other ways.

Sixty-nine hugs in a lifetime are too few. Sixty-nine kisses in a year may not be enough to fill a heart with love.

Sixty-nine days isn't a lengthy measure of time in one's lifetime. Even if it feels as if it is.

It's only taken me sixty-nine days to fall in love with Gavin Vaughn.

Maybe it will only take me sixty-nine more to bury that love in a dark and deep grave.

I can hope, anyway.

We've known each other for years, attending the same schools since we toddled our way into Mrs. White's kindergarten class. My first memory of

Gavin is of him helping me up from a fall after a vigorous round of hopscotch with Katie Wheeler. I'd scraped my knee bloody, and he walked me to the nurse to get it cleaned and bandaged.

Our circle of friends was once the same but has fractured and split over time. Gavin is a jock; a hockey playing hotshot. While his crowd grew to include more athletes and cheerleaders, mine veered toward artists and misfits.

It was inevitable. Kids used to call me "Oddette". They probably still do. I wouldn't know, as I stopped paying attention to such things a long time ago. I wear clothes only from thrift or vintage shops, mixed and matched in quirky but fun ways. It's my style, but not really on trend. It makes me stand out in ways most teenage girls don't want to. But I like who I am and the individual I've become through my short life experiences. If I'm odd, then odd is a good thing.

For sixty-nine days, I thought Gavin believed the same.

The consignment shop I work at sits across the street from the local ice rink. Sixty-nine days ago, I locked up after closing the store and ran into Kyle Langford. He's always been a bully and a lot of an asshole. I ignore him because I don't think he learns so well and teachers early on passed him just to get him out of their classrooms. His stupidity shouldn't be an excuse for being a dick, but I feel bad for him. In our small upstate New York city, everyone knows everyone's business. He was picked on when we were younger, then he had a growth spurt that gave him the courage to flip the script.

Kyle had been drinking; I could smell the beer wafting off him from a few feet away. The strong bitter odor overtook me as he grabbed my arm when I tried to walk to my car. I'd told him to let go, and shook myself loose, but then Gavin was there—his wide build pushing between me and a belligerent Kyle.

"Leave her alone, Langford." Gavin's voice, guttural and direct, sent a shiver down my spine. Not in a bad way. In a good kind of way. The way that makes me want to rush home and shove a hand down my pants.

I'm a damsel in a damned great dress, not one in distress. Doesn't mean I don't like a big, strong guy standing up for me. It's never happened before, so maybe that played into my reaction some. Or that Gavin is outrageously good-looking with his dark hair consistently on the messy side and his confident stance. I'd bet he's never felt awkward a day in his life.

That night started a trend. One that lasted sixty-nine days. Not one of those days passed without either Gavin waiting for me to lock up after my closing shift or calling me from wherever he was to make sure I made it home safely.

He and Caroline Crow had just ended their three-year relationship. He said they never should have dated to begin with. That they'd mistook their close friendship for something more and succumbed to the pressure of friends and family to make it romantic. They still cared deeply for each other and were the best of friends. But Caroline would be heading to college in Michigan soon and Gavin would be playing hockey for Boston College. He said the timing felt right to end the relationship and enjoy one summer, single and free, before heading to their prospective universities.

Except Gavin didn't spend it single and free. He spent it with me.

Working had been all I wanted to do in my spare time, saving up for my move to New York City. Then he showed me attention and I made room for him in my life. So much room that he eagerly filled. He snuck in through my bedroom window more nights than not. Several nights a week he'd either bring me dinner or take me out, depending on how our schedules aligned. I was charmed by him. Maybe I always had been, to some extent. He never was like the other athletes who made fun of me and my friends at every opportunity. Gavin was kind when he was forced to interact with us.

Every time he took me out, he was the perfect gentleman, holding doors, pulling out chairs, and the like. It was a princess treatment I'd never gotten before.

"The train from the City to Boston isn't too long." He'd told me that after the third time we'd had sex, and we were languidly wrapped in each other's arms. I'd agreed, thinking, just maybe, we could make something work between us. Hopeful that we could keep a connection without it interfering in either of our studies.

One of the things we bonded over so quickly was our mutual dedication to our futures. Gavin is determined to play for the NHL. I'm destined for the fashion industry, in one way or another.

At the time, I'd thought I was willing to travel further than the few hours' train ride if it meant seeing his crooked smile and getting a blissful orgasm out of it. Gavin Vaughn is infinitely better at sex than any of the other guys I've been with. There have only been two, anyhow. Both a bit awkward and bumbling. But they were nice, and I don't regret my time with either of them. Though, neither gave me the same electric charge I feel when I'm with Gavin.

My grandmother always said, "When you know, you know." I didn't understand what she meant until I'd spent weeks with Gavin. Then I understood. I knew. I *know*. Or so I thought.

We'd begun making plans for our moves. He'd even gone into the City to look at my three prospective apartments and helped me evaluate the pros and cons of each. One he ruled out immediately, not liking the building's outdated security.

"I want my girl safe," he'd said, and then kissed me with more passion than I'd ever known. *My* girl. I liked being claimed by him, more than I cared to admit.

In return, I'd helped him make a list of all the necessary items he'd need for his dorm room in Boston. We even shopped for many of them together. It was comfortable and very domestic, but it solidified the feelings that had been forming a new life in my heart. Our excursions cemented those future fantasies I fell asleep to at night.

Ones that played visions of a future power couple; him the NHL star winger and me styling all the most famous celebrities while I travel around the country to watch him play during the season. And cozying up together in our Manhattan high-rise home in the off season.

Youth makes us all a little stupid in love, I suppose. Maybe no eighteen-year-old should count on love to last and all I've done is set myself up for disaster and heartbreak. But age doesn't make my feelings less valid.

What's the saying? *Love loves its youth.*

Love *is* what I feel for Gavin. It's not just lust, though there is that. And it isn't only a strong liking that will easily fade with separation. The thought of losing this relationship sends a sharp pain to my chest. As if it's shattering into a million tiny fragments, exposing my heart to every painful detail the world holds.

I guess that's why they call it heartbreak. Even if that doesn't sound as horrible as it feels. Looking down to check I'm still whole, my hand rubs at the pain. It's useless, of course. I can't ease this pain or untie the thick knot tightening in my stomach.

I've had crushes before. Even a few boyfriends. It didn't skew my entire existence when we broke up. I fear losing Gavin will. Life won't be the same without hearing his deep rumbling laugh, or without the way he rests his free hand on my nape as he drives.

The curtains, ones I made myself from old tablecloths I found at the thrift store for a dollar, flutter from the breeze wafting in the open window. Sun shines in, only highlighting the vibrant colors I've decorated everything with.

It's a small space, the smallest of the three rooms in our trailer. Dad once offered up his home office for me, but I declined. My room is tiny, but it's the only one I've ever known, and each piece has been carefully curated over time. Like the throw pillows trimmed with felt balls that I worry with my fingers when I'm thinking. And the landscape painting that my friend Tiffany did for me in the eighth grade before she moved to California. I decoupaged a frame I found in a dumpster with magazine cutouts, so it's a little bit of me surrounding a lot of her.

The colors can't penetrate the bleakness overtaking my thoughts, though.

Gavin has been radio silent for days now. Five, to be exact. The first day I didn't hear from him made me concerned. By the third, I was stressed out, calling and texting in regular intervals.

Yesterday, I received a response.

GAVIN:

I'm so sorry.

Nothing more than that one text, despite my attempts to get him to explain.

I know the reason now. I know we're over. What I don't know is how. Or why. Well, I guess I know why, to some extent, thanks to Dad's stubborn refusal to stop his subscription to the *New York Times*.

An explanation would be nice, though.

The last time I spoke to him, he said good night and that he'd call me the next day. The next day turned into the next and the next. Each without a word. Until those three words.

I'm so sorry.

For what, I've been wondering.

A tear spills out from the corner of my eye, and I angrily swipe it away. I won't cry over this. He duped me, played with my heart and my trust. That doesn't deserve tears. It deserves anger and rage.

Sixty-nine days shouldn't be so hard for me to incinerate in the hellish depths of my soul. It's a short span of time at the near beginning of my life's line. One day, I'll forget Gavin Vaughn, the love we made, and the hurt that followed.

Staring down at the wedding announcement printed in the *New York Times*, the one my mother quietly handed to me with sadness, I make myself a promise.

Never fucking again.

1

GAVIN

"**O**h. My. Fucking. God. DAD?"

"In the kitchen," I holler, trying to be heard over my daughter's screams as she barrels down the stairs. I think it's excitement. I *hope* it is, anyway. But who the fuck knows. Tori is a nineteen-year-old tornado. I can never keep track of her trajectory.

I wouldn't change that for the world, though. This past year has been rough on both of us, and for her mother. The divorce was long overdue, but Tori didn't realize it. Caroline and I sheltered her from that as best we could. In hindsight, maybe we should have given her a heads-up. We threw a lot at her in a couple of years' time.

Starting with our move from the East Coast to Seattle when the Blades picked me up in their expansion draft. Tori was sixteen. Leaving behind all her friends and her dumbass boyfriend, Richy, was a lot to ask of her. I can feel bad about ripping her away from her girlfriends, but not about Richy.

That kid was the douchiest of all douchebags. He had big dreams of being a DJ, but the kid couldn't keep a beat if it was hitting upside his stupid bleached-blonde head. I was tempted to dump her into therapy, convinced something major had to be wrong if that asshat was who she was bringing home for dinner. Caroline talked me down, saying he was "just a phase".

A phase Tori cried over for two weeks after our move. Luckily, her eye caught some new guy when she started high school here and things eased up.

Until she graduated and Caroline chose to leave me and move back to New York. Tori went with her, but she's back now. After a gap year, she's decided to go to school here in Seattle. I think she feels bad about the attitude she's given me since the separation from her mother. She shouldn't, but I won't complain about whatever reason sent her back to the West Coast. I love having her around.

Maybe she's making a mistake not attending school in New York. She is studying fashion, after all. But the school she was looking at there has a satellite program here in conjunction with one of Seattle's universities. So, she can always transfer if it doesn't work out. Though I'll miss her face if she does.

Professional hockey is a hard life. I've missed so much of her childhood by being on the road. Now that I'm close to retirement, it's hitting me hard just how much I wish I would have been there for.

"Oh my god!" It's definitely excitement in her voice when she slides on socked feet up to the breakfast bar.

"What's up," I ask, looking over my shoulder as she sets her laptop on the counter, flipping it open.

"You *have* to see this."

"Let me finish this up," I say, cracking a few more eggs into the bowl. "You want ham and cheese?"

"Yes, please."

Continuing to make our omelets, I smile when I hear her chanting under her breath.

"Oh my god, oh my god, oh my fucking god."

Victoria has always been animated and theatrical. A trait I think she picks up from her mother. Her determination is from me, though. One hundred percent. There has never been anything in her life that she wanted and didn't work hard until she got it. She's privileged, sure. My career offers a lot of financial comfort. Her being an only child meant she was fairly spoiled her whole life. But she's never been a brat about it. If we put limits on things to help her grow into a responsible adult or evoke some work ethics, she never complained.

She's a smart girl. Smarter than her old man, that's for sure. That's probably something she got from her mom, too. Caroline was supposed to attend Michigan State University after high school. She'd earned a full academic scholarship, wanting to go into biomedical sciences. That changed because of Tori.

Caroline maintains that her decision to become a mother instead of a college graduate was her decision, and her decision alone. That's never stopped me from blaming myself, though. My career path didn't really allow me to be the primary caregiver for a child, leaving her to take that roll on. I've tried to get her to go back to school on numerous occasions, but she always declined.

"I'm a full-time mother until she's an adult," she'd say every time I brought it up. How else could I respond to that but with acceptance? Tori has always come first. Motherhood wasn't on the top of Caroline's to-do list at eighteen years old. Of course, it wasn't. But from the day she found out she was pregnant; the baby was the most important thing in her world. Mine too, despite everything.

The day she told me is a day I'll never forget. I didn't know shit about being a dad. Fuck, I didn't know shit about being an adult, a man. You learn quick when you're suddenly responsible for another human. Or two. And I was responsible for both Tori and Caroline. Her whole world altered because of sex with me; I wasn't about to abandon her. She's been my best friend since we were seven years old. You don't turn away from a friendship like that. And although I may have been a dipshit teenager, I was never the type of guy to turn my back on responsibilities.

Well, mostly, anyhow.

To say I've always made the right decisions would be a boldfaced lie. There are regrets, things I wish I could change. But I have never been malicious. I've always cared about the people around me. Despite the circumstances, I think I've been a good dad and was the best husband I could be to Caroline.

"Oh my god, oh my god."

I chuckle as I fold over her omelet. My skills in the kitchen aren't many, but this shit, I have down. When I take Tori out to breakfast, she never orders omelets because they don't make them as good as mine. It's a small thing, but my dad-ego swells every time, like she's just handed me the Stanley Cup of parenting or some shit.

She'll be moving into her own place in a couple of weeks. One closer to campus since she doesn't like driving in Seattle. I can't blame her; this whole city was built on a cliffside. I'm going to miss having her here. It's been nice not being alone. I've always had nights to myself when I'm on the road, but until Caroline moved out last year, I'd never come home to an empty house. The adjustment wasn't the easiest.

Cillian, my teammate, tried to convince me to get a cat. It doesn't seem right to leave a little furball home by itself while I'm away for days on end, though. Maybe I should buy some plants—I can name them and talk to them like they're real-life friends.

Jesus. Is this what loneliness does to a person?

Looking back, I've been lonely in certain ways for a very long time. It was something I never focused on, though. Instead, I'd push the thought to that dark spot in your mind that you only peek into when absolutely necessary. It became necessary when Caroline left. Or inevitable, anyway.

I'm thirty-eight. Evaluating things I have avoided is imperative now. I'm young, but old for the sport, so this will be my last season. This time next year, I won't only be a divorcee and the father of a grown daughter, but I'll also be unemployed. Or retired. Whatever. It feels like the same thing. It feels like I'll be useless. Purposeless. Not needed.

There is no plan after retirement. Some may look forward to that sort of life. One without plans or structure. The only part of it I look forward to is waking up without an alarm. The rest feels daunting.

Who am I if not a hockey player, a husband, and a dad? I'll always be Tori's dad, but it's different now that she doesn't need me on a regular basis.

I plate the omelets and turn to my girl. Her mass of dark hair is a nest atop her head. What looks like a messy bun to me is really something I know she spent at least fifteen minutes on. I like it when she wears it up, though; it lets me see her face better. It also shows off her new tattoo. A sample of black leaves creeping up from her shoulder and stretching up her neck. It's pretty and reminds me of her mom, who has a similar tattoo on her side.

"All right, what's all the excitement about," I ask as I push her plate next to her laptop.

"Oh my god, Dad, you'll never believe this," she starts off dramatically. "You know it was, like, the weirdest decision to come to school here instead of attending in New York. Or even in Los Angeles."

"I do," I admit. "And I love having you here, but I won't be mad if you decide you aren't getting out of it what you need."

"I know," she says, rolling her eyes because we've gone through this abundantly. "And I told you that this decision felt right. Now I have confirmation that it was."

"How could you possibly have confirmation when school hasn't even started yet?"

"Because they just emailed us all to let us know of some major staffing changes and a new mentorship program that they're rolling out this term." Her eyes sparkle with the same enthusiasm her voice carries. "They've hired an industry professional to basically work as an advisor for us this year. Someone who will check in with us on at least a weekly basis to give us pointers, or whatever. And at the end of the year, we'll have our own student fashion show that will be filmed and streamed to industry insiders."

"So, something like a university version of *Project Runway*?" I may be a big bad hockey player, but I sat through every season of that show with Tori.

"Exactly. They're promising that not only will design houses see it, but fashion magazine editors, celebrities, and celebrity stylists, too. Like, everyone! It could land us jobs straight away. The exposure is huge."

"This is only for the Seattle campus?"

"Yep, they're trying it here first since we don't have the same access to the industry as the New York campus does. I think they want to establish a better rep for this campus or something. I don't know. I don't really care the why, you know? I'm just so excited!" She pauses to eat a few bites of her breakfast, happily humming around every fork load. "This is really good, Dad. Maybe you should open a breakfast spot or a food truck. That could be fun."

"For who?" I ask with a grimace. Sleeping in is the best thing I have to look forward to. After retirement, I'm only getting up early to make breakfast for her, if she's here. No other reason.

"Yeah, I guess that's a lot of stress," she considers. "But you'll need something. Golf, maybe? A lot of your teammates like that."

"No, thank you." That's never been a favorite pastime of mine. Tori isn't wrong, many of the guys play golf during their downtime. Or video games. Mine was spent with my kid and doing whatever she wanted to do. Even if that meant tea parties where she made me wear shiny plastic necklaces or letting her play beauty parlor and dotting my hair with seventy-two tiny ponytails. Because of that, other than workouts and crime documentaries, I don't have much in the way of a hobby.

"You could just throw yourself into dating," she hedges. I haven't done any of that since the divorce. Honestly, it's a daunting idea. I wouldn't even know how to go about meeting a woman. Other than the ones who hang around the team in the hopes of catching one of our eyes. They've been coined "puck bunnies". Mostly they're no different than band groupies. They're fans. They just happen to be fans that are maybe actively looking to bed a pro athlete.

Many of them do. The younger single guys take them up on their offers often enough. I've done it a few times since the divorce. Each time was weird, the first, especially. I'd only ever been with two women, and I've been with Caroline since we were fifteen, minus the short break up we had before her pregnancy. Even then, I'd thrown myself into another relationship and fucked it all up. I don't know how to be single.

I'm not even sure I know how to navigate a casual, sexual relationship. My dick doesn't have a problem with it, but my head does.

"Why do I need to date?"

"Mom is," she says, albeit with hesitation.

"That's good, Tori. She deserves that."

"So do you." She sounds far stronger than I know she feels. This hasn't been easy for her. Caroline and I put on a good show. From anyone's perspective, we had a great marriage. We were a solid team, working well together to create a great home. But as a couple…we lacked a lot.

"My schedule is crazy," I remind her. "Who has the time?"

"Dad…"

"Tori," I say, mimicking her slightly annoyed tone.

"Fine. But you at least need a hobby."

"I bought a book the other day. Maybe that will be my new hobby."

"You going to start a BookTok?"

"I don't know what the hell that is."

"You're getting old, Dad." She rolls her eyes dramatically, but a wide smile plays on her face.

"If you stop getting older, so will I. Deal?"

"Yeah, sure. Deal," she answers easily.

"How did we end up talking about me anyway? We're supposed to be talking about you, future Miss Fashion Designer." I reach over the kitchen bar to tap her nose, something I've done since she was a toddler. Another thing I'll miss now that she's growing into an independent young woman.

"Do you really think I'll make it?"

"Of course. Why wouldn't I? You've been making your own clothes for years and nobody has the style you do."

We bought her a sewing machine when she was eight. It's been upgraded twice over the years, and added to with other contraptions that I don't understand the function of. She can make garments from scratch, but she prefers to dive through "the bins" at Goodwill. Tori enjoys finding that diamond in the rough, or whatever, and turning it into something on trend. Or ahead of it? I don't know.

I do know that she is extremely talented, and I don't think that's my bias talking. The kid always looks amazing, her friends and random strangers we run into while out are constantly complimenting her. That's got to count for something.

"But of course, *you'd* say that. You're my dad, you have to."

"Have I ever lied to you?"

"No," she says thoughtfully. "Though, you could have, you know? It was fucking hard being the only kid that didn't believe in Santa and the Tooth Fairy."

"You survived it," I say, laughing. That was more Caroline's idea, but I backed the decision wholeheartedly.

"I did," she agrees. "But still. I'll be more convinced of my future if Odette likes me."

Odette. That name. I haven't heard it in years. I knew an Odette once. A long time ago, when I was young. When I thought I was free to know her. When I thought I'd finally had a chance.

Before Tori.

"Odette who?" I already know the answer, but I ask anyway. There is only one Odette in the industry who could cause this type of reaction from my daughter. There's only one Odette in the world that could have my heart cartwheeling in my chest by just the mention of her name.

"Dad," she sighs. "She's only the hottest celebrity stylist. Like, ever. Odette Quinn."

Fucking hell.

"That's your new mentor?"

"Yes! It's so exciting. Isn't it?"

Yes. It sure is fucking exciting.

2

ODETTE

S uccess is a strange creature. Arbitrary and subjective, it's different for everyone. I wonder how many people didn't recognize it once they achieved it. I sure didn't. After all my years of working endless hours to build a business, the moment I'd "made it" passed me by. It went entirely unnoticed. I didn't see the numbers in my bank account for what they were, my friend list being mostly A-listers wasn't impressive, it was part of the job.

The first apartment I bought in Manhattan cost me nearly a million dollars, but that was inexpensive by my peers' standards. It was a two-bedroom housed in an old building where most of the residents had lived there for decades. Small and quirky, but it fit my personality and had a view of the Hudson. Tiny as it was, it was still a substantial upgrade from the fifth-floor walkup studio I had before in Bushwick. I loved it so much I never left it, even when my finances allowed me to purchase a much larger, sleeker place to live.

Perhaps it was because I came from such meager beginnings and something in my subconscious was telling me to be grateful for what I had. My parents were hardworking blue-collar workers. My mother was a hairstylist, my dad an insurance adjuster. We lived humbly so that we could enjoy the occasional meal out or road trip vacation.

When my net worth swelled, I didn't see it as something to use for splurging. I did move my parents into a house eventually. Nothing new and flashy, they wouldn't have liked that. But it was an upgrade that they deserved, and it helped to set them up for a comfortable retirement.

That was success for me. Mom and Dad moving into a home completely paid for by me was the moment I realized I had accomplished what I set out to do. It's also the moment I decided I could ease back on how hard I worked. My fourteen-hour days dropped. At first, it was only a couple hours less a day, but eventually, I quit taking meetings on Sundays. I even started taking vacations, something I'd been very reluctant to do before.

If I traveled, it was for work, shopping all over the world for my clients. Trips to Paris and Milan were plentiful enough, but there wasn't any downtime. Other than a nightcap and possibly a passionate one-night stand with a handsome foreigner. Rest and relaxation haven't been in my vocabulary for the past twenty years.

Now I'm settled in my ridiculous seven-thousand-plus-square-foot Mission-style home on the Seattle historical registry. It's all dark beams and intricately carved woodwork, but with feminine details like gold filigreed wallpaper and pretty green-tiled and copper-hooded fireplaces. It's downright gorgeous and absolutely too fucking large for just me. I couldn't pass it up, though. When Rhonda, my real estate agent, sent me the listing, I knew from the first external snapshot that this would be my new home.

My new schedule as mentor at the Fashion Institute will allow me for much more downtime, now that I've taken a liaison from styling. Well, mostly, anyway. I'm keeping a handful of clients, but the rest have been gently given over to my protégé, Fallon. He's worked with me for years and is more than capable. In fact, he's eager and confident in his abilities. I am, too, otherwise I'd never hand my small empire over to him.

Finding Fallon wasn't easy. Most young ingénues in fashion are only focused on the most talked about, or the most unattainable fashion designers. It's an industry built on expense and excess. But it doesn't have to be. I've maintained my habits of taking something old and making it new and have been lucky enough to find people to work with that share the same drive. There's room in the industry for folks like us now, and more and more sustainable designers are hitting the scene each year. Fallon wants to make responsible fashion waves just as much as I did at his age.

Now, I want to teach that to others. Seattle is a far better place to start than the designer-lined streets of Manhattan. I'd only visited here a couple of times. There's a local designer who got her start thrifting for old designer items and reimagining them into something new. I'd come to her shows when it fit into my schedule. The city was always welcoming with its perpetually laid-back attitude. Seattle embodies the work hard, play hard attitude. Probably because it's knee-deep in the tech industry, a sharp contrast from the world of fashion and celebrities that I've been swimming in.

Here, you put in the hours to get your job done and finish the day with some sort of outdoor activity. Even if it's raining, you'll see people casually outside. No one scurries from place to place to avoid it. When Vanessa Andrews, the director of the Seattle campus, first contacted me about this position, I laughed at moving to Seattle. She told me she'd felt the same when she first considered moving here. All the talk of rain was daunting. But she's now found it to be therapeutic. Cleansing, she called it.

I get it now. It's almost a natural reset, washing the day's grit and grime away. Never in a million years would I have believed I'd be embracing rainy weather. I was never the woman who would walk to the office in tennis shoes and change when I got in. I couldn't afford to be spotted in such a casual manner.

Things change, though, and now I'm planning outfits around Hunter rain boots and Birkenstock sandals. Well, maybe I'm not taking it that far. The point is that I feel like I can without it being career suicide. It's a weight off my shoulders I hadn't realized was even there. I mean, I love fashion, I live and breathe it. That doesn't mean I don't like the occasional moment of just living without worrying about my appearance.

There were many pros and cons to moving to Seattle. I weighed each one carefully. The cons were far fewer but heavier. One nearly stopped me from accepting the position. However, the pros were too great to pass up. The work-life balance is too appealing. Especially given my recent diagnosis.

About a month before Vanessa called me, I found out I have an autoimmune disease. Supposedly, Hashimoto's is manageable with the proper medication, but I'm not there yet. It's still too new and I'm trying to find the right combination of medications, supplements, and life changes to make a difference.

Basically, I'm tired. Physically and mentally. Vanessa had given me two months to ponder the decision. Unfortunately, those months were filled with red carpets and after parties. I was swamped and riddled with flare-ups that made me erratic, and honestly, a little frightened. I was losing hair in clumps, and it was impossible to feel any sort of calm. Not to mention that I couldn't get warm even if I planted my ass in front of a raging bonfire.

After several frantic calls to my doctor and my therapist, it was clear I needed major changes in my life. A successful career isn't a replacement for a healthy life. Or so everyone tells me. It's not easy to hang up workaholic habits or tell clients that you've worked with for years that you can no longer be at their beck and call twenty-four-seven.

So. Seattle.

After only two weeks here, I already feel better. As I walk into my new office space in perhaps the most nondescript building on the block, I consider how ordinary it feels compared to all the sleekness I've known.

I almost feel overdressed in my vintage blue and cream Claire McCardell dress. But Vanessa greets me just inside the doors, dressed in equal style. Because of course she is like me—the woman who lives and breathes fashion.

"I have that same dress in my closet," I tell her, gesturing to her black mini Stine Goya dress. "We'll need to coordinate from here on out."

"I'm so glad you're here," she greets with a laugh. "I've missed you, my friend."

Vanessa and I met in college. She was the posh to my eccentric. Though our backgrounds couldn't have been more opposite, we became fast friends. Our paths have rarely crossed these past twenty years, but we've always maintained our friendship.

"I'm glad to be here, it's already feeling like home."

"Well, with that amazing mansion you just bought, it ought to."

"It's a big place, but mansion," I ask, skeptical.

"Odette, that place is huge and you're coming from that tiny apartment that couldn't even fit your wardrobe."

"True." I laugh. "That's not a problem anymore. I converted two spare rooms into my closets."

"I'd expect nothing less." She grins. "Come on, I'll show you around, then let you settle in before your first meeting."

The group I'm mentoring comprises of twenty-two freshmen students. This week, I'll be meeting with each of them to talk about aspirations and look over their portfolios. Vanessa sent over their applications to me, but I didn't look through them. They're in the most exciting time of their lives and I want to live that with them. Besides, it's good experience for pitching themselves.

Nothing about the interior of the institute fits the bland exterior. It's bright, natural light seeping in from windows, along with thoughtful lighting conducive to the large open workspaces. No expense has been spared on the sewing equipment or the computers that students will be able to use to design and fabricate their own textiles. Everything is clean and bare now, but I know it won't take long before it's covered in swatches, scraps, and spools of thread.

I can't wait for it. As stressful as it can be, there's something endlessly exciting about the newness of it. I haven't been offered the chance to experience cutting-edge fashion from its infancy since I, too, was a student.

"Your office is upstairs." Vanessa points up to a bank of windows that overlook the workspace. "Come on."

We ascend a set of stairs to a lobby containing a small reception area and a large coffee bar. *Priorities.* Down the hall, we pass several offices. Vanessa introduces me to my new peers, a few professors and a couple of admin. Mostly women, but one professor, Jake, reminds me of a younger Tim Gunn with his three-piece, perfectly tailored, suit. The other two, Feng and Jolene, are equally as pleasant.

My office is at the end of the hall, sitting on a corner with dual aspect windows that overlook the mountain in the distance.

"Well," I muse, dropping my handbag onto the large desk, "a lady could get used to this."

"That's the idea, anyway," Vanessa responds. She had tried to get me to sign a five-year contract. I refused, not knowing if this was the right move or not. We haggled and settled at two. From there…who knows. I should have known she'd continue trying to tempt me in any way she could. This view does that, for certain.

My house sits on a lake but it's at the wrong angle to get a mountain view. Looks like I'm being spoiled with that, too. I'm not complaining.

"You're starting off strong," I tell her. "This place is great."

"It is," she agrees. "It's the start of something great, I think."

"I can feel that."

"Again, I'm glad you're here, Ode. I'll let you get settled, but we're doing drinks this Friday."

"That sounds divine, Vanessa."

"Great! Everything you need to log in is in the folder on your desk. I'm just across the hall, holler if you need anything."

"Thank you," I say. "I mean it."

"You're welcome," she tells me with a knowing smile. "Don't go easy on the newbies today."

She laughs as she leaves me, but after meeting the first three students, it's clear I can't go hard. So far, they're all amazing with endless potential oozing from every pore.

Benji was first up, aspiring to be a ready-to-wear designer like Ralph Lauren or Michael Kors. He has an eye for color and comes up with unexpected combinations that somehow work beautifully.

Celine was next and is edgier. She'll easily have a career in haute couture. Her pieces were works of art and she's leaning into unconventional material choices.

Jun-Li was my third student and the first one to proudly admit she only works with neutrals, no color whatsoever. A bold move, as it can lend to the finer details of a garment not carrying over so well to the runway or magazine layouts. But she had talent in spades.

The knock on my office door signals my fourth student's arrival.

"Miss Quinn?"

"Hello," I call, waving her in. She's tall with dark hair and darker eyes. She could model, honestly. As I scan her style, I don't recognize a single item on her, though it clearly isn't an ensemble she picked up at the local shopping mall, either. "Call me Odette, please."

"Odette," she tries out. "Okay. Hi, I'm Tori."

"Have a seat, Tori." I wait for her to sit in the chair opposite me. She nervously places her hands in a few different positions before laying them on her thighs with a soft sigh. "You're nervous."

"Yeah, sorry. You're just…well, sort of my idol." The olive skin darkens on the apples of her cheeks.

"Oh? Do you want to take the styling route?"

She shakes her head. "I want to design my own line, but more like how you design."

It's no secret that I design many of my own outfits and some for a few selected clients. But I never did take it as far as starting my own fashion house. That may have been my dream at the young age of eighteen, but the more jobs I acquired as a stylist, the more I fell in love with it.

"Seldomly?" I tease the question.

"No," she laughs, some tension leaving her shoulders. "I want to design full-time, but I want to do it as responsibly as possible. No fast fashion, no overseas child labor, and no waste."

"A lofty goal. Do you have a plan for it?"

"The beginnings of one. I need to learn more about the industry before I hammer out the finer details, but I believe I can accomplish it."

"I like your confidence, Tori. Show me what you've got," I say, nodding toward the portfolio set in the chair next to her. She hands it to me, and I flip it open to the first page. It's a collage of photos, not drawings like the students before her. "Tell me about these."

"These are all fits I put together using thrifted items that had seen better days and giving them new life. Most garments are a combination of three or four thrifted ones."

"Your use of patterns is exceptional," I compliment. Again, it's a display of unexpected combinations, florals mixed with geometrics or stripes. Her use of color is bold but softened by feminine touches of lace or bows. It's almost coquettish at times, but without the girlish aspect. I can see women of all ages in the clothes. Hell, I'd wear several of them. "Where did your inspiration come from?"

"When I was eight, I saw my first episode of *Project Runway*. I was a goner from there. My mom bought me a sewing machine and some fabric. But my dad told me about a friend they'd had when they were younger. She'd gone to secondhand shops and redesigned the items she found into her own style," she says. "I fell in love with the idea and never really looked back."

"Their friend sounds a lot like me," I say, flipping the page. I stop when I notice the name embossed on the inside of the cover. Victoria Vaughn. I pause and get a better look at her face. Holy shit. "Vaughn? Daughter of Caroline and Gavin?"

"Yes," she says, her eyes widening in surprise.

"I grew up with your parents," I tell her, leaning back in my chair. "I probably am that friend your dad spoke of."

Gavin Vaughn was at the top of my cons list. I'd convinced myself that this city was big enough for the two of us and I wasn't likely to run into him at all. Who would have expected his daughter to be sitting in my office on my first day at work? Not me, surely.

Tori looks like them both, now that I take a moment to consider it. She has Gavin's eyes and Caroline's high cheek bones and petite nose.

"Oh my god," Tori whispers. "That's so badass."

Badass? I'm not sure. Fortuitous? I sure hope not. Just my luck? Fucking probably. Tori seems as shocked by this revelation as I am. I guess her parents never mentioned they knew me. Why would they, though? Who was I to them? To Caroline, I would have been one of the artsy girls that never rated her attention as part of the elite high school student body. To Gavin… well, I was probably only a mistake he made that one summer. The girl he slummed it with while on a break from the girl he really loved.

It's all water under the bridge, now, and thoughts that Tori never needs to hear. She's not her parents and I won't treat her any differently due to the pain they caused me all those years ago. My job is to nurture her talent and this young woman has that in spades.

"Why Seattle," I ask her, knowing her roots match mine in New York state. With this portfolio, she could have gotten into Parsons.

"I missed my dad," she says with an easy shrug. "He's here, so I am, too. Besides, I don't think the evolution of sustainable fashion will start in New York."

I've avoided run-ins with Gavin and Caroline for damn near twenty years, but now, it may be inevitable. For the first time since I deplaned at SeaTac airport, I'm questioning my decisions.

3

GAVIN

"**I** cannot believe you didn't tell me," Tori chastises me as she bounds through my front door, using the key I told her to keep when she moved out last week.

I cannot believe she's already moved into her own apartment just a couple of blocks from school. It doesn't seem right; she was just born. Or so it feels like. Time moves too fucking quickly for my liking.

In a couple of years, I'll be forty and she'll be old enough to have a drink at my birthday. How in the hell did this happen?

"I mean, she's huge in the business. I've talked about her with you and Mom, and neither of you said anything. Not even when I told you she'd be my mentor. What's up with that, Dad?"

"That's complicated, kiddo," I say, attempting to dismiss the conversation altogether. I should know better than to think she'll so easily drop it.

"I'm not a toddler, I can handle complexities."

"You're a complexity."

"I'm not, I was the easiest kid, and you know it. Now quit diverting, Dad."

"That's true, except when you were three and started bossing us around like you ruled the roost," I say, trying another route away from her destination.

"Odette Quinn. Spill the tea or I'm going to jump to all the wrong conclusions," Tori demands.

All her assumptions would probably hit closer to the truth than not, though. Telling her the story of her dad being an asshole to the kindest girl he ever knew isn't something I want to do. I've made a lot of mistakes in my life, ghosting Odette is the biggest. It's the one that keeps me up at night, even now, thinking of all the ways I could have handled the situation.

All the ways I *should* have.

I wasn't upfront and honest with her. And now I'm not being either of those things with the most important person in my life. Again.

I'm not sure how Tori will handle the whole story. Will she feel guilty for her unwitting part in the story? I'd never want that. I've never wanted her to know the truth of our family and those we've hurt along the way.

Then again, maybe Odette didn't drown in the same sea of sorrow I did. She was strong, so independent. She had the world waiting to fall at her feet. Maybe that's what happened. I've long tortured myself with the idea that she moved to the city, made a name for herself, and had some wealthy, well put together man who'd follow her wherever she wanted to go. Odette deserved nothing less. I wanted to be the man who gave her everything. Or everything that she couldn't attain by herself, anyway.

"I cared about her once. A great deal and a long time ago," I finally say, unwilling to lie. She'd see through it anyhow.

"Before you and Mom?"

Fuck.

"No, kiddo. Not exactly."

"Not exactly? What does that mean, Dad?"

"It means that for a time before your mother and I were married, we weren't together."

"How much time," she asks, more concern in her tone now than the disgust that was there a moment ago.

"A couple of months. For the summer before we moved to Boston."

"Why weren't you together then? I thought you'd been together since you were fifteen or something."

"Your mother and I," I start, then think better of what I was about to say. "We were young, Tori. We had plans for colleges in different states. Maybe she never told you, but she had a scholarship to Michigan State. Our plan wasn't for her to follow me around the country watching me play. We made the decision for a clean break at the beginning of the summer."

"And that's when you began to care about Odette?"

Began? No, that's not so accurate. She'd always been there, somewhere in the periphery. Always noticeable and unforgettable. I was damn near obsessed with her, but I kept that to myself.

"We spent a lot of time together those months," I say. "She was different than anyone and everyone in our town. Confident, but awkward. Beautiful, but strange. Smart, but quiet about it. And so fucking ambitious it rivaled my own dreams of the future."

Every spare moment I had that summer, I wanted to spend it with her. Watching her sew or draw, listening to her ideas and plans. She was the first real feminist I ever met and made it clear she didn't need a man in her life, though she'd smile playfully at me as she said such things. It was like a form of foreplay for her. A cat and mouse game where I was the mouse. Fuck, I loved that; knowing that she could just as easily spend her time alone but instead chose to spend it with me.

She taught me to be more grounded, less excessive and showy. Odette appreciated quality over quantity, a novel concept to a spoiled teen like me. She labored over every purchase, even the small ones, like what to have for lunch. Taking anything for granted was beyond her.

"I learned a lot from her. About myself, people, and life in general. I'm sure she'll teach you even more."

"You loved her," Tori says in a quiet gasp, her eyes shiny with tiny pools of sympathy.

"There wasn't enough time for all that," I dismiss, but it tastes sour on my tongue. I didn't know what love was then, I guess I still don't understand that kind of love. It's not what Caroline and I had throughout our marriage. I love my ex-wife; I have since we were very young. But it lacked the passion and yearning I imagine a marriage is supposed to have.

I know fatherly love, which mostly consists of stress and the thought that I'd put myself in front of Victoria to protect her from absolutely anything. Being a parent changes you, or it should. If it doesn't, you either started out a fucking saint or a complete piece of shit.

Brotherly love, I know well, too. I feel it for my teammates. As one of the older players, many of them have become like younger siblings to me. Being an only child myself, it's been great to have a sort of family with me no matter where we are.

But romantic love? That's something I only came close to once.

"Did Mom know about her?"

"Your mother and I have never had secrets, kiddo."

"Then why did you get back," she starts to ask the question. "Oh."

"Kiddo," I hedge, watching her face fall.

"Mom was pregnant." Tori's hand starts to rub at her chest. "You guys got married because she was pregnant with me."

"Hey," I say, pulling her to the couch and wrapping my arm around her. "It's not a decision either of us regret. We'd make the same one a hundred times over."

"But you weren't in love. It all makes so much more sense now."

"In love? No, maybe not that. But we did love each other. We still do. She's been my best friend for most of my life. We've had a great life, Tori. Haven't we?"

She pulls her knees up to her chest, hugging them to herself as she snuggles further into my arm.

"We have. You guys are the best," she says. "Is that why she wanted the divorce? Was that always the plan? To split when I grew up."

Possibly that's what we both thought when we went into it, but it wasn't something we discussed.

"The only plan we had was to raise you the best we could. We'd been broken up for weeks when your mom realized she was pregnant. She immediately knew she wanted you and that college wasn't as important to her. I thought the best way to take care of you both was to get married right away. It gave us some special privileges on campus in Boston and later with the NHL. We didn't consider anything past that. Past you."

"Why didn't you tell me this when she filed for divorce? I was so mad at you."

She was, and that was pure hell for me. The divorce wasn't either of our faults, it was the natural progression of things, really. Tori couldn't understand without us telling her the rest. But then we risked her being mad at Caroline, and placing blame on herself, too. I preferred to take the brunt of it, knowing it would pass eventually.

"It was a big change for all of us, you, especially. We didn't want to add to it with our messy past."

"But I'm part of that messy past."

"No, you aren't, Tori. You're the best thing that ever could have happened to us." I press a kiss to her crown. "You believe me, don't you?"

"Yeah," she says, her voice a little shaky still. "But what was the cost?"

"What do you mean?"

"Did it cost you your happiness? Or Mom hers? What if you both missed out on the love of your life?"

"You're breaking my heart, kiddo," I say into the dark messy bun atop her head. She smells like she always does, some combination of fruit and sugar. "Don't you know you are the love of my life?"

"You know what I mean, Dad."

"Listen really carefully, Tori. I could not have been happy if I wasn't coming home to you while you were growing up. Your mother has always felt the same. Okay?"

The last thing I want is for her to wear any blame or guilt. Our life has been great, regardless of how it all started. It's why we always sheltered her from the hard truth that Caroline and I haven't had the most traditional marriage.

It wasn't an open relationship or anything extreme. But it was more of a partnership than any sort of love match. That doesn't mean we didn't find happiness in it. There was camaraderie, caring, and a shared sense of something bigger than us. We had fun as a family.

"I just want you to have someone," she tells me, peering at me so she can read my expression better. "The thought of you here all alone bothers me. You should have a partner. You should have love, Dad. A real relationship."

"Do you tell your mother these same things?"

"No, she already knows. She's already looking."

Tori maps my face, looking for signs that I'm concerned about this news. But I'm not. Caroline deserves to live the rest of her life with someone she loves and who loves her back equally. She's still my friend, even though we've tried not to be too reliant on each other anymore. We don't speak daily but several times a week. Which is probably still too much, but habits are hard to break, and we do share a daughter.

She hasn't mentioned dating to me, though. I can't figure out a reason why she'd omit that from our conversations. Maybe she shares some of the same concerns Tori has about me. This is my first attempt at bachelor living, and they don't seem confident in my ability to thrive in it.

I've done okay, though. Caroline always handled the household since I was the one bringing in the income. I have a housekeeper who helps me keep up on this place, but I do know how to clean my own toilet. Jasinda comes in twice a month to scold me and laugh at my novice abilities. At least I try, she always tells me. And sure, I suck at cooking, but I'm getting the hang of it. I've nearly mastered baked ziti and can unbag a salad with the best of them.

Some of the team wives looked after me when Caroline left. I had a freezer full of prepared meals that lasted me a month and gave me time to settle into a new way of life. Tori suggested I hire a chef but my days of being that dependent on someone else for my most basic needs are over.

I want to take care of myself more. Maybe even take care of someone else, if the right woman comes along.

My mind immediately conjures images of Odette Quinn. Except they are images of her at eighteen, not who she is today. I don't know that version of her at all. Would I feel the same way about her now as I did then? Even if I did, would she give me a chance?

Doubt it.

I fucked up. I know I did, and I can only blame my age and circumstances for so much of it. The biggest problem was me and how poorly I handled the situation. Odette deserved more.

Maybe I'm the man now that I should have been then. Maybe I'm enough.

Maybe she'd never give me a second chance to prove that, though. Who could blame her?

That's even if she's single, which doesn't seem likely. Not at our age and not with who she was. Odette probably has always had a trail of men standing in line for her attention. Not only because she's gorgeous, but because she's different and caring. Or was. Is she still?

Regardless of whether she is or not, a relationship with anyone isn't my priority just yet. The season starts next week. My team and my performance this season are my top priorities. It's my last season, after all.

Fuck.

That will never sound right to me. Later, I'll have a lot of changes to face, but I'll also have the time to devote to a partner. There's time. At least, I hope so.

4

ODETTE

"**W**ell, what did you think of your first week?"

It's the first question out of Vanessa's mouth when I slide into the booth opposite her at a trendy bar a few blocks from the school. It's my type of place and looks like it could be a setting in *Peaky Blinders*. The drink menu has an impressive array of handcrafted cocktails. After a quick perusal, I settle on one called the Spumoni Negroni.

"It was great," I say, flipping the page to the dinner side of the menu. "You've picked an impressive group of students."

"I'm glad you think so," she says with a wide smile. "We have special plans here, and it starts with them."

"They're all talented, but there are a few that have potential to make substantial changes in the industry," I say. Vanessa said she picked this place because they have a decent gluten-free menu, something she knows I'm struggling with. I love bread and I miss it daily. I could live off croissants and coffee, two things I'm not supposed to be consuming now.

I've become a tea drinker. It's not so bad, but it's not coffee.

"A friend is meeting us here; I hope that's okay."

"Of course," I say, dismissing her concern. "What friend?"

"One of the professors at Seattle U, Preston Wyatt."

"If ever there were a professor's name," I tease, and she laughs.

"Am I missing the fun already," a deep voice asks. He's tall, attractive, with dark hair, a strong jaw, friendly eyes, and who looks like a professor, dressed in a tweed jacket. But it's tailored to perfection, and he wears it so well that he doesn't look outdated or stuffy. Quite the opposite. In fact, he looks…appealing.

"Hello, Preston. Glad you could make it," Vanessa greets him. "This is Odette Quinn."

"Lovely to meet you," I say, sliding farther into the booth, allowing him room to sit.

"Likewise. Vanessa has spoken quite highly of you."

"All lies." I laugh. "I promise I'm much more of a stubborn twat than she's let on."

"That's nearly verbatim what she said you'd say," he tells me with a smile that's just slightly lopsided. A small, faded scar sits at the upper corner of his mouth, and I wonder how this pretty man could have possibly gotten it. It reminds me of Gavin Vaughn, whose body had many marks from years of hockey.

Truthfully, the short time I spent with Gavin has been wreaking minor havoc on me all week since meeting his daughter. It was a formidable time in my life, and he had a larger impact on me than I like to admit. But I shake those thoughts away in favor of the man currently sitting beside me and eyeing me with the same appreciation I have for him.

"I may not see much of her, but I know her well enough," Vanessa says. "Preston teaches art history."

"Really? Are you only into the history or do you have an eye for it, as well?"

"I have a meager appreciation for it."

"Now that's a lie," Vanessa says. "Preston has an amazing eye for talent. I'm jealous of a few pieces he's managed to acquire for his personal collection."

Preston holds his palms out in surrender as the server arrives to take our orders.

"Maybe you could come by my new home and help me find some pieces. I'm only barely settled and there are a handful of spaces that need artful attention," I tell him.

"Ode bought the Denny mansion," Vanessa adds.

"No shit? Do you know the history of the place?"

"Very little," I confess. "I was told the original owner was a descendant of one of Seattle's founding fathers, and it's been owned by a corporation since the seventies and only occasionally used."

That was obvious in my first walkthrough of the home. It felt sterile and impersonable, nothing in it felt handpicked with care to an overall aesthetic or personal feeling. It made it an even more appealing property for me to buy. It's a bit of a clean slate inside an amazing historical shell. Something I can give renewed life with my personal taste and style.

My mother says I'm replacing my clients with the house. I can't argue it, she's probably right. An outlet for my own creativity has always been something I need. Only so much of that can happen through my own wardrobe.

The house is massive, it's going to take me the better part of a year to give it the life it deserves, but I'm up for the challenge.

"The corporation was the Unification Church," Preston says.

"The Moonies," Vanessa asks, and Preston hums in acknowledgement.

"Wait, wasn't that the church with AR-15s?" I can't hide the shock, nor the humor in my voice. Of course, the agent I worked with left out that "minor" detail.

"That was the Sanctuary Church, which was an offshoot started by Moon's son. Unification Church was most notorious for its mass weddings in South Korea."

"Hmm, well, I guess it adds some spice and history to the house," I say, shrugging it off. It does explain a few things about my new home. "Maybe I'll sage a little, though."

"The historian in me would love to take you up on the offer, if you wouldn't mind me poking around your house."

"Oh, not at all. The place is fabulous and deserves more than just my attention," I say. "I was thinking about hosting a welcoming party for the students. I want them to see me as more of a peer than an instructor of any kind. Perhaps a casual get together will help their comfort with me."

"It's not a bad idea, if you don't mind them knowing where you live," Vanessa says.

"I'm in one of the most famous houses in the city, I'm not sure I could hide it even if I tried."

"True," she agrees.

"You live there alone?" Preston raises one eyebrow. They are neatly trimmed, as is his matching short beard. He's a well-manicured man from what I can see. While he's without the signs of someone who's worked with their hands their entire life, he's not necessarily soft, either. His hands are large, shoulders wide, and his burnished hair is styled in a way that suggests he's done little more than run his fingers through it as it air-dried. I bet his students love his lectures.

"I do."

"Odette is the consummate single," Vanessa says, taking a sip of her drink that has just arrived. "I've never seen her in a relationship."

Side-eyeing her, I see the spark in her eye. The one that says she's up to something. In this case, matchmaking. It's not her first attempt. This is a regular habit of hers. I love her, but it's misplaced.

A relationship gal I am not.

"Never," he asks.

"Not since I've known Vanessa anyway," I confirm.

"And you met in college?"

"We did." I nod, taking a big sip of my drink. It's good, hits like a balm to my most vulnerable spot that feels just slightly exposed right now. "The last relationship I was in ended right before I moved to New York City for college. It hasn't been a priority since."

"That's a long time to be single," he says.

"Maybe," I say, shrugging. "I have had seven different men ask me to marry them, if that counts for anything."

"Seven?" Preston throws his head back in laughter. He has a nice throat, a prominent Adam's apple below his strong jawline.

"And I turned down every single one. What about you? Family?"

"I have a son, Victor. He's twenty-four and living his best life on the East Coast."

"Married?"

"Separated." He says it with a slight shrug, but there's a pursing at his lips that tells me it might not be a safe topic to explore just yet.

Interesting.

Besides not being interested in relationships, I'm not entirely a good woman, either. I don't fuck with men who are available. Which, of course, leaves me with a long line of narcissistic assholes and men in dire need of therapy.

If you're an emotionally unavailable guy, pull up a chair and let's get to know one another for a night. On the other hand, if you're healthy and looking for love…no thank you. I don't make time for men that might get attached, because I won't reciprocate and then things get messy.

I'm not on the prowl for love or commitment, only a good time and a better goodbye.

From a young age, my father taught me that anything a man could do, I could do better…while bleeding. Men should fear me, he said, and I shouldn't ever forget it. He probably didn't expect me to embrace that motto in my sexual endeavors, though he's never chided me for it, so maybe he did. My parents were never conventional thinkers, really. They're quite progressive, which is likely why I've ended up the way I am. I have never bowed to societal norms. Not even when choosing my bed partners.

Preston is my type of man in many ways. Smart, handsome, well-built, and most importantly, not entirely available. I don't care that he's still married, that's his business, not my vagina's.

"Where's George," he asks Vanessa, a clear attempt at changing the subject away from his marriage.

"Beijing. For another few days."

Vanessa has been married to her very distinguished and much older partner for over a decade. George is in some sort of finance that bores me to death, so I've never much cared to learn the ins and outs of his specific career. It takes him to every part of the world. Vanessa used to travel with him more, but she's become more discerning over the years. Choosing to go only to new or favorite places.

They're complete opposites, but you couldn't find two people more enamored with one another.

"If I plan the party for next weekend, will he be home? I've missed my friend," I say. George and I have always gotten on well. He's French and says I should have been born there because my outlook and lifestyle are more European. He once said I was never destined for a "stodgy, prudish American life".

Criticism of how I live isn't strange to me, so I loved George instantly for his lack of judgment.

"You know he'd change his schedule to accommodate anything you ask for," she says with a playful eyeroll. "The man loves you almost as much as he loves me."

"Hardly." I laugh.

"He likes you?" Preston asks me. "I'm convinced George hates me."

"Oh no, why do you think that?"

"He gives me that look. Do you know the one?"

"I do," I say, giving Vanessa a wink.

"He gives that look to every pretty man. George likes to pretend I'll leave him for a younger man," she explains.

"George thinks I'm pretty?"

"Do you avoid mirrors, Preston?" I ask.

"You think I'm pretty?"

"That's not the word I'd use," I purr before finishing my drink in one large swallow.

Everything is ready. Thanks to the caterer I hired and has handled nearly every detail for me. We've kept it simple enough, hors d'oeuvres and canapes. We opted out of a bar since all the students are underage, but there will be fancy non-alcoholic drinks being passed around.

I'm giving myself a once-over, making sure my Halston pantsuit is still wrinkle free and the double-stick tape is holding the plunging neckline where it should be. I want the students to see me as "one of them", in a sense, but I don't need to be flashing them the goods.

Preston might get a peek if things go well, but he's the only exception. We exchanged numbers the night we met. He's texted me a few times this week, mostly to ask how my day was. There was some implied intent on wanting to see me again. I'm not looking for exclusivity, so I've been cagey on the subject. At least until I understand where his head is at. Though I did reiterate my invitation to him for tonight's gathering.

Preston Wyatt, though he's caught my eye, is not my focus tonight, however. The kids are. This past week was another great one. While they haven't been let loose in the workroom yet, they've been sketching like mad and it's amped up my excitement. I've been missing this for too long; the birth of so many new ideas and the feeling of just starting on the path of something life-altering. It hasn't been a big part of my life since I first hired Fallon and he had that same wide-eyed enthusiasm.

Before that, it was when I first started college, everything between the two events is a blur of long days and sleepless nights repeated over and over for so many years. It's no wonder my body rebelled.

I fasten on a fine gold chain and make my way down the sweeping staircase to the foyer. I've been here nearly six weeks now and am still not used to the space and grandeur of this house. I can already hear George's laughter before I make it to the front door.

"Odette, my second love," he greets me with air kisses. "What in the world have you gotten yourself into here?"

"It's large, but she's the classiest house in this city. You, shoosh!" I raise on my toes and wrap my arms around him. "It's good to see you, friend."

"You, as well. It will be good to have you so close. Vanessa needs the company when I'm away."

"I do just fine alone, thank you," she says, pushing him aside to enter the house. "There are cars pulling in right behind us, so you're going to have to let me explore this place on my own."

"Of course, enjoy yourself."

"We'll catch up when you have a moment to breathe," George promises.

They wander off and leave me to greet the students and their dates. I issued invites with a plus-one option, not wanting anyone to suffer from the anxiety of showing up alone. Benji has his girlfriend with him, Jun-Li is accompanied by her girlfriend, and Celine is alone. I expected that from her, she's a bit like me, I think. Confident, independent. I show them all to the dining room where the libations are set up.

"This house is amazing, Ms. Quinn," Celine says, spinning in a slow circle to take in the ornate ceiling. Her skirt, an array of black angles, twirls around her

"How many times do I have to tell you to call me Odette?"

"A few more, I guess," she answers. "It doesn't feel right."

"We'll work on that," I tell her, patting her shoulder. "And yes, she is an amazing house."

"This is the dream, though. Right?"

"For some of us, it is, sure. It's taken me all this time to realize that, though. Dreams change, Celine. Don't ever stop chasing them."

"Yes, ma'am."

"Oh, darling, that's even worse." I laugh.

"Sorry," Celine says with a surprising giggle of her own. "Your outfit is fabulous, too. That's Halston, isn't it?"

"You know your fashion history, Celine. Enjoy yourself," I tell her, as the doorbell rings again.

Opening it, I find a few more students and Preston. Greeting the younger ones first, I send them in to find their cohorts before I turn to Preston.

"Hi, I'm glad you could make it."

"Thanks for inviting me," he says, placing his hand on my waist and leaning down to kiss my cheek. His cologne permeates the air around us—it's neither strong nor unpleasant. Though I prefer the smell of a man.

The faint hint of sweat, or dirt, or oil. A sign that says they've been physical at something. I don't meet many men like that in my line of work, unfortunately. My memory fails me on the last time I had that in life, something other than posh and clean.

"Of course. I hardly have any friends in this city, it was nice to meet someone new. And I would really like help to find some art pieces. Especially if you know of any great local artists."

"Sure," he says, his face falling slightly. I didn't invite him strictly for the help, but I don't mind that he's hanging on that hook a bit. "Any style in particular?"

"No, as long as it's as fabulous as this house. Feel free to look around. Every place there is a blank space, needs to be filled. This house needs life again. Especially the primary bedroom," I say with a flirtatious smile, pumping his ego back up again. It's not a ploy though, my bedroom has been something of an afterthought in the design sense. It was painted a yellowish-white when I moved in. I had the painters cover that with a peacock blue, but that's where the work stopped.

"I'll let you play hostess and catch up with you later," he says, winking before he walks away as another few people walk through my front door.

I lose myself to the crowd for a time, mingling, meeting all my students' partners or friends, and answering the variety of questions about this house. What made me buy it? What are my plans for it? How do you even fill so much space? A few of the students know some of its history and ask me about that, too.

She's a great conversation starter. Luckily, the weather has been pleasant today, and many of my guests are enjoying the large yard that overlooks the water. Watching from the windows, I smile as I see George talking to Preston, giving him that look.

"Odette?" I recognize Tori's voice from behind me. She still carries a hint of New York with her. Turning to greet her, I freeze. An unfamiliar tingle races up my spine as I come eye to eye with her father.

Gavin Vaughn, as I live and fucking die all over again.

5

ODETTE
THEN

"**W**here are you taking me?" It's been three nights since the incident with Kyle outside of work. Gavin asked for my number that night and he's called every day since. Last night, he was even waiting for me outside the shop when I closed. He followed me home to make sure I got there safely, then he asked if he could take me out today.

It might be a bad idea, a big mistake, but I said yes. Resisting those eyes and that crooked smile is hard. Gavin is charming without even trying to be. It's no wonder the whole student body loved him all throughout school. Even though he runs with the elite, nobody ever had a bad thing to say about Gavin Vaughn.

We've had minimal interaction with each other, a few classes together, is all. But it isn't like we had group projects together, or that he ever gave me a second glance. That's probably for the best since he was with Caroline, and had he focused even a small amount of his addictive personality on me, I'd have been crushing pretty hard.

It's only been a few days and I already am. Like I'm a thirteen-year-old girl instead of an eighteen-year-old young woman about to start a life of her own.

"Watkins Glen."

"The state park?" I roll my eyes over my outfit; high-waisted yellow shorts, ivory Swiss dot blouse. At least I have Keds on, but they're white.

"I promise you won't get dirty."

"How do I know I can trust you, Vaughn?"

"You think I'm taking you to Watkins Glen to what? Murder you and bury your body in one of New York's prettiest places?"

"I mean, I deserve to be buried in a gorgeous place. But I was more concerned about my outfit. These shorts are from the 1940s."

"Irreplaceable?" he asks me only after a moment of laughter at my obvious lack of self-preservation.

"Very," I confirm.

"I got you," he says, reaching a hand over to grasp my own. He twines his fingers in mine, and I feel the faint callousness, I assume from years of hauling hockey gear, taping and waxing sticks, and whatever else it is he does. I don't know that much about the sport, to be honest.

Our joined hands don't look as strange as it feels. Guys have never held my hand before. I've never been romanced. As his thumb traces a pattern on my skin, I think that's exactly what he's trying to do.

"Why?"

"Why will I make sure you keep your one-of-a-kind shorts clean?" He glances across the cab of his SUV at me, a little confused.

"Why me? Why now?"

Gavin squeezes my hand, not answering for a minute. The silence pricks my skin, nervous little needles poking me by the millions. It doesn't matter what he says, this is all temporary anyway. I move to the city in a few months, and he'll go…somewhere else. My mom would tell me to try and enjoy the moment, live without worry of what the future holds.

That's harder to do than she makes it sound. My dreams are too big to push aside, even for a date with Gavin Vaughn.

"I don't think there's a way to explain without me sounding like a real douchebag, and the last thing I want is for you to think I'm an asshole."

"You should try," I tell him. I slide my hand from his, but he squeezes it again, halting my progress.

"Give me a chance, please?" I nod at him, and he continues after he swallows. "I love Caroline like a sister. She's my best friend. I think I've known that for a long time now. But I didn't know if she felt the same. For two years, I've been dreaming about breaking up with her, but I didn't want to hurt her. Or lose her friendship. For two years, I've been dreaming about someone else." He looks at me, then quickly looks away, his cheeks turning a soft rosy color.

I just made him blush.

"You're right, that does make you sound like a creep."

"Does it freak you out?"

"That you crushed on me for two years? No, not so much. I just feel sorry for Caroline."

"Really?" Gavin cringes as he asks the question.

"Sure. I think I'd feel bad for anyone that thought they had someone, but that person was somewhere else, either in their mind or heart. You know?"

"That makes me feel worse," he admits. "If it makes it any better, it turns out she more or less felt the same."

"More or less?"

"She's not in love with me, either. But she hasn't been crushing on anyone all this time. I think that's why she never broke up with me, she was…I don't know. Content with having something over nothing."

I can see how it would be nice to always have someone in your corner, a person to hang out with every Friday night, or whatever. I can see Caroline's point of view, because she didn't have anyone she wanted to be with instead. But, apparently, that isn't Gavin's truth.

"That's sad, but I guess I get it."

"Do you still want to get to know me?"

He asked me that last night, before he asked if I'd go out with him today. He'd said he wanted to know me but only if I wanted to know him, too. It was as if he was making clear that my boundaries mattered. He caught me off guard with that; teen boys don't understand things like that. Maybe Gavin is wiser than the average jock.

Or maybe I'm reading too much into it.

"I do, Gavin," I tell him, honestly. We've only spent an infinitesimal amount of time together, but he already has me curious. And a little turned on.

Okay, a lot. It was images of him that I touched myself to last night.

"Thank fuck," he mumbles, and I laugh. The conversation continues for the rest of the drive, but not with any sort of heavy subject. Gavin asks endless questions about me, from the mundane favorite color and food to things that spark more conversation, like where my love of fashion came from.

"My dad loves old movies. Musicals, specifically. I grew up watching them with him and people were different then, most dressed up every day. A causal day was still a man in a button-down and a woman in at least trousers and blouse," I explain. "While Dad would laugh at the cheesy one liners or songs, I obsessed over the fashion. Always imagining ways I could take those old pieces and wear them in a modern way."

"You're close with your parents?"

"I am. I'm an only child, so that helps. But they're also great."

"That's good. My dad is great, but my mom can be hard. She's sick a lot, depressed. With me gone for hockey so much, it puts a lot of pressure on all of us."

"I'm sorry, that must be hard."

"It is, but we manage. The time that she's feeling good makes up for the bad days."

Now it's my turn to squeeze his hand. He changes the subject again, and I let him because it's only our first date. If he doesn't feel like deep diving into his family dynamics just yet, that's okay.

The drive is another forty minutes, but the time flies with our conversations. We occasionally pause the talk to turn up the radio to sing along to some of the songs that come on. We have similar taste in music, and both sing along dramatically when Eminem's latest hit comes on. When "Beautiful" by Christina Aguilera is next, he indulges me while I belt it with my chin resting on the open window.

My hair will be a windblown mass of black tangles, but the sun shining on my face and the knowledge that Gavin wears a big smile is worth it.

"Has anyone ever told you that you're tone deaf?"

"Yes," I say, snickering. "Thanks for letting me sing anyway."

"I liked your version better." He pulls my hand up to his lips and presses a sweet kiss to the inside of my wrist.

"Liar," I tell him, a little breathlessly.

"I'm a lot of things, Odette. But that's not one of them. I promise."

"You're making me a lot of promises today, Vaughn."

"Only the ones I know I can keep, Quinn."

A picnic. Gavin has planned a picnic with views of the waterfall. Since the weather has been nice, the two-mile trail hasn't been too mucky. But whenever there was a chance I could get dirty, Gavin would either pick me up over his shoulder or tell me to hop on to his back so he could carry me through it.

He's as ridiculous as he is sweet. By the time we get to what he deems the *perfect spot*, my entire outfit is still pristinely clean. And he did all that while still carrying a backpack full of food and a blanket.

"You're strong," I muse, as he spreads the blanket out.

"I won't make it to the NHL any other way," he says with a shrug.

"That's the dream?"

"It's the plan."

I like his confidence. He's sure of himself but not in a cocky way that turns me off.

"Thank you," I say as I sit cross-legged on the blanket and help him unpack the food.

"You're welcome. I told you I wouldn't ruin your outfit."

"I mean, for this," I say, looking around. It's a busy day here, but that doesn't detract from the beauty of this place. The sound of the waterfall drowns out all the talking around us and I feel cocooned in an invisible bubble with just him. "It's really pretty here."

"It is," he agrees. "We used to bring my mom here for her birthday."

"Not anymore?"

"No, she doesn't like crowds so much these days."

"That must make it rough for her to go to your games."

He nods, then pulls out a few different containers: one has berries, one with cut-up vegetables, and one full of cubed cheese. "She tries pretty often, though. I wasn't sure what you liked."

He pulls a few sandwiches out next, all labeled with black marker on the baggies. His handwriting is horrific and makes me smile.

"Turkey is my favorite."

"Oh good, that one's for you then."

We eat in a comfortable silence. Gavin's bare knee rests against mine and I like the small contact of our contrasting skin. My legs are pale and smooth, while he sports a light tan and soft hair.

When we finish all the food, I crawl onto his lap and sit with my back to his chest so I can lean my head back on his shoulder and watch the water shower the rocks. It's nice, and it feels right when he wraps his arms around my midsection.

"Thank you for coming with me today," he says, and I turn my face to his.

"You're welcome." I study him as he stares back at me with a flame in his eyes. "What is this to you, Gavin?"

"It's a lot of things. A dream, a possibility. A chance to see if there's something here."

"Something more than a crush, you mean?"

"Definitely more than a crush."

"And when the summer ends?"

"That's months away. Can we see what happens between now and then?"

I should say no. It probably can't end well, after all. How could it with me in New York and him in Boston? That small two-letter word won't come, though, I can't force it out of my mouth no matter how hard I try. Because the truth is, I want to agree. I want to take it day by day and see where it goes. The chance at something is better than the guarantee of nothing.

Right?

"Kiss me, Vaughn, and let's see what happens."

6

GAVIN

"This might be a bad idea," I tell Tori as we take the last turn according to the GPS. Odette's house isn't far from mine. I've been in Seattle for a handful of years now, but I don't know the different neighborhoods well, unless it's one a teammate lives in. Even then, I only frequent a few of their homes.

Cillian has a fancy-ass floating house in Eastlake. Fane's partner, or one of them, anyway, is wealthy and has a nice house on the other side of town. Most of the other guys have condos spread around, but I don't know anyone who lives in the Windermere neighborhood.

"The plus one didn't have stipulations, Dad."

"A plus one usually implies a romantic partner, though."

"But I don't have one of those. Besides, Odette is really cool, and you already know her. She might be excited to see a blast from the past, or whatever."

Tori sounds confident, but I don't miss the way she's fingering the hem of her skirt.

"You're probably right," I say, pushing a little more cheeriness into my tone in the hopes of easing her. "Holy shit."

The house we pull up to is not an ordinary house. At all.

"Wow," Tori whispers beside me.

"Yeah. Wow." We park and walk up to the porch of the enormous white mansion. I know she's been working with the rich and famous, but somehow, it didn't cross my mind that Odette is one of them. I guess I still imagine her as the girl I knew as a kid. The one who shopped at thrift stores and drove a dented car that was twice her age.

Hell, I'm a professional athlete and I don't know if I could afford a place like this. Definitely not after all the money I paid Caroline in the divorce. I'm not bitter about that, though. She deserves to be comfortable. She says I paid her too much. I disagree, though, because she doesn't have a career. Her skillset is that of a stay-at-home mom and that deserves a great salary.

The door is open, but I still knock as we walk through the foyer. It's circular, paneled in dark carved wood topped with a floral wallpaper in different shades of green and purple. A huge bouquet of fresh flowers sits on a round table in the middle, the smell permeating the whole space.

Tori sneezes twice, her allergies in full swing.

"You okay?"

"Yeah, but let's find everyone else," she says, leading me through the arched opening and further into the house.

That's where we find her. Standing at a large bay of windows overlooking the expansive backyard. Her hair was shorter when I knew her, cropped just below her chin. Now, it's long and flows down her back. I wouldn't recognize her from sight, at least from this angle, but the hair on my arms rises in some unseen recognition.

This pull can't be ignored.

"Odette?"

"Tori, glad you could—" Odette starts and abruptly stops when she sees me standing next to my daughter. "Vaughn."

"Quinn." I mimic her tone, a combination of awe and apprehension.

"I hope it's okay, I brought my dad. I don't have a boyfriend, and since you know each other," Tori starts to ramble.

"Of course," Odette says, painting a bright smile onto her face quickly. I see through it, but I doubt Tori can. "Gavin, it's been too long, darling."

Darling?

"Far," I say, and Tori side-eyes me, but I can't pull my gaze off Odette. She's a pillar in royal blue from shoulder to toe. Whatever she's wearing has a slight shimmer, and when she steps closer, I can't tell if the dazzle is her clothing or her. She always did scramble my brain.

Her hair isn't the only thing that's changed. She's curvier, her body fuller but her face more defined with angles. Her lips are like I remember, bright and heart-shaped. The most kissable I've ever seen. If circumstances were different, I'd say fuck it and take them right now. I want to. But I'm not that kind of asshole.

Then there are those eyes. Hazel and piercing…they've always been transfixing but now they look at me with a directness I never knew from her before. Distrust, likely. I can't fucking blame her there.

"You look fabulous, my dear," she says to my kid, making her beam with pride. I know she fretted for hours about what to wear today. I hate the pressure she puts on herself, but I also understand it.

"Thank you."

"Everyone is outside but grab a drink and a plate before you head out," Odette says, gesturing to the next room where I can see a spread of food.

"Thank you," Tori repeats, taking a few steps in the direction of the dining area. She looks at me to follow, but I give her a nod, suggesting she go ahead without me. She can't hide her knowing smirk.

"How have you been, Odette?"

"Fabulous."

"This house is great," I say, taking a step closer to her and fighting every urge to touch her. We don't know each other, not anymore, but our chemistry is alive and fucking well.

"Mmm, yes, she's fab…"

"Fabulous?" I smile but don't laugh out loud at her obvious fluster. She's as affected by me as I am by her. Probably more so because I'm sure she didn't expect me to walk into her house today.

I give her a moment as she looks at her shoes, and she eventually releases a long breath.

"Hi," she says when she looks back up at me. "Gavin."

Besides my grandmother and teachers, Odette was the only person as a kid that called me by my full name. To everyone else, I was Gav or Vaughn. Still am, in most instances. I loved the way she said it, though, how her teeth almost bite her lower lip when she pronounces the V. She says it slow and cool, and it makes me anything but.

"Hi, Odette. Sorry to surprise you like this."

"It's fine," she says, except I see her throat move like she's swallowing down what she really wants to say. "It's good to see you. How's Caroline?"

All hope of casually catching up with Odette flies out the wide-open French doors behind her. Maybe I shouldn't have expected anything different. Sure, it's been twenty years, but the way I handled things back then was abysmal, at best.

"She's good. Better than ever, happy back in New York. I hear she's dating."

"Are you divorced?" Odette blinks a few times, her long lashes as black as her hair.

"For over a year now."

"I'm sorry to hear that," she says. It sounds genuine. Which makes sense, honestly. Despite how we ended, I never knew Odette to be bitter or vicious. Though I wouldn't blame her for hating us.

"Don't be." I offer no other explanation. This isn't the place. "You look… fucking amazing. And this place is something else, Odette. You've done well for yourself."

"In some ways, sure. And thank you," she says, running a hand down the fine fabric at her hip. "You have, too. Your plan came off without a hitch."

"In some ways, sure," I throw her words back at her. Most certainly not in others. I had planned on a passionate and loving marriage, after all. "How are you liking Seattle?"

"So far, I'm loving it. But everyone tells me to wait for winter."

"Not much different than New York winters, in my experience."

"That's good to hear," she says, averting her gaze back to the windows.

"Sorry, I'm probably keeping you from your guests," I say, touching her shoulder as I move to step around her. "I'll catch up with you later, Quinn."

I don't give her a chance to say anything else. I don't want to hear her say no, nor do I want to monopolize her while she has a house full of guests. I grab a water and wander the main floor. It's not what I would imagine her living in, this grandeur. I'd have expected her in a small bungalow, busting at the seams with art and kitsch. Those are present here, but the scale feels wrong, somehow.

I check in with Tori and meet a few of her classmates. None are overly impressed by me, which is probably a breath of fresh air for my daughter. There have been too many times in her life when she thought she had to fight for attention around me. For all the privileges my career brings her, there have been plenty of downsides, as well.

After about an hour of aimless meandering, I settle into a chair on the back patio and watch the sun play over the lake. It's a comfortable silence until an older gentleman sits in the chair next to me.

"I hear this is your last season," he says.

"It is. I'm practically geriatric by NHL standards," I confirm.

"George Andrews," the man says, holding out his hand to me.

"Gavin Vaughn. Nice to meet you."

"Likewise. What brings a star of the Seattle Blades to my friend's home today?" he asks with an edge of possessiveness that draws my curiosity.

"That's my daughter." I nod my head toward Tori, who's laughing with a couple of her cohorts. "She thought she should drag me along today because Odette and I grew up together, oddly enough."

"You're kidding?"

"Not at all, we come from the same smallish town in upstate New York."

"You're telling me you knew the most enigmatic woman in all of fashion before she was the enigmatic woman? I thought my wife was the only one," he says, smiling ear to ear. He leans closer to me, elbows on his knees. "What was she like as a child?"

"She was mysterious then, too. Kept to a small circle of friends, mostly artsy types. Which I guess you'd expect. She made her own rules in life. According to my daughter, she still does. And she always had a smile that drew you in."

A memory conjures from one of the few classes we shared in high school. It was creative writing and we had to read our short stories for the class. A guy named Jerry was reading his, a fantasy tale about visiting a sideshow and running into a womanly snake creature with huge tits. Odette burst out laughing, unable to contain herself. I couldn't take my eyes off her. I'd never seen her display her joy so unabashedly before. Half of the class probably fell for her at that moment, her head thrown back as she snorted, not trying to control herself at all. I'm sure she laughed like that with her friends, but it wasn't something the rest of us saw much of.

Fuck, she had a great laugh. Does she still?

"You haven't stayed close?"

"No, we haven't spoken in almost twenty years," I answer. The last time I saw her is imprinted on my brain. Our last conversation haunts me like a recurring nightmare. It's difficult to remember things I talked about last week, but I remember every word that was passed between the two of us that night. Our *last* night.

More than anything, I remember the smile she wore purely for my benefit because it was a complete fucking lie.

"That's not something she shares with just anyone these days. Her real smile," he muses. "Count yourself lucky."

"Oh, I do." Our short time was special, and I cherish it, even if I hate that it had to end. Watching her now, how she moves through the crowd with a self-assuredness I've only ever seen in other athletes, I wonder if there's a possibility of a second chance for us.

Is it too late to see if that connection is still alive? Or is it long buried? I don't think it is because I still feel something when I look at her; a remnant of what pulled me to her in the first place. A desire to be close, to know all her secrets, and to be the one she trusts them to.

"You have a daughter," George says. "Is there a wife?"

"An ex-wife," I say, not taking my eyes off her.

"Oh, you poor, poor man," George says before rising. His laughter fades as he walks away.

What the fuck just happened?

No matter how hard I try, I can't pull my eyes off Odette. She's speaking with Tori, who is animatedly telling a story, her hands waving. My daughter is comfortable with her, only after a couple of weeks of school. Tori's grown up around minor celebrities, maybe that helps her be at ease with someone she idolizes the way she does Odette. Hockey isn't on the same level as fashion, or even other sports. We can live our lives mostly going unrecognized and unnoticed. We don't make Page Six headlines. Odette has. I know because I can never go long without my curiosity getting the best of me and typing her name into my search engine.

One time, Caroline saw me reading about her. She didn't say anything, just placed a hand on my shoulder and a kiss to the top of my head. We never discussed it, but I'm sure she knew that a part of me was never present in the room with me. I left it with Odette at the young fucking age of eighteen.

Whether she knows she has it or not. Whether she's kept it safe or not. The gorgeous woman talking to the most important person in my life has held whatever part of me causes the tightness in my stomach. My other half, my soulmate…I don't know what to call it, but I've only ever felt it with her.

Or maybe that is just my guilt speaking.

A man walks up to Odette, stealing her attention away from Tori, who glances around until she sees me. I smile and throw her a small wave. A few minutes later, she's climbing the stairs to the patio with a boy in tow.

"Dad, this is Drake," she introduces him as they take seats of their own.

"Hey, Drake. Nice to meet you."

"You too, Mr. Vaughn."

"Call me Gavin. Mr. Vaughn makes me feel old," I say. "Do you go to school with Tori?"

"Yeah. I moved here from Kansas, terrified and alone. But Tori's work-station is right next to mine and she said that meant we were destined to be friends. I haven't been able to shake her since," he teases with a wink.

"Sounds like my girl," I tell him. "She's a good friend. You're in good hands."

"Drake also knows hockey," Tori says.

"Oh yeah?"

"Yeah, my grandfather played in the NHL for a few years. Joshua Jensen."

"Seriously? Jensen is in the Hall of Fame," I say, and Drake nods. "Do you play?"

"Nah, my coordination doesn't allow."

"Same," Tori says. Which is true, athletic abilities were never in her wheelhouse. "Odette says she's never seen you play."

"She probably doesn't have a lot of time for sports," I say nonchalantly, but it stings some, the knowledge that she surely hasn't had the same level of obsession for me that I have for her.

"You should get her tickets for a game."

"I doubt she'd want that," I start, but Tori interrupts.

"You could try, Dad," she insists, and I get the feeling she's trying to matchmake.

I wonder if it'd work…

The way Odette is speaking with that man tells me it wouldn't. Her hand rests on the lapel of his stuffy jacket. It's nearly eighty degrees out today, so why is he wearing a blazer? Then again, maybe that's what Odette is into. Maybe he knows more than I do. She leans in whenever she says anything to him, and I don't like it. Not one bit.

I'm jealous.

Is she dating him? Are they something to each other? Does he make her come?

Fuck.

A familiar feeling takes over me. One I know well, it's in my blood and my bones.

Competition.

I welcome it, and like every time I take the ice, I play to fucking win.

7

ODETTE

The card is attached to a large bouquet sitting on my doorstep when I get home. It's like the one I had in the foyer the day of the party. But bigger. Enormous, really. He must have spent a pretty penny. Gavin's number is written below his name.

Regardless of how pretty the flowers are, regardless of how pretty Gavin Vaughn is, and good grief has that man aged to perfection, he's not my fucking type.

He's single. Unattached. Available.

Which can only lead to strings, complications, heartache.

I think I'll pass.

Even though I rub my finger across his name and number, remembering those weeks we spent together…I can't make myself call him. My time with him was happy and stress free. I bloomed into a woman with him. But those memories are tainted by something else. By the sharp pains of rejection and heartbreak. That's not who I am anymore, though. I reject; I don't get rejected. Avoiding situations that cause me any kind of hurt is a specialty of mine. It's how I maintain sanity with what's been a busy lifestyle.

It's not so busy anymore. Fallon is succeeding in his attempts to take over my client list. He hasn't needed me, and the amount of downtime I have now far exceeds what I anticipated.

So much so that I'm now trying to find hobbies. *Hobbies.* Something I never had time for before. Vanessa has been firing off ideas, but none have stuck. I'm not a yoga class type of girl and the only thing appealing about a wine and painting night is the wine.

Odette Quinn is quickly becoming a homebody, it seems. If only New York City could see me now. I've gone from rarely eating in to rarely eating out. Granted, I eat a lot of takeout because my skills in the kitchen haven't been honed over the years. That was another thing Vanessa suggested… take up baking. With eating gluten free, it wasn't a bad idea. So, I bought some cookbooks and went on a horrifically expensive grocery trip. I can't believe how much more it costs to live allergen free. What kind of bullshit is it when poison costs less than actual healthy sustenance?

I know I've been privileged with the amount of wealth I've amassed in a relatively short time. Truth is, I've done little with it. For myself or for others. I ignored it, mostly, pretending it wasn't there unless I was buying myself some rare and expensive article of clothing or pair of shoes.

Or this house with more history than most. Some would say I squandered a fortune on this place, and they'd not be wrong. I'm committed to her now, but that doesn't mean I don't still have money to put elsewhere. Somewhere needed, someplace that helps others. I've been a workhorse and a socialite for twenty years, maybe it's time to be a philanthropist and use my meager superpowers to make a difference in more than just making people look and feel fabulous in their clothing.

Charity can be one of my newfound *hobbies.* It's long overdue.

I suppose I could say the same thing about Gavin. Our meeting again is long overdue, but that doesn't mean it's a good idea.

After reading the small card a few more times, I deposit it in the trash and try not to think of it again. Seattle is a fresh start for me, a chance to change my life, and bringing old stresses in won't help me.

PRESTON:

> There is a showing at a local gallery Friday night. Promising new artist. Accompany me? There is a piece I think will be perfect for your dining room.

My phone chimes with the text message.

Whatever relationship Preston and I are nurturing hasn't progressed much. In some ways he's been brave, texting me often. In other ways, the man is far too timid, as if he's afraid to make any advancements. Whether he's afraid of me, himself, or his estranged wife, I'm uncertain. Which only keeps me holding him at arm's length. While I'd love to fuck the man, I don't think he's ready for that. I don't chase any man.

My mother once told me I fight for what I want in every aspect of my life except the one that involves love. It's a hard truth to swallow, but I know that some battles aren't worth waging. Some wars you are destined to lose.

Some things you don't deserve, anyhow.

ME:

> Sounds fantastic. Send me the details and I can meet you there.

This is not a date; I mentally add to my response, then head to the kitchen to try my hand at double chocolate cookies.

"Coming," I holler to whoever is knocking at my front door while I frantically try to figure out a way to pause. Not finding one, I drop the controller on my couch and rush to the door. "Gavin?"

"You didn't answer my question," he says, stepping in and leaning against the jamb.

"Which would imply the answer is no."

"Would it? It could just as easily be a yes." He smirks, and like last weekend, it does something to me that I'm choosing to ignore.

"How?"

"Fifty-fifty shot that it was a yes?" He grimaces, charming as ever.

"It wasn't."

"But it could have been, and I wouldn't have known had I not shown up."

"In your experience, does this kind of bullshit work with women?"

"I don't have much experience," he says, and I nearly feel bad for asking. Of course he hasn't; he's been married since he was eighteen. He holds up a large bag in offering. My stomach growls, making him smile wider.

"I'm not dating you, Vaughn."

"Who said anything about dating? It's dinner between two people who grew up together, Quinn. I know you want to say yes."

"To the food, yes. To you, I don't know."

"Fair enough. Let me feed you."

"What's in the bag?"

"Let me in and I'll show you," he says in more of a question than a demand. My stomach rumbles again.

"Fine, but don't think this will work again next time, Vaughn." My intrigue, and hunger, apparently, overrule my disdain for his presence. I don't hate Gavin. I never could, though I tried. It was only the circumstances I hated, and the pain that I felt alone in. I hated that the most.

"Deal."

I open the door and step aside so my biggest mistake can walk through it. The smell of the food follows me as I lead him to the kitchen.

"I hope Thai food is okay? Without knowing your preferences or allergies, I ordered a variety figuring something would be safe."

That's surprisingly thoughtful. Or maybe it's not, he always was before… until, well.

"Pad Thai and fried rice are both good options for me. I need to avoid gluten," I answer as he takes out and opens box after box.

"Avoid or eliminate? Are you celiac?"

"No, just avoid. I was diagnosed with an autoimmune disease recently. Apparently, gluten is the devil and I need to make it my bitch." I pull the plates out of the cupboard while trying not to stare at him too much. He's big and takes up a lot of space. And air. And attention. I can't help but trace the lines of his body, taking in his casual outfit. It's my job, after all. "Did you just roll out of a workout, or do you always dress down for dinner with…whatever the hell we are?"

"I came straight from practice." He chuckles. "What autoimmune?"

"Hashimoto's. It's a thyroid thing," I say, and Gavin stops unpacking food and turns to me. "What?"

"Shh." His hand comes to rest on my collarbone, his thumb at the base of my throat. Slowly, he moves it up, stretching my neck taller, forcing me to look up at him while he studies the column he fingers. Gavin's tall, six feet or more. I'd forgotten. Or it's something I repressed, like the feel of his touch and what it always made me feel.

"You can't see my disease," I snark.

"I can see if it looks enlarged," he murmurs. "How are you coping with it?"

"I have my good days and bad," I say, blinking a few times, confused by the tender voice and the heated touch. "I was having more bad than good before I made the move here."

"Were you living too fast, Odette?" His voice is nearly a whisper when he leans down and settles the question in my ear. Blood pools in places it shouldn't, and I hate my body for it. I battle it enough with my disease; I don't need to fight sexual urges on top of it.

"Yes, and it was fucking delicious," I purr, stepping back from his body heat.

"But you're paying for it now."

"Everything decadent catches up to us at some point, Vaughn."

"I hope that's true," he says, piercing me with his light eyes—a contrast with his dark hair and the light scruff at his jaw. I don't think we're talking about the same thing, though. Or maybe we are, but our perspectives are worlds apart.

My stomach makes another low rumble, and Gavin grins.

"Sorry," I say, rolling my eyes.

"How often do you eat? You're so thin."

"I work in fashion," I remind him with a raised brow.

"Doesn't mean you should waste away. It can't be good for you."

A busy schedule and societal pressure have a way of taking a toll. For years, I only ate one meal a day, typically dinner with friends or clients, accompanied by booze or wine. Yeah, that kept me slim enough to fit into all the great fashion but at a price.

"I'm working on that."

"Maybe I can help," he says, going back to the food and distributing portions on each plate.

"I'm still not getting on ice skates, so I don't see how you could be of any benefit." It was something he'd tried to get me to do several times. Each time he asked, I'd laugh it off. Athleticism isn't in my wheelhouse.

"My whole career depends on me being healthy and in shape, smartass. I know a thing or two about healthy weight gain."

"Why would you help me? We aren't friends."

"We were once," he says, his eyebrows dipping together.

"We were never friends, Gavin." He finishes plating food without responding. "What would you like to drink?"

"Just water, please," he says, so I fill up two glasses and motion my head toward the living room. The dining room is large and formal, and I think it will only add to the awkwardness of this night. He follows me but stops when he sees the television. "Are you playing *Animal Crossing*?"

Clearly, he's trying to hold back his laugh, his shoulders bunched as he tightly holds on to the plates.

"Fuck you, Vaughn. It was your daughter who suggested it."

"Did she now?"

"Yes. I needed a relaxing hobby and she said this was all about decorating homes and collecting clothes," I huff, dropping the glasses on the coffee table and taking my plate from him.

"So, right up your alley," he teases.

"Your mouth would be better full of food," I mumble as I switch the television to a local station. We eat in a strange silence for a few minutes. Why is he here? What's the end game?

If he wants a second chance, I'm probably the wrong woman for that. I don't even give most men a second night. It's never worth it.

While I may not hold grudges, I learn my lessons with people. That whole "fool me once" thing is a good motto and I live by it.

"Just say it, Ode. Whatever you're thinking."

Ode.

He used to call me that in more intimate moments. My heart clenches, but it's in a different way now than how it affected me then.

"What do you want, Gavin? Why are you here?"

"I told you already. I want to catch up. Our past wasn't something I wanted to bring up tonight, but if that's where you want to start, we can," he says casually. As if this is normal dinner conversation for him.

I like to think I read people pretty well, but this man confounds me with his level of ego and confidence. Maybe it's a hockey player thing. I wouldn't know, as I've never known another one besides him.

"We said all we needed to say on that subject twenty years ago," I say, looking directly at him.

"I disagree."

"Why?"

"So, you do want to talk about it?" he asks between bites of Pad See Ew.

"No."

"Then I'll wait to say it until you're ready to hear it. Until then, I'm offering a friendship, Odette."

"Can I decline your offer?" We both realize I'm avoiding whatever he was alluding to, but like I said, I don't want to talk about how I fell in love with him, only to watch him marry someone else.

"You can fucking try," he says, his voice low and guttural. I shouldn't find it sexy, but damn it, I do. "Why didn't you ever start your own line? Or fashion house? I'm not sure what to call it. But why did you head into styling instead?"

He's back to casual in a flash, as if he didn't nearly growl at me a second ago.

"It was easier to get a job as a stylist. New York is expensive, and money mattered. I thought design could come later, when I was making a decent living. But I fell in love with styling. It allowed me to be more creative because I was working with different personalities and body types. Designers are too often pressured to create for certain sizes, or lifestyles, and limited to one cohesive collection per season. I wanted something different. Besides, I still design, they're just very limited runs," I tell him. It's the question I'm asked most. I've spewed this answer so many times over the years, it feels almost rehearsed.

"That makes sense. You always were ridiculously creative," he says, taking his last bite and setting his plate down. "I knew you'd succeed at whatever you did. Never would have dreamed you'd leave New York, though."

Is that part of the reason he chose her over me? Because she'd follow him, and he thought I wouldn't?

No. No, that's not right. It was because of Tori. I *know* this.

"Tori is wonderful, by the way," I say, diverting the conversation from myself. "She's sweet, spunky, and so talented. You two raised her well."

I should get bonus points in the form of a chocolate chip cookie, gluten free, of course, for saying something nice to him. It's not like I hate him, but I didn't sign up for him to be in my living room comfortably eating dinner, either.

"Thank you," he says. "Though, Caroline gets most of that credit. I was gone so much with hockey; I feel like I missed a lot."

"She's just as much you," I say before I can catch myself.

"How would you know? We aren't friends, right?"

"You're right," I say, standing to collect both plates. He stands, too, and follows me to the kitchen. "I thought I knew you once, but that wasn't the truth."

"Odette." Gavin traps me as I drop the plates into the sink. He cages me on either side. "You did know me. It wasn't a lie. The me you knew, was the most honest I ever was."

"I don't." My voice catches on the rest of the words, fingers tightening on the edge of the sink. I don't want to talk about it, but mostly, I don't want to remember. The cuts, the hurt, the scars…

"I know. I'm sorry," he whispers into my hair. "Upsetting you wasn't the plan. I just want to be in your world, Ode. However you'll let me. I'm fighting for it. This time, I'm fighting for it."

8

GAVIN

"**F**uck, Wylder. Take it easy on me, I'm old."

"You're ancient, but we both know you can take it," Cillian says, shoving me once more before skating away.

Tomorrow night is the home opening game of my last season, making today, officially, my final offseason practice. Technically, skate is over, but some of us stayed on the ice for a friendly scrimmage. Coach watches with an eagle eye from the other side of the boards, ensuring we don't get too carried away. The last thing we need is an injury before the season even starts.

This isn't how we usually blow off steam or jitters or excess energy, but our goalie, Blom, wanted more time on the ice today. Instead of handing him over to the trainers and coaches, we took it upon ourselves.

Things feel different this year, like we've found a new sense of solidarity in ourselves. Last season ended with some drama around our rookie's sexuality. The team rallied around him and we're better for it. We're a cohesive unit now, an actual team rather than a bunch of bucket heads who just happen to wear the same logo.

I steal the puck from Lehtinen and quickly glide down the ice, taking a shot on Blom. He blocks it and laughs like the maniac he is as I skate around the net. Goalies are weird as fuck, ours is no exception. But we all love the guy and he'd be the first to jump in and defend any of us. If all that padding didn't get in the way, anyhow.

We get another ten minutes before Coach Cole calls it, telling us all to get the fuck off the ice and enjoy our last night. But not too much.

Every player has different rituals and superstitions. Some won't have sex the day of a game, while others will. Some won't have it the day before, either. I played with one guy who wouldn't eat meat from season start to end. My quirks have never centered on sex or food. Though I do tap my stick twice on the ice every time I go into warmups. It's dumb, but I've done it since peewee hockey, so I'm not going to stop now.

I do like having someone in the stands on opening night. Whether it be a home or an away game, it connects me, knowing there is someone there *for me*. Tori will be here tomorrow, just as she was last season. But I wish another dark-haired woman would be sitting with her.

I fucked that up last night. Odette's cell phone had been sitting on the coffee table while we ate. While she didn't notice the text that came through, I saw it when the preview flashed on her screen. That stuffy dude from her party said he was excited to see her Friday night.

Should I have paid that much attention to it? Nah. But it was right fucking there. And because of that, I snarked at her, and she went even further into offensive mode.

Odette fucks with my head, but no more than I fuck with it myself. After her party, I got the idea that the universe was giving me a second chance. I'd planned on last night to be light and casual, then I was going to ask her to come to my game on Friday.

Instead, I acted like a twat and upset her. She wouldn't even exchange phone numbers with me. She's so stubborn, and fuck if that doesn't turn me upside down.

Last weekend, she was elegant and classy, taking care of her guests with a charming smile. Last night, she was more the Odette I remember, a little reserved, as if she couldn't read the situation. I made her nervous and she lost the shell she wears for everyone else.

That means something. I know it does, she can't deny it.

But I'm an idiot with no experience on how to charm any woman, let alone one like Odette Quinn. We aren't shithead teenagers anymore.

"What's up with you, Vaughn?" Fane asks.

"What do you mean?" I almost call him rookie, but he isn't that. This is Zander's second season and he more than proved himself worthy of the team last year. Kid has more guts than most and enough talent to back it up.

"You've looked like you need to take a shit all practice. You're very scowly."

"Scowly isn't a word," I say, laughing.

"Words weren't words until someone invented them," he says with a shrug. "I'm inventing this one, just for your face. What gives? Tori okay?"

"She's great." I sigh as I sit, unlacing my skates. "It's me, I'm the problem."

Blom starts singing from a few lockers over. Wylder throws a towel at him, trying to get him to shut up.

"What do you mean?" Zan takes the bench next to me, starting to strip out of his own gear.

"I don't know how to date," I finally admit to an uproar of laughter. "Fuck off, the lot of you. Especially you, Cillian, your history with women is downright abysmal."

"That's the fucking truth," Coach says as he walks through. Cillian is married to our coach's oldest daughter, but it was a rough history. Weirdly enough, Zander is in a relationship with his other daughter. I play with some brave-ass motherfuckers. Never in my life would I have dreamed of dating a coach's kid. But Cole is one-of-a-kind, for sure.

"Yeah, yeah," Cillian says. "I fixed it, though. Figured my shit out."

"How did you manage that, anyway? She didn't talk to you for, what? Five years?" I ask. Isla, his wife, broke up with him when she found out he was getting "friendly" with a psycho who used to work for the team that drafted him into the NHL. Still, she eventually forgave him. But they had years together before he fucked up, while I only had weeks with Odette. "Mine hasn't spoken to me in twenty."

"What the fuck, man?" Blom asks. "You been hung up on some bird since childhood?"

"Something like that." I nod. "She and I were together for a little while after Caroline and I broke up. Then my ex-wife found out she was pregnant."

"Dude," Zander says.

"Oh, shit," Cillian chimes in. "You broke it off with her and married Caroline?"

"Yeah," I confirm. "Caroline was giving up an education to keep the baby. I thought it was the right decision. I don't regret that."

"But you've been missing this other woman for all these years?" Zander asks.

"Fuck, I love a good love story where one is pining away for the other. You're like Jane Eyre or some shit," Lehtinen says.

"How the hell does a neanderthal like you know anything about Jane Eyre?" Blom asks him.

"I watch movies like the rest of you! I just don't stick to action and sci-fi. I like drama, too. I'm a sophisticated man." The whole locker room laughs at that.

"Pining might not be the right word. But I've thought about her a lot. She just moved to Seattle."

"She single?" Blom asks.

"Yeah, that's not really the problem. I mean, I think she might be dating some guy, but she just got here, so it's too new for that to be a concern."

"What's the issue then?" Zan asks. "She hate you?"

"Maybe not hate but strong dislike. Or distrust." Both, most likely. And I deserve that, but we're different people now, in different circumstances. I'm not the one who needs convincing of that, though, she is.

"You need to grovel," Lehtinen says.

"He shouldn't have to grovel for choosing his child," Cillian says, the dad in him taking over. "But you're definitely going to have to pull something swoony out of your ass."

"You're an NHL player, it shouldn't be that hard," Blom adds.

"You'd think that, but not with this woman. She's way more famous than me, man."

"Who is she?" Zander looks at me with renewed interest. All the guys do, but he's the one who asks the question.

"Odette Quinn. She's a big name in the fashion industry."

"Fuck off," Lehtinen says. "You know Odette Quinn?"

"How do *you* know her?" I ask, surprised. As well-known as she is, I didn't expect any of these guys to recognize her name.

"She's often a guest judge on that modeling show."

"Who are you?" Blom asks him, just as surprised as the rest of us that he watches model reality television.

"Hey, I'm the smart one in the room," he argues. "You all spend time watching men get sweaty and bloody, while I watch beautiful women. Dumb motherfuckers." Nobody has an argument for that. Letty is our class clown, our goon. He doesn't let you see much past that, but maybe the guy isn't quite what we all think.

"If you haven't talked to her in twenty years, how do you know you want a second chance?" Leave it to the youngest in the room, Zander, to be the wisest of us all.

"Saw her last weekend," I tell him. "Everything about her has changed but she still felt so familiar. Like, I remembered how she smelled, and it felt like coming home. Brought dinner to her house last night and the chemistry is still there, even though she fights it."

"If she is already letting you bring dinner over, then what are you worried about?" Cillian asks.

"She didn't let me, per se."

"Dude's taking the heavy-handed approach," Blom says, laughing.

"Sometimes that's all you can do," Cillian says. He'd probably know. From what I know of his situation with Isla, she, too, was reluctant to give him the time of day. But he shared more than a sordid past with her—they also shared a child.

That's something I need to be careful of, too. I don't want to complicate anything for Tori and her mentor.

"You want my help, buddy? I'd be more than happy to go to her house and put in a good word for you."

"You can stay the fuck away from her, Letty."

"Hey, man, just offering help," he says, holding his hands out in innocence. All while wearing the biggest shit-eating grin I've ever seen.

"No, man. I'll go. All the ladies love goalies," Blom chimes in.

"Lies," several of the guys say in unison.

"She didn't kick you out when you showed up with food?" Zander asks, bringing us back to the topic at hand. I should have known better than to bring this up with all the chuckleheads, but honestly, I don't really have anyone else to go to. I could call Caroline, but I've purposely been trying to keep boundaries there.

I still think of her as my best friend, but if we're going to move on, we can't be the first person either of us run to. That won't work for future relationships.

"No, but I think I just caught her when she was hungry."

"Doesn't matter, she let you stay," Cillian says. "That's something. If she hated you, she'd have at least made you leave."

"Or called the cops on you. That's what I'd have done if it was me," Blom adds with a wink.

"Ah, thanks, buddy. Love you, too."

"I could give you the same advice these meatheads gave me when Isla was consuming me. Grand fucking gestures."

"Is that what worked with Isla?"

"Nah, that's not really her thing. I chipped away at her by constantly putting myself in her way and making sure she could see I wasn't the same dumbfuck she'd dumped all those years before," Cillian says. "If you broke her heart, she's scared you'll do it again."

We played a great game. The fans will be more excited for the rest of the season because of it. It felt great to be back on the ice in competition.

So why am I at home alone, acting like a sad sack of shit?

Because I sent two tickets for the game to Odette's house, only for her to give them to her friends, Vanessa and George. They told Tori that Odette was on a date and didn't want the tickets to go to waste.

A date.

A motherfucking date.

With another guy.

I showered at the arena, but I strip down again anyway, stepping into the steam and letting the hot water work at the internal tension. She's fucking with me. Not intentionally, but she is all the same.

It's not different than when we were young, and I'd steal looks at her every chance I got. There were so many days when I thought I should be with her instead of Caroline. High school pressure and expectations from our families got in the way. Everyone saw us as the "it couple" and we went with it. But it was Odette I fantasized about.

My mind plays back that night at her house, her standing at her sink in that flowy short dress. I tried not to be obvious in my ogling then, but now, I can appreciate her long legs. Toned with just a hint of sun-kissed glow. She was barefoot, toes painted a shade that matched her dress. Her hair pulled up in some intricate knot.

If things had been different, I'd have tangled my fingers in it and pulled it loose to flow down her back. Then I'd have slowly pulled her dress up and panties down with a soft touch that would drive her crazy, to keep her on the edge between titillating and tickling.

She'd have leaned in with her ass, bowing her back as she gripped the sink and widened her legs to give me the access I'd need to bury my face in her cunt and lay out every apology there.

I'd have made her come the first time like that. The same way I made her come for the first time when we were younger.

Fuck, I remember everything about her then. I remember more about her than I do most parts of my own life. How she tasted, how she sighed in pleasure, and groaned in release. How I always left her trembling and out of breath. So bold and unashamed with sex, even then.

I would have turned her around then, lifted her onto the counter to fuck her face-to-face. Eye to eye, equals in our need for each other. I'd have ripped that flowery dress right off her, had her bare before me when I thrust in the first time. She'd have pulled at my hair to keep my face close, her heels digging in to my ass as she wrapped them tightly around me.

My hand tries to imitate the pressure of her pussy, but it can't, so I dive deeper into my made-up vision. Odette's head thrown back, her neck there for me to nibble and suck. Fuck, I'd sink my teeth in as deep as my cock, pinning her to me.

We'd have come together, her name on my lips and only mine on hers.

I come in my hand at the thought of her stuffy, professor boyfriend watching as I make her come harder than he ever fucking could.

9

ODETTE

Mundane.

That's how I'd describe sex with Preston. Dull somehow feels more insulting. Mundane has a more romantic flare to it.

Either way, that's what it was. He's a nice man. Too nice, too sweet and gentle. We could be great friends; he'd be an exceptional one, I think. He's interesting, intelligent, curious about the world.

"So, it's not a love match?" Vanessa asks. We're having brunch together, along with George, since he leaves tomorrow for another business trip.

"What *is* love, darling?"

"By definition," George answers, "an intense feeling of deep affection, or great pleasure in something."

"Then, no. It's not a love match," I confirm. "The pleasure was good, at best."

George laughs, while Vanessa only looks concerned.

"He can learn to be a better lover," she says.

"He's forty-two, and not my student."

She laughs. "I'm aware. But he's been married since he was twenty. Perhaps he didn't have the opportunity to learn. His wife is very reserved."

"You've met her?"

"A few times, she's quiet. Timid, even."

"My exact opposite."

"Sounds like it," George says. "If he couldn't let loose with you, he might be a lost cause."

"Whose side are you on?" Vanessa asks him.

"Odette's," he answers. "I want her to find her match just as much as you do, my love. We only disagree on who that may be."

"Who would you suggest?" I ask him, curious as to why either of them puts any thought into my lack of love life. They weren't always like this, but they see the changes I'm trying to make, and I think they believe that means I must be ready for love. I'm not as convinced as they are.

"Well, Vanessa would line up an endless array of scholars and intellectuals. I, on the other hand, would lean toward a more rugged type. Someone good with their hands, not just their mind. Someone who would challenge you, make you brave."

"I *am* brave," I challenge, pointing my fork at him as if to threaten him to say it again.

"In so many ways, yes," he agrees. "But you aren't brave enough to be vulnerable again. Preston doesn't strike me as the man who can encourage that out of you. He's more mouse to your cat, a plaything. A game."

"Aren't they all," I tease. I do treat the men in my life like toys. And like a toddler, I get bored with them so easily. None get to know me, none break through my shell.

Not since *him*.

"Someone more like that hockey player friend of yours," George suggests like he's reading my thoughts.

"Gavin isn't a friend."

"What is he then," Vanessa asks. "Besides the boy who once broke your heart."

Vanessa knows my history, thanks to our first drunken night together in college. I spilled it all and swore her to never speak of it again.

"A memory."

"A bad one?" George asks.

"A bittersweet one," I clarify. "A beautiful one, followed by a sorrowful one." I could never regret those days with Gavin. I've tried, but I can't. New love…no, *first* love is an amazing thing.

"You loved him," George states.

"I thought so at the time. But I didn't know anything more about love then than I do now."

"Because you don't let yourself," Vanessa says. "I'm sorry, I don't mean to push. If I didn't see the things you don't, I wouldn't."

"What does that mean? What do you see?"

"We both see you desperately searching for changes," George answers. "But I also saw the way you looked at him when you thought no one was looking. And I saw him doing the same."

"Curiosity is what you saw. It means nothing. We don't know each other anymore."

"Maybe you shouldn't waste the opportunity to get to know him then. What's the harm?" Vanessa asks with that same concerned look.

Another broken heart, I answer her in my head.

"This is good, Drake. But be mindful of adding too much here," I say, gesturing to the floral applique at the hip of the dress. "You don't want it to distract from the silhouette."

Drake steps back to analyze his design, I stand next to him, waiting for his conclusion. I've made it clear that while I make suggestions, they are in no way obligated to take them. My opinions are to provoke thought, nothing more. These students have loud voices, they need support, not influence.

"It's adding too much bulk," he finally says. "It will make her hips wider. If I move it up and turn it..." He unpins the applique and adjusts it to a position farther up. "Here, it will accentuate the waist."

"Well done," I tell him and move on through the workroom. Mostly, the students in their first year aren't designing for class. Their coursework is more on learning sewing skills or patterning, along with fashion history and the like. But the workroom is a free space for them to come and work out their creative needs in between or after class. My office is just down the hall, so I spend a lot of time here. Even if there is only one student here. Today, there are four, including Tori, who just walked in with a big bag.

"What do you have there?" I ask.

"A new haul from the thrift store," she says, excitedly dumping the items onto her station.

"I hope you don't mind me watching the process?"

"Not at all," she says.

"Glad I don't make you nervous."

"Well, I didn't say that." She laughs. "I'm here to learn, though, and you have the best eye."

"You flatter me, Ms. Vaughn. Talk me through the process?"

"Sure."

She lays each piece out, pointing out what attracted her to every one. One is the color, one is the quality of the denim, one is the art deco-style print. There are a dozen different pieces as she starts to rip stitches and make cuts. She doesn't discard anything, just sets the scraps aside for "future projects" she says.

Two hours pass like minutes, and she has three new garments laid out and patterned. I'm not the only spectator anymore, either. Benji and Drake have both pulled up stools next to me.

"That was fucking impressive," Benji says.

"Agree," Drake chimes in.

"Did you envision these pieces while you were shopping or while you were laying out the garments here?" I ask her.

"I usually get an idea when I see something at the store. Half the time, it morphs into something else when I start to rip everything apart," she says, surveying her work. She picks up one of the discarded scraps, holding it up for us. "I already have several ideas for this."

The guys make more remarks, further boosting her confidence, before they leave the workroom.

"You know, that one is my size," I tell her, pointing to a mini dress she has laid out with the denim and two different prints, hinting that I'd wear it. It's not a lie, I would wear it proudly.

"Dad says you're too thin," she blurts. She immediately regrets it, looking appalled at herself. "Oh my god, I'm so sorry."

"It's fine." I laugh. "He said the same thing to me."

It's been a couple of weeks since Gavin showed up at my door with dinner. That hasn't stopped him from reminding me he's around, though. Like clockwork, every three days, a new floral arrangement is delivered to my house. Each one accompanied by a note signed with his name and his phone number.

Each one asks a question, too. They aren't to ask me out, instead, he's trying to provoke conversation. He's trying to get me to answer. So, he asks silly things like what animal I would choose to be if I could shapeshift. It's all quite ridiculous and I haven't answered any of them yet, but he still tries.

"I think he misses you," she says. "I hope it's okay for me to say that, and that I'm not crossing some line. But I think he misses you as a friend. He says you're the most interesting person he's ever known."

What do I say to that? I don't know how much Tori knows of the situation with me and her father.

"That's sweet of him," I tell her, going for a neutral response.

"I get why you'd be reluctant. He does, too. But he's determined. Just so you know," she says. "He's really going to try to…I don't know, be a better person to you this time."

"He doesn't have to," I start to say.

"I know, but he thinks he does," she insists. "How things happened with you? That's his biggest regret. Maybe he just wants to know the woman you've become despite it all. I can tell him to stop, if you want me to. He'll respect that."

"You don't have to do that," I say. "You've got enough on your plate here making these fantastic garments. Stay focused."

"Will do," she says, easily dropping the subject. I get the feeling she wants to encourage me without pressuring me. Much like Vanessa and George.

I don't know how my love life has become such a hot topic. They all come from a place of well meaning, so I'm not holding it against anyone, but I'd be happy enough if it would simmer down.

There's only one thing to do in moments like this.

Shop.

That's exactly what I do. I forgo all the big designer names and scour the internet for the best boutiques in Seattle. All my spare time here has been shopping for home goods and furnishings. I haven't bought any new clothes in far too long. My friends in New York would hardly recognize me.

The first shop is owned by a woman in her sixties. She's had the store since 1988. She curates its eclectic collection herself, bringing items in from all over the world. The next is a lingerie store owned by a couple that hand makes all the products in the back of their store. They show me around, and I end up buying way more underwear than a single woman could need.

After that is a jewelry store, then a local handbag designer, before a few more clothing stores. I don't leave a single shop without purchasing something beautiful. Like everything I've been buying for the house, these items all inspire something in me.

Tori did that for me today, too. Watching her work makes me miss the days when I created in a similar way. She's better at it than me, much better.

So much more talented. She'll go far, and I'll be proud to have played a small part in her success.

The conversation with her plays in my mind throughout my shopping spree, and at some point, I decide to send a text. Maybe what Vanessa says is true. I'm here in Seattle making big changes with my career and for my health. Why stop there? Why not make some changes with the way I treat men and sex?

Sometimes a lady wants to be fucked without putting a lot of work into finding a guy.

A new arrangement might be exactly what I need. I won't know until I try, anyway.

I arrive home to another bouquet. It's large, like they've all been. Unlike the rest, this one is made up of dark florals. Blacks and purples with soft dark greenery. There's a card attached, of course, but I don't open it. Tonight, it doesn't matter what question Gavin has for me.

Noting the time, I take my bags to my room, dropping them in my closet and pulling out some of the new lingerie. I take a quick shower before donning it and covering it with a dressing gown that was gifted to me by one of the men that once proposed.

Stephen was the type of man who always got what he wanted. He thought he wanted me, but I suspect it was only because I didn't want to keep him. He was an excellent gift giver, though, and it would have been rude to send back such beautiful things like this.

The knock on the door comes just as I walk down the stairs. I open it to his smiling face.

"I was surprised you texted," he says.

"I should have sooner. I've just been busy."

"Understandable. Honestly, I didn't think you were going to give me a second chance," he says. "What made you change your mind?"

"Memories," I say. He looks confused but doesn't ask. "Come on in, Preston."

10
GAVIN
THEN

I've been spoiled in my life. My family, while not wealthy, has always been comfortable. My parents are kind, caring, and always treat me with the same respect they expect in return. Every dream I've ever had has been met by nothing but support from them. I was born with a talent I can only take so much credit for. Sure, I've put the work into hockey, but so much of it has come naturally.

School has never been hard. I'm not a genius, but I'm smart enough that nothing has been particularly challenging. I'm surrounded by friends and never lack for something to do or people to do it with.

All that aside, I feel like I've won some kind of lottery by dating Odette.

We've been together for weeks now. There haven't been any labels or declarations made, but I think of her as my girlfriend. She's mine. Just as I'm hers.

Everything about us is different than the relationship I had with Caroline. It's exciting instead of comfortable. She makes me think differently because we're so different and our circles have never really collided.

Each morning, I wake up eager to talk to her and antsy to see her. It's not how I've ever felt about Caroline. My adoration for my ex-girlfriend slash best friend is different on every level. We grew up together, there isn't anything we don't know about each other.

Odette is like getting a present every day and being continually surprised by what is inside the box.

While I love that for her and I, it also makes me feel some kind of remorse for all three of us. Caroline could have had this with someone else, and Odette and I could have had this earlier.

But it is what it is, and I'm not trying to look at the past. We have big futures ahead to focus on. I want Odette to be a part of that. Besides hockey, I've never been so confident in anything. That's probably stupid, we're both so young and this has just started. But I know how I feel. Even if I'm not sure she feels the same.

We've gone out a lot these past weeks. I've taken her to dinner more nights than not, we've been to movies, we've picnicked. I can't get her to ice-skate or hike with me; her refusal always makes me laugh because she says she's "not that kind of girl", as if I'm asking her to let me bang her in public or something.

Tonight, I'm going to push her boundaries some and take her camping. But, like, fancy camping. It's only one night; she'll survive and not hate me for it. In fact, I'm banking on her loving it.

Fuck, I hope she loves it.

"Wake up, baby. We're here," I say, when we finally arrive. The drive was a few hours to get just outside of the city. A hockey friend of mine lives here and he has private roof access which overlooks Manhattan across the river. I thumb her temple, and she sighs as a smile grows. She hasn't opened her eyes yet, though. "You were sleepy."

"Somebody has been interrupting my beauty sleep," she says, slowly waking up and looking out the window. "Where are we?"

"Weehawken."

"Why?" she asks, laughing. And yeah, this is why I left it as a surprise. Weehawken isn't exactly a big destination city.

"You'll see," I tell her, leaning over to press a kiss to her cheek. "Don't judge just yet."

"No judgment, but maybe some shock and awe," she says. "Weehawken, New Jersey, for a date night is definitely a choice."

"Trust me," I say when I rush around to the passenger side and open the door for her.

"I do," she says, her eyes shining with what I think is honesty. I stare down at her in a silent vow that I feel the same.

This isn't something she does easily, the whole trusting someone. I caught on to that early enough. She keeps her cards close to her chest. It's not from any past trauma, we've had conversations about that, and she doesn't have any, she's just cautious with herself. She's a planner, things that veer away from that plan put her guard up.

Things like me. I'm chipping away at it little by little, though. Her trusting me feels like a huge step.

"Come on then," I say, grabbing both of our overnight bags with one hand and tangling my fingers with hers to lead her into Jack's building. It's a walk up and she's throwing me side eyes by the time we get to the fifth floor. Odette doesn't voice her complaints, and again, it makes me laugh.

"Are you laughing at me?"

"Nope, I wouldn't dream of it."

"I'm on to you, Vaughn."

"I hope so, Quinn," I say, slow and quiet. Jack opens the door when I knock, and after a quick introduction, he points to the stairs. Odette's still looking confused, but as soon as we walk out on the roof, her face morphs to surprise.

He found me a company that set up a big white canvas tent furnished with an actual bed and some cozy sack chairs and string lights everywhere. They catered food and left a cooler. We're set up with anything we could need.

"Gavin."

"I know you aren't the camping type, but this is only barely camping."

"It's perfect. Really."

"I thought it would be cool to watch the sun set on the city that you're going to be calling home soon. The one you're going to take by storm," I tell her, taking a seat in one of the chairs and pulling her down on my lap.

"You think I will?" She stares out across the river. It's quieter here, but I think we both imagine the noise there. The people, the cabs, the life, it's much more than what we've grown up with.

"I know you will. They're all going to fall at your feet, Odette," I say. "As they fucking should."

"You're very confident in me," she says, turning in my lap to see me better. "I like it."

"I like you," I say, though other words form in my head. Words I'm not sure she's ready to hear, or I'm ready to say. It sits on the tip of my tongue, though. Not heavy, but making its presence known.

"I like you, too, Gavin." She snuggles down into my chest. "You're special. Do you know that? Has anyone ever told you?"

"Coaches have."

"I don't mean just hockey," she says, placing a hand over my heart. "It's more than that. You're more than just that."

My breath hitches, because no, nobody has ever said anything like this to me. That word wants to slip out even more, but I swallow it down with the emotion she evokes and instead tighten my arms around her.

"You're more than just your dreams, too, Ode. You're thoughtful and kind, but tough and honest, too. My mom would call you an old soul."

"I like your mom," she says.

"She likes you, too," I say, showing some of my own honesty but keeping out the fact that both my mother and Caroline's were upset by our breakup. They've been friends since they were teenagers. I think they always had this grand plan for our families. Maybe I went along with it, in part, to try and keep my mom happy. I know now that nothing I can do will help, and it isn't my responsibility.

"She's going to be very sad when you leave for school."

"She will," I agree. "But at least I'll be close. I had opportunities all over the country and considered one farther west. That would have been trickier; she doesn't like long flights."

"And I'll be there," she says, looking at the horizon as daylight starts to fade and the lights of the city start to shine.

"Living your best life and maybe visiting me on the occasional weekend."

"You sure you'll have time for that in between all the puck bunnies?"

"Are you jealous of these nonexistent women, Quinn?" I ask her, thumbing her chin to make her look at me.

"I don't do jealous, Gavin. I'm not that—"

"Type of girl," I finish for her. "I know."

"I guess I'm just saying that I know it might not be as easy for you as it will be for me when we're apart."

"Why do you think that?"

"Because you're a hotshot jock with huge prospects. You'll always have women throwing themselves at you. It won't be the same for me, that's all."

"You don't think I would be faithful?" While I understand what she's saying, I don't think I've done anything that would give her the impression that I wouldn't, or couldn't, stay true to her.

"Well, we've never actually defined that we're a couple or anything, for one. Secondly, of course I think you would be faithful to me, if that's what we decide we're doing. I'm asking if that's what we're doing," she says. "Are we?"

"I want that," I say, resting my forehead on hers. "In my heart, we're already there."

"You're sure?"

"Never been more sure of anything in my life."

———

"We need to talk," Caroline says when I answer the door.

We haven't spoken much since our breakup, a stark departure from, well, really, our whole lives. She and I both thought it was best to try and sever the ties some. Of course, we still want to be friends. But we don't need to be attached at the hip going into the next stage of our lives.

"Sure, come on in," I say, examining her red, puffy eyes. "What's wrong?"

"Are your parents home?"

"No, not for another hour or so. What's going on, Caroline?"

She walks past me into our living room and falls into the corner of the sofa. Immediately, she covers her face and starts sobbing.

"Caroline? What the fuck?" I kneel, trying to wrap my arms around her to console her. My first thought is that someone hurt her. My second is that I might get brought up on charges if they did.

"I'm so sorry, Gav. I don't know how it happened," she says through hiccupping cries.

"What's happened?"

She wipes at her cheeks and eyes, eventually lowering her hands to her lap.

"You've been getting close to Odette. Spending a lot of time with her?"

"Yeah," I hedge. I'm not sure what she could have to do with anything that would make Caroline cry like this. "Why?"

"Do you love her?"

"I'm not sure. It's early still. I like her a lot, definitely."

"I thought so. I could tell the last time we talked."

"What does this have to do with me and Odette?"

"I don't want to make things harder for you," she says quietly, her fingers visibly shaking.

"Caroline, tell me."

Sometimes, I think if we pay enough attention to what's going on around us, we can see the world giving us warnings. Like, the air around you changes when you're about to be thrown on your head. It's not like a lightning strike, it's quiet and subtle, but I believe it when people say they felt the sudden dread. I feel it now, like my whole life is going to change by whatever Caroline is about to say.

"I'm pregnant, Gav. And I'm keeping it."

Surely, I didn't hear that right. The blood pounding in my ears must have distorted her words. She can't be pregnant since we've always been so careful.

"Repeat that," I say.

"I'm pregnant. Four months along. And I'm sorry that this is happening right now."

"It's not your fault," I say, my voice feeling far away. Or maybe it's my voice here in the room with her, but my body and soul are somewhere else. Floating above us, watching as our lives change irrevocably. "It's not something you could have done on your own."

"No," she says, laughing a little but in that nervous way we use humor to mask our real emotions. "Sit, let's talk it out."

Caroline pats the cushion next to her, and I join her.

"Fuck, Caroline."

"I know." She sighs. "It had to be that last time. Isn't that just the craziest kind of luck? I've known for a few weeks, but I wasn't sure what I wanted to do. It's a big decision and I didn't want to rush it."

"No, I wouldn't want you to, either," I say, still shocked by all this. "What about school?"

"I'm not going." Her answer comes quickly but there isn't any sadness with it.

"You're sure?"

"I've never been surer," she says, and it reminds me of what I said to Odette only last night.

This is why Caroline asked about her. Because how do I start a relationship that already had so many obstacles in front of it, when I'm about to be a father with another woman? How am I even supposed to navigate college and hockey through all this? It's not going to be easy living in Boston for the school year and having a baby here in upstate New York, let alone a girlfriend in the City.

My focus was supposed to be school and the sport. Odette was going to be the prize in my free time, but now, I'll be prioritizing differently, and she'll be left where? As an afterthought? She's not somebody you put at the bottom of your list.

"Fuck," I say, leaning my head back against the cushion and staring up at the ceiling fan as it whirls as fast as my heartbeat. "I'll have to break it off with Odette. Won't I?"

"I don't know, Gav. I really don't know. I hate that for you, though, you know that, right?"

"And I hate that you're putting off college and a career." Caroline is smart, she always has been, it's come easy to her. She never struggled in school, every year ending it with a perfect four point. Cheerleading was the extracurricular she chose to help impress colleges because she wanted to have choices on where to go. I've never had any doubt that she'd be amazing at whatever she chose to do in life. "You're going to be a great mom."

"I know," she says, confident but still somehow sad. "It feels right. Keeping the baby? It feels right, like I'm meant to be this baby's mama. I don't want you to worry about that."

"I would never. I'm more worried about how I'm going to fit in."

We talk until my parents come home. Then we talk more, including them in the conversation. My mom cries with Caroline in her arms, while my dad, the more rational of us all, helps me work out plans. We painstakingly work through every angle like it's a hockey game rather than a pregnancy. I feel oddly detached from so much of it but, halfway through the night, I make a decision of my own.

Caroline made hers, and now, I've made mine. She agreed with it. Are either of us truly happy about it? Not entirely. But it isn't about just us now, we have a baby to think about. We're young and naïve, yet we know what's most important here. And that is giving this child a good life, filled with love and opportunities. We both had that. We still do. The proof is shown by how both our families are behind us now.

For better or worse.

11

GAVIN

I'm about to pop the bread loaf into the oven when the text chimes on my phone. It's an unknown number, of course, but I know who it is.

If I answer your last question, will you stop sending flowers, it reads.

ME:

If you continue to answer some by text,
then maybe I'll consider stopping.

ODETTE:

I'm not sure I can agree to that deal. I like
the flowers. Especially the dark ones.

Despite her now glamorous life, it seems she hasn't changed all that much. She's still playful and likes banter.

ME:

Is that a request?

ODETTE:

> No. They're beautiful, but you
> should stop. It won't work.

Except it already has, she's texting me. We're having a conversation. I have her number now.

ME:

> What won't work?

ODETTE:

> I'm not going to date you.

ME:

> I only asked for friendship. Out of curiosity,
> why wouldn't you date me? I'm one of
> Seattle's most eligible bachelors.

ODETTE:

> Which is exactly why I won't date you.

ME:

> Explain?

ODETTE:

> No, thank you.

ME:

> I'm making you something.

Maybe a change of subject will keep her talking.

ODETTE:

Why?

ME:

Because I'm thoughtful and helpful. A genuinely
nice guy. You should get to know me.

ODETTE:

Do I not already?

ME:

No. I don't know you, either. Not
anymore. We should change that.

She doesn't answer, and though I could take that as a bad sign, I don't. It's good that she didn't immediately dismiss the idea.

ME:

It's my teammate's birthday this week.
Party at his house on Saturday. Mostly
just teammates and their wags. Will you
go with me? Just friends, I promise. I can
introduce you to some more locals.

I'm not holding my breath that she'll say yes. I've thought of her as stubborn before, but I'm not sure that's quite right. It's more that she's confident in who she is and what she wants. She's not the type of woman who lets anything get in her way.

I guess that includes me. Can't say I don't deserve it, exactly. But I'm hoping we're beyond that now.

ODETTE:

Just friends, Gavin.

ME:

Just friends, Ode.

There's no telling what made her change her mind. I'm not going to question it because her agreeing to go with me feels a lot like winning the Stanley Cup.

ODETTE:

As for your last question. Edgar Allan Poe. I feel like he could use a hug.

I'd asked her if she could meet a dead historical figure, who it would be and why. If I'd bet on her answer, it would have been that it would be some famous fashion designer that I'd never heard of. That's the thing about Odette Quinn, she's always unexpected.

ME:

Good answer. I'll pick you up at six on Saturday, friend.

Dropping my phone to the counter, I go back to making my loaf of gluten-free bread. Caroline says the store-bought shit is trash and suggested I try making my own for Odette. We spoke a few days ago, after weeks of relative silence. Tori had told her about Odette and now she's just as eager as Tori to force me and my old crush back into each other's orbits.

No more eager than me, really. But Caroline has always carried some guilt over how things happened, despite me telling her none of it was her fault. I guess we both think we've stolen one another's happiness in some way. Tori makes up for it, so it doesn't really matter.

I want the same for her. She's closer to it than I am since she's met back up with the guy she met while we were married. It was obvious to me that she'd fallen in love with him then, so I'm glad they're getting their second chance now.

Even though his name is Brock, and I can't picture him as anything but a huge muscle head. Apparently, he owns a nursery. The plant kind, not the baby kind. Which Caroline loves; she's become earthy and spiritual the past few years. Looking back, I think she saw the shape of things before I did and took the proper steps to ensure she would come through it healthy and content. Whereas, I threw myself into work and ignored the fact that my life was going to change drastically when my kid graduated high school.

I always knew Caroline was smarter than me. I'm catching up now and can focus on both my last season as an NHL player, and seeing if whatever was between Odette and I may still be there.

The woman fucking confounds me. Something she said sticks with me while I watch the bread bake. I took particular care with this loaf, as the last three came out as hard as a hockey puck.

I feel very…domesticated. Oddly enough, I thought the guys would give me shit for this, but they didn't. They've been encouraging me, in fact. This one already looks better than the last, as it rises like a cloud above the pan.

Odette won't date me because I'm eligible. What the fuck does that even mean? Pulling up the search engine on my phone, I type in her name and the word boyfriend. Keeping tabs on her over the years, I never let myself explore too far into the men she was rumored to be with. I didn't want to know if she had found some great love with some rich or famous man.

Within seconds, I'm given a long list of headlines connecting Odette to various men of wealth or fame. Actors, entrepreneurs, a rock star, even an extended member of the British royal family, at one point. A person could look at this list and feel insecure about their own status.

I don't, though. I know what I have to offer. And I know, at one time, I meant something more to her than all these men she quickly moved on from. My aim is to have her remember that. To remember me, and us, and how amazing we were together.

Clicking through them one by one, I quickly find a common thread. Not all the men, but so many, are married. Estranged, or rumored to be in troubled marriages, a couple very recently divorced at the time they were spotted with Odette.

The minority of them are single and free.

What in the ever-loving hell?

Odette opens the door and every question I've wanted to ask her vanishes from my head. *We're just having a friendly outing.* I can't haul her over my shoulder and carry her to bed. Though that's all I fucking want to do, seeing her right now in her form-fitted skirt that lands just below her knees. A couple of inches of her stomach are bare below a fitted top of the same color. Dark plum that complements her skin, glowing and smooth and damned lickable.

I can't wait to peel her out of it…

"Hi, Gavin," she says, holding up a bottle. "I didn't know what was best to bring. Wine, bourbon, or these fantastic mini cupcakes I found the other day. I ordered fresh ones for today, but then thought I should ask you. Honestly, I don't know much about athletes' parties. Do you all even drink? Or eat sweets?"

"Wine, the wives will love it," I say, still perusing her body, taking in every curve. "How are you the one nervous?"

"I'm not," she starts to argue, then stops. "What do you mean? Why would you be nervous?"

"I wasn't before. But here I am trying to be friendly, and you open the door dressed in that."

"There is nothing wrong with what I'm wearing," she says with all the confidence she should have. She is the expert, after all, she knows what she's doing.

"Nothing at all," I confirm. "You're the most gorgeous thing I've ever seen. And now I have to take you to a party filled with dirty-minded hockey players."

"You're dramatic," she says with a sigh. "Has anyone ever told you that?"

"No. Never." I laugh. "I'm the most down to earth man I know."

"Doubtful," she says. "Is there anything I should know about these people?"

"These people?" I ask as I follow her around while she places the bottle of wine in some fancy bag and grabs her purse. "I'm not taking you to an island of pariahs."

"Dramatic," she accuses again. "I meant, are there subjects that shouldn't be spoken about or quirks I should know about. I hear goalies are unique. Is it okay to look him in the eye?"

"Now who's being dramatic? Of course, you can look Hugo in the eye. But only the left." I wink at her, and she can't help the smile that grows. "Barring walking in there and declaring you're a Vancouver Canucks fan, any subject that comes up should be safe."

"Considering I don't know what that is, it shouldn't be a problem."

"You wound me, Odette," I say, this time purposely being theatrical and pressing a hand to my chest. "You know so many famous people, how have you never rubbed noses with pro athletes?"

"I've met a few. Worked with a baseball player's wife once. That just isn't the world I've been in, though. Today will be good at widening my circle," she answers, as I load her into my car, trying not to let my hand linger on the smooth skin at the small of her back.

"Is that why you said yes?" I ask when I'm in the driver's seat and start the engine.

"Partly. I do need to meet more people here. I'm afraid my social life is meeting an early demise."

"Quite a bit different than life in the Big Apple?" I ask, ignoring how it makes me feel that she isn't here entirely for me.

"I rarely spent time at home there. Here, it feels like I'm rarely away from it."

"You haven't been going out?"

"Some. I meet Vanessa for brunch most weekends, and Preston has taken me out a couple of times."

"Preston?" I ask. "The stuffy dude from your party?"

"He's not stuffy."

"He is the definition." I wonder if he's married, but I don't ask. Not yet, not when we're just starting out our time together. My curiosity is piqued by what I found online, but if I'm realistic about it, I already have an inkling of why she chooses the men she does.

"In looks, perhaps," she says, implying there's been some intimacy that hasn't been at all stuffy. My knuckles whiten on the steering wheel, but I let the comment pass. It's not my business. *Yet.*

"Do you get back home much?" I ask, changing the subject.

"I still go home for Christmas. Dad would be broken-hearted if I skipped that."

"I can imagine." Odette's house was always a hit during the holiday season. Her dad spent days setting up decorations on the lawn and lighting the house to perfection. The scene grew a little every year; and by the time we graduated high school it was an entire Santa's workshop in her front yard. "I don't get to go back that time of year, so I haven't seen how it's evolved."

"They moved a few years back; he has more yard to work with now."

"Maybe I'll get to see it next year," I say. "After I retire."

"Why are you retiring?" She sounds surprised, and maybe…disappointed. Or sad? I don't know why she would be, though.

"I'm old, Ode. I can't keep up."

"We are not old," she says. "I've never seen you play."

She used to talk about watching me when I was in the NHL, during that short time we made future plans. When we had dreams that included each other. We talked about her first NHL experience being my first professional game. I can't count the number of times I played in a game in New York and thought about trying to send her tickets. I never did. Of course, I never did. It would have been presumptuous and cruel after what I did to her. That never stopped me from wanting that part of our dream to come true, though.

I never forgot Odette. Maybe she didn't forget everything, either.

"I know. I did try to give you tickets," I remind her.

"I was otherwise engaged," she says elusively, and I get the impression it was with the stuffy dude. "Maybe try again."

"Really?"

"Why do you sound so surprised?"

"Because I've been trying to get you to give me the time of day for a month now and you've been ignoring me."

"It's hard to break years of practice," she says quietly as she watches the houses we pass outside the window.

"Odette, I'm…"

"No, Gavin," she interrupts. "We're not talking about it."

"Whatever you want," I say, reaching for her hand. She doesn't pull it away, a small win, but I'll take what I can get. We will have to talk about it, sooner rather than later. I'll give her more time, though, since she's giving me some of hers.

We fall into silence for the rest of the short drive to Zander's house.

"Stay put," I tell her before rushing around to open the car door for her.

"I can get in and out of vehicles on my own, Vaughn," she snarks.

"I'm aware," I tell her, standing close enough that our bodies brush against each other when I help her out. I don't move right away, opting to breathe her in instead, watching the way her lips part ever so slightly and the vein at her neck pulses harder.

I may not be a married man like she prefers, but I still affect her.

Game fucking on, Quinn.

"Oh, fuck. She's here," Lehtinen says as soon as we walk in the door of the house Zander shares with his partners, Damian and Willa.

"Is he talking about me?" Odette whispers to me, eyes wide.

"He's a fan."

"You're kidding?"

"You don't think you have fans?" I ask, and she shakes her head. "You're gorgeous and adorable, Quinn."

"Hi!" Lehtinen says loudly, rushing up to the two of us before we've barely taken three steps inside. "I'm Oliver. Olly. Or Letty. Or whatever you want to call me. Future husband, maybe?"

"Shut the fuck up, man," I say, as both Odette and I laugh. "Odette, this is Oliver Lehtinen. Your biggest fan, evidently. And the Blades' resident shithead."

"That's me," he confirms, aggressively nodding his head without looking away from Odette.

"It's nice to meet you, Oliver."

"Likewise. You're beautiful. Has anyone told you that? Dumb question, I'm sure you hear it all the time."

"It never hurts to hear it again, though," she says playfully.

"I'll tell you all the time," he says, holding out his arm to her. "Come on, I'll introduce you around."

What the fuck? I'm being cockblocked by my own teammate.

"Oh, yeah. Okay. You'll catch up, Vaughn?" She hands me the bag with the wine.

"Sure," I say, letting him take her around to some of the others while I head to the kitchen to find Willa and Isla. Sisters, my coach's daughters, and both partners to teammates. Isla is married to Cillian Wylder, and Willa is with Zander. The Cole family is the heart of this team. Coach is stern, capable, but cares about his players like family members. Isla, who also works for the organization, knows everything there is to know about hockey and isn't afraid to impart knowledge to help any of us out. And Willa has become something like the team's mother over the past year, consistently hosting gatherings to keep us all unified and cared for. We're a lucky team, and we all know it. "Hey, ladies."

"Hi, Gavin. How are you?" Willa asks.

"Doing great, how is everyone today?"

"We're good," Isla says. "Seems like you just made Letty's day even better."

"Fucker stole my date right out from under me," I say, handing the bottle to Willa. "This is from Ode."

"Ode?" Willa teases.

"Date?" Isla chimes in.

"Well, she doesn't see it that way. But I'm working on it."

"She's even prettier in person," Willa says. We all turn to where Odette laughs with Oliver and Hugo. It's the same as when we were school kids, her head thrown back slightly. Watching her laugh feels like the first day of summer or Christmas morning. It makes me giddy with excitement and I can't pull my eyes away.

"Ah fuck, you're a goner already," Isla says. "How long have you known her?"

"My whole life, really. Give or take a twenty-year absence."

"She feels like home," Isla muses.

"Is that what it was like for you when Cillian came back?"

"Yes. But those feelings were tainted by a lot of anger and fear, too. So, it was hard to see it right away."

"Or it wasn't, and you just fought it," Willa says.

"Yeah, there was that, too," Isla admits. "I don't know your story, but if I can offer some advice?"

"Absolutely."

"Don't waste any more time. It's precious and you can't get it back." Isla's eyes are watery as she says it, and I move to wrap my arms around her.

"Get off my wife, asshole," Cillian says, stepping into the kitchen.

"No," I say. "She's too smart for your dumb ass."

"Don't I fucking know it," he says, leaning down to press a kiss to her lips. "You okay?"

"I'm good. Just feeling a little sad for our friend here."

"Don't be sad," Cillian and I both say in unison.

"I'll get it figured out," I add, looking up to see Odette watching us. Our eyes lock and I swear our hearts dance in time with each other. For someone who plays a very physical sport for a living, I've become a fucking cinnamon roll.

I wink at her and mouth, *"You good?"* She smiles almost bashfully and nods. It's a long moment before she looks back to Hugo, who is asking her a question while Letty stares at her like a lovesick puppy.

Can't blame the guy. It's the way she carries herself, confident and classy but without the air of superiority, like she doesn't realize her own status. She's friends with some of the most famous people in the world, but you wouldn't know it because she doesn't flaunt it. Or think she's one of them.

"I don't know, man, Oliver might beat you to it," Cillian says.

"No way," I say. "She won't admit it yet, but she's mine."

Odette surreptitiously glances my way a couple more times, each one making my smile grow. I fully expect to battle with her, she's far too stubborn to just give in, and I still have that stuffy dude to contend with. But she'll come around, I'm sure of it.

12

ODETTE

I can't remember the last time I laughed this much. Which must really say something about my life, right? The crowd I've ran with my entire adult life doesn't have birthday parties like this. They aren't casual and relaxed with everyone teasing everyone else. They don't reminisce about the silly adventures they've had in the past because they'd be more ashamed or afraid of appearing uncouth. Class and sophistication are everything in high fashion.

Here, with all of Gavin's friends and teammates, it's another world. I'm realizing that maybe I played the part too well, but never really had fun. I had success, I made money, and while I had plenty of great moments, overall, my life hasn't been *fun*. That wasn't something that mattered much before, I was focused and driven. But now?

Everything is different. With more time on my hands, will my life be boring without friends like these? Will *I* become boring? What a horrible fucking thought.

When I said yes to coming here, I had a vision in my head of what it would be like. Hockey players are wealthy and that typically comes with a certain way of life. But these men and their wives have tossed that on its head. The women are all polished and beautiful, but they're also down to earth and *real*.

Then there's Gavin.

He hasn't been clingy, instead he's let me be pulled from one conversation to the next naturally. Though he's checked in on me in subtle ways. His attention is never fully averted. I guess mine hasn't been, either. He's so easy-going with everyone. How the men respect him, and the women seem to genuinely care about him.

It's a stark reminder of why I fell in love with him. *Before.* He's kind, he's endearing, he's loyal. So loyal that I lost him because of it.

When he asked if I would come with him today, my initial reaction was to tell him no. Of course, no. But something Tori said made me reconsider. She thinks he's lonely. It reminded me of a conversation I had with him once.

He said it was hard living with his mother and mental health issues. He saw the toll it took on his dad and he worried about the decisions he made because of it. His dad loved his mother, but he was lonely at the same time. She wasn't the same person she'd been when they fell in love, and he missed her. Gavin had once come home to find his dad drunk and crying about how he'd almost had an affair.

He'd told Gavin that lonely people do stupid shit.

Aren't I living proof of that?

I can't trust my heart to Gavin. But I can be his friend. And maybe, in the process, neither of us will be as lonely nor as stupid.

Just maybe.

I've spent so much time pretending I hate him for my self-preservation that when he came back into my life, I forgot it was a lie. I never hated him, I hated how it hurt to lose him.

Or maybe this is the biggest mistake I'll ever make.

"Do you have any embarrassing stories about Vaughn growing up?" Axel Wallin asks. He's one of the handful of single men on the team, they've all been very upfront about their status, and I get the feeling it's for Gavin's benefit in some way. They've hardly let him get close to me, every time he tries another one of the guys comes to grab my attention.

"He hasn't told you about the time he and a few friends were dared to streak across the field at halftime during a football game?"

"Odette," Gavin says from the other side of the room, hanging his head.

"He did not," Cillian says. "The Vaughn we know would never. He's the classiest twat out of all of us."

"Oh, he did. He was known to never back down from a dare. Four of them stripped behind the concession stand to nothing but a sock on their dicks and ran from one end zone to the other. The principal tried catching them, but she was in heels that kept sinking into the grass."

"She broke her ankle," Gavin says amidst the laughter. "For whatever reason, she didn't suspend us, but we had detention every day until she was out of her cast."

"I bet it was a small sock," Letty says. "Like one of those baby ones."

"Fuck you," Gavin says.

"She's not denying it," he says, pointing at me. "It's okay, you can tell us, Odette. We won't tease him too much."

"It wasn't…" I start to say, when I feel the heat on my cheeks. Being well endowed is one of Gavin's gifts, something I remember all too well.

"Well, fuck," Letty says. "That's no fun."

Gavin is suddenly standing behind me.

"Thank you, Ode," he whispers in my ear. His hand comes to rest low on my hip. "I'm glad you remember. I remember some things, too. Like the way you taste."

His whispered words send a shiver down my neck. I'm sure he didn't miss it, just as I don't miss as his palm slides slightly lower to the curve of my ass before he walks away.

"Have we ever tried daring Vaughn to do anything?" Axel asks Oliver.

"No, come to think of it. We'll have to change that."

"Oh no, have I started something?" I ask.

"Are they being too much?" Isla asks, handing me a glass of wine.

"Thank you," I tell her. "Not at all. This is all…refreshing."

"Come sit with me?" she asks, gesturing to two chairs off in a corner. I nod, follow, and sit with her. "I imagine these yahoos are a lot rowdier than your usual crowd."

"It's night and day," I agree. "But I'm having a great time."

"I'm glad. Cill told me Gavin was bringing you and I worried their razzing would be too much. They can't be reined in, though, not even for Gavin's sake."

"I get the impression he's very respected," I say, looking to confirm what I've already caught on to.

"Every one of them plays a role for the rest of the team. Letty is the clown, with a little help from Hugo and Axel. Gavin is the veteran on the team, he has more experience in the game. But also, the life experience of being a father and husband. He's been there to help guide many of the younger players through the rough life during the season."

"That tracks with who I knew him to be," I admit.

"Cillian said the two of you grew up together?"

"We did. And now I mentor his daughter in college."

"Do you miss it? Your life in New York?"

"Just between the two of us, because if this got out it would demolish my reputation," I say, and she laughs but nods. "I thought I would miss it so much more than I do. Honestly, I think I needed the change for a long time and was too stubborn to confront it."

"Oh, I understand stubborn better than most," Isla says. "I'm kind of a professional at it."

"We all have our strengths," I say.

"You might be the first person to ever imply it's something to be proud of," Isla says. "I may have just fallen a little in love with you, Odette."

"I do love a fan club, so that works out just fine for me."

We chat for a while, with some of the other ladies coming to join in. They talk about some gala that the team has every year to benefit a charity. A few of them, Isla included, perk up when I offer to help with dressing them for the event. After a time, most start to disperse and it's just me and Willa standing alone talking. She's smart, funny, and passionate. She and her sister would be impossible not to like.

Her eyes light with curiosity when she notices Gavin approach us wearing a strange look of his own. Excitement mixed with trepidation, maybe.

"Are you about ready to head out," he says, stepping up close to me. His hand once again finds purchase on my hip. "I have to be up early in the morning."

Then he pulls me close, and his mouth hovers over mine, so close. My body reacts, my breasts brushing his chest and heat pooling low in my stomach. My heart frantically chants, *We can't, we can't, we can't. We won't survive this.*

It's just a kiss between old friends. It's just a kiss. It doesn't mean anything.

We can't.

"Yes." The word barely escapes, and his lips meet mine with feverish heat. Gavin doesn't hold back; he's not starting slow and building up. He's picking up where he left off. His hand skates up my back, supporting me as he leans in, leading with his tongue. It's passion, desire, a need to be closer, further, deeper. *Connected.* He doesn't let up until I'm practically gasping for breath. After I fill my lungs, staring him down eye to eye, I realize it only lasted a matter of seconds. Though it felt like a lifetime. I mentally shake away the butterflies that have taken up residence in my chest and secure my armor back in place. I'd been so at ease here today that I'd forgotten it all together. "Did they dare you to kiss me?"

"No, Ode," he says, looking wounded. "Those aren't the games I play."

Gavin takes my hand and weaves us throughout the house to say our goodbyes. I trade numbers with Isla and Willa. Letty tries to give me his, but Gavin shuts the idea down quickly. I play along with his possessiveness because, in truth, I don't want to call him out on anything in front of his coworkers and peers. It feels good to have made a couple of friends today, people who don't know me as a socialite but as just a woman, a teacher, an old friend of their old friend.

"You have great friends," I tell him when we're in his SUV. Gavin hums but doesn't say anything. He hasn't said anything to me since the kiss. Perhaps accusing him was mean spirited, but I'm sure I didn't give him any signal that it was okay to pursue a kiss, either. No matter how much I liked it. My feelings for and about Gavin are so tangled and still so raw. Maybe a friendship with him isn't possible. "I'm sorry."

"I'm sorry," he says at the same time.

"What are you sorry about?"

"I shouldn't have kissed you."

"Why did you?"

"Because for hours today, I watched you wrap an entire house full of people around your finger by doing nothing but just being you. Those guys aren't easily impressed, everyone there is accomplished in their own right, and every single one was completely enamored by you. Did you have a single conversation today that didn't have you and the person you were speaking to laughing?"

"I don't know," I say. "That's just conversation, though."

"Sure, for some, but not everyone. You strode in and dove right into the deep end like you've lived there your whole life. All while dressed incredibly sexy but not in a way that made you seem unapproachable or that had the other women jealous. I'm not sure you know what a feat that is."

"I have lived in similar settings for a long time now. It's not that difficult to navigate when you know what you're doing. That doesn't explain the kiss."

"I'd say I couldn't help myself, even though I know that makes me sound like a giant asshole. I crossed a line you've been clear about. I apologize. Next time, I'll make you beg for it."

"That's never..." I say, but he interrupts.

"What are you sorry about?"

Initially, I was apologizing for anything I might have done to give him false hope, or an impression that I was looking for more from him. Now...

"I don't think I'm sorry, after all," I say, leaving a little petulance in my voice. "And for the record, I never beg."

"We'll see about that," he says, as I turn to watch out the window. "We need to stop by my place. I forgot to grab your gift before I came to pick you up."

"You don't need to get me gifts, Gavin."

"I wanted to, Odette. Some things I'm not going to ask permission for."

"Like all the flowers you've sent?"

"Yep, just like that."

"Has anyone ever told you how insufferable you are?"

"No, but you can as much as you want to," he says.

He parks in the driveway and once again tells me to stay put so he can open my door for me. The house is newer, an ultra-modern build that is unexpected with its stark paint, clean lines, and no outside embellishment.

"I didn't picture you living in a place so...posh."

"You imagined where I lived?" he asks with a sly smile. "Come on in, it's not as unwelcoming inside."

He's right, I realize when we step inside. It's decorated with overstuffed furniture in warm colors. It's cozy and quaint but still somehow works with the architecture.

"Tori helped you decorate," I guess.

"I gave her a budget; she basically did the rest," he says. "In here."

He walks into the kitchen, stopping when he arrives at the shiny white countertop. A large wicker basket sits there, a bounty of baked goods spilling over the top.

"What is this?"

"Bread, blueberry muffins, apple cinnamon muffins, snickerdoodle cookies, vanilla scones," he says, pointing to the various items. "All gluten free and organic. I was very careful with the ingredients."

"You made all this?"

"Yeah, and a few other things that tasted like shit and got thrown out. These all turned out pretty good, though. You can freeze some, so they'll last longer."

"Gavin."

"Caroline said good gluten-free bread is hard to get and who the fuck can live without bread? I get restless sometimes when I'm here alone, so it seemed like a good way to spend my time." He's rambling and rearranging things in the basket, all while I stand in awe. "When I finally got the bread right, I figured I might as well try muffins and then it all snowballed."

What kind of man learns to bake for a practical stranger, because we are that, aren't we? Even if it doesn't always feel that way.

"Gavin," I repeat, as a sudden wave of chills grabs hold of me. I wrap my arms around me as if it can ward off the cold, the emotion, the exhaustion that wants to creep in. I've had a few Hashimoto flare-ups that have felt similar, but I think this is more than just that, it's different. Foreign, even.

"Hey," he says, stepping close and cupping my cheeks. "You okay?"

"No," I say, staring up at him with a vulnerability I haven't felt for so, so long.

"It's just bread, Odette." He rubs his thumbs along my jawline and it's the most soothing thing I've experienced since being sick as a child and my mother would lay my head on her lap and pet my hair.

"It's not just bread, Gavin," I tell him. "It's you being considerate and kind when I've been the opposite to you."

"The bread, the flowers, they aren't transactional, Ode. You don't have to be nice to me because I do things for you. If I didn't want to do them, I wouldn't," he says. "I understand why this is hard for you."

Try as I might to keep the tears at bay, I can't.

"You don't, Gavin. You can't possibly understand what it's like to watch the only person you ever planned a future with wait at the end of the aisle to marry someone else. I watched you kiss your bride and smile while my heart broke in real time," I say with a voice that sounds steadier than it feels. "You can't know what it was like to lie in bed alone that night and wonder how their wedding night was spent."

"Ode." His forehead rests on mine, his eyes closed. He can try not to see but I'll live with those memories forever.

"I can't give you much of me, Gavin. There's so little left of me."

"I don't believe that, and I'm so sorry."

"Don't. I don't need an apology."

"What do you need, Odette?"

"For you to abandon any expectations," I say. His handsome face was happy and hopeful all day. I've now ruined it because I won't hold in my own truth. I don't know if it's fair to share my pain with him but it's too hard to keep it to myself right now. "Friends is all I can give, Gavin. And I fear I can't be a very good one to you."

"I won't ask for more than you can give, Ode," he says after a steadying breath. "Just let me be some small part of your life."

13

ODETTE
THEN

"Gavin is here," she says warily. "I'll tell him to leave if you want me to."

"No. I'll talk to him," I tell my mom.

"You sure, honey?"

Am I? No, not at all. What outweighs that is my need to hear his reason. I nod and crawl off my bed, the place that I've been spending too much time in these past days. Instinctively, I reach for the sweatshirt that I've been wearing for weeks—the New York Ice Wolf's logo emblazoned on the front. Gavin lent it to me one chilly night and wouldn't let me return it. It's the only thing I have of his and I debate whether I should return it or not.

I leave it and grab a cardigan that's seen better days if the piling at the sleeves says anything. It's thick and cozy, though, and that seems more important just now.

My mother didn't let Gavin inside. I step out on the front porch. He's sitting on the steps. He doesn't look up, but his shoulders tense. We both know this won't be easy or kind, the weight of it stifles the summer air.

Taking a seat on the same step, I keep to the far side, leaving as much distance between us as I can.

"You're marrying Caroline next week."

"I'd hoped you hadn't heard. I wanted to tell you first. Our mothers were…anxious to get the news out."

"Was I nothing but a hall pass? One last fling before you locked it all down?"

"No, Odette," he urges, finally looking at me. "How could you think that?"

"How? Be real, Gavin. You're the star couple and I'm the awkward girl that gets no attention. I know how it plays out; I've seen all those movies. What I don't know is why me? What did I ever do to either of you?" Emotion clogs my throat, turning my words into something less than the strength I was hoping for.

"Fuck," he curses, standing to pace in front of the steps. "I can't believe… is that really what you think of me?"

Of course not, I want to scream. But I can't tell him I'm in love with him now. So often people don't understand what they have until it's gone. I knew, though. I knew and I continued on with the relationship with hope in my heart. I happily pretended that the next four years of our lives wouldn't be as hard as they seemed. That a long-distance relationship wasn't something that would break us.

How can he think that anything I just said is truth? How can I be in this much pain and anguish, and he not feel it like a cold wind? It's all I feel. I pull my knees higher, resting my head on them and cocooning myself in my sweater.

A small sob escapes, and I hate myself for it.

"Ode," Gavin says, sitting next to me and pulling me close.

"Don't. Don't touch me."

"Please, Odette. Let me hold you while I explain," he pleads, finally giving me the same sadness I've been feeling for days. "Caroline's pregnant. I got her pregnant before we broke up and she wants to keep it. She's not going to school. With my scholarship, the only way she can come with me is if we're married. Plus, there's insurance and everything. It's all I could come up with."

Gavin isn't the type of guy to not take responsibility. He's a team player. Caroline has been on his team for a long time, so I'm starting to wonder if I ever got past tryouts.

"When did you find out?"

"She came to tell me the night after we got back from the city."

"Why didn't you come sooner?"

"Will you look at me," he asks. I don't think I can, though, not if I want to keep myself held together. So, I shake my head, burying it further into my knees. "I was coming to terms with the decision I made. If I'd come sooner, I don't think I could have gone through with it. I wouldn't be able to say what I need to say to you."

Goodbye. He means goodbye. I might die, here and now. The hurt is too sharp. My limbs vanish under its force, like my whole body becomes nothing but the throbbing in my chest. Just the breaking of the heart of a girl who never should have dared to believe she stood a chance.

"My mom saw the announcement," I tell him.

"You shouldn't have found out that way. I didn't know they had done that until it was too late."

I want to tell him that he should have come to me days ago, but how does that make me sound? He's dealing with a life-changing event; I'm only dealing with heartache. Our problems aren't on an equal level.

I love him. I love him enough to support him, even if I hate everything about it. I love him enough to not add to his own pain. It wouldn't be love if I hated him for choosing a child or for supporting his family.

And that's how I know what I feel is true.

Turning my head, I see him matching my position. We stare at each other in silence. I imagine he's waiting for my reaction. He looks tired and weary.

"I don't want this to be my last memory of you," I say. Gavin closes his eyes in relief, probably thinking this conversation would go a different way.

"Will you go for a drive with me?" I nod and go back inside to tell my mom and get some shoes.

Gavin drives in more silence. It's not a long drive, only about fifteen minutes before we stop at a fishing pond that's been used by locals for decades. He pulls out the blanket he keeps in the trunk, the one he used on our first date at the waterfall. A poetic ending, maybe.

Still, we don't speak as he takes my hand and leads me to the water's edge where he spreads out the blanket. We lie there, staring at the stars that freckle the sky, not touching, not talking. Just being.

A single tear spills, and I roll over to my side to watch him. It's hard not to touch him when all I want to do is crawl inside him and find comfort. I'll need to find that on my own, though.

"Come here, Ode," he whispers. "Let me hold you one more time."

Five days later, I'm at Gavin's wedding. I wasn't invited, but I had to see. This closure has become an obsession the last few days. So, I stand in a side hallway of the church they chose, unseen and unnoticed. But I have a partial view of the nuptials. This was a rushed event, but they've still made it pretty with pale yellow flowers everywhere. They could have gone to the courthouse, had a private ceremony.

Except that they're doing this for real. It's not a shotgun wedding with the intention of it ending anytime soon. I imagine Caroline wanted some semblance of the wedding little girls dream about. Or maybe it's for their families' benefit.

It's not information I'm privy to, of course. I mean nothing in all of this.

I feel that all too hard when Caroline steps into the room with her dad at her arm, and Gavin's face lights up in a broad smile. My stomach sinks. There's joy there now, not like the smile he wore for me on our last night together. I pasted on mine when I told him I understood his decision. That I didn't hate him for it, I never could. That he was a good man and should be proud of that.

It would be easier if I could. It would be easier to bury this pain in anger.

Life can prepare you for a lot of things, but not watching the person you're in love with vow their life to someone else. I hear every word over the blood rushing through my head. To have and to hold…'til death.

They're planning on forever while I can't imagine what tomorrow looks like.

I shouldn't be here.

I'm not supposed to be here. If he wanted me here, he'd have asked. Not that he would have.

I'm alone in this, I'm on the outside, an intruder.

The uninvited.

After they seal their vows with a kiss more passionate than you'd expect from friends, I sneak back out the way I came. I live within walking distance and run all the way home, barging through my front door to find the house as empty as I feel. But even alone, it feels confining and I rush right back out through the back door until I'm at the far corner of our small lot where my mother's dainty yellow flowers bloom.

I drop to my knees and pull them out by the roots until I collapse in sobs, dirt caked under my nails. There, I bury this hurt. I bury this love. I let my tears dry and lock down my poor, battered heart.

14

GAVIN

*F*uck, that hit is going to hurt later.

I shake it off and race down the ice, succeeding in getting the puck back from Jenkin. Keeping control of it, I get a pass off to Wylder, who takes a shot at goal. It's blocked but Fane gets the rebound goal.

Getting to the bench, I roll my shoulders, trying to release the tension. I just can't take the physicality like I used to. These younger players are hungry and tough. While I'm still fit as fuck, I don't recover the same as a twenty-two-year-old. Some of these guys are closer to Tori in age than me, and it's a bleak reminder of how old I am in this game. Like, she could be dating one of these chucklefucks.

I pop my neck to the side and hear it crack, feeling instant relief in my body, if not my mind. But I keep my head in the game. We're on a streak and I'm determined to have a winning season to retire on.

Once I'm back on the ice, I take another check to the boards that I'm sure is going to leave me bruised. That's just part of my life now, though. Again, I shake it off and keep my eye on the puck. This time, it's Letty who has control but no clear shot. I position myself just outside the crease so when he passes it off to Axel, the latter can pass on to me as I partially blind New York's view. I shove it toward the net, the light goes off, and we've scored another goal.

Up by three, we have a little more room to breathe, but hockey moves fast, and you can lose a lead as quickly as you gain it. We manage to keep it, though, winning our fifth game in a row.

I feel like a tenderized piece of meat afterward, but the ice bath the trainers push me into helps some.

"Doesn't look so big to me," Blom says, peeking over the rim as he walks by.

"Fuck off," I laugh, tossing a piece of ice at him. The guys have been razzing me relentlessly since they met Odette. She's liked by them all and I wish we were in a place where I could bring her around more.

We're not, though, and I have to accept it as a consequence of my own decisions. She doesn't understand why I chose the things I did. Why I chose to marry Caroline. Not past the point of not wanting to abandon my kid, anyway. While I'd love nothing more than to try and explain it all to her, it's obvious she doesn't want to hear it. Or can't.

Would I be able to hear it if I was in her shoes? If I'd gone to her wedding and watched her marry someone else? The thought of that knots my stomach. If that's the effect that idea has on me now, I can only imagine what it would have been like for her then. When our feelings were all so fresh and raw.

I was in love with Odette. I know that now, even though I didn't ever say the words to her then. But she doesn't know it. And I doubt I could convince her of it today.

She was there at my wedding. I can't believe she came.

I lean my head back and let the cold eat away at me. I deserve this for everything I put her through. Even now, I'm still causing her turmoil, when all I want is to get to know her again. To finally have the chance we were denied the first time around.

That might be out of reach, but I can't give up yet. I didn't fight for her before, I won't make that choice again. If I'm the cause of why she spends her life alone, and I suspect I am, it's my responsibility to try and fix that. Or help her heal from it. Because when I needed it most, she was kind and gracious, even while she was breaking.

It's a favor I need to return. Somehow.

Fuck, it hurts to think of her the day of my wedding. It physically hurts like a knife to the gut, stabbing over and over. What she said the other night plays on repeat in my mind. I can picture her lying in bed that night imagining me and Caroline entwined together in newlywed bliss.

That's not what happened. But she doesn't know that. Odette doesn't know how scared we both were, or how horrible we felt about so many things. She doesn't know that I mourned our relationship like it was the death of half of me. Or that I didn't really feel like I was living again until I held Tori in my arms for the first time.

"Time's up, Vaughn," Coach says, knocking me back to the here and now.

"Thanks, Coach."

"You feel okay? You took a couple hard hits."

"You know how it goes, shake it off and get back out there. I'll be ready for the next game," I answer. We don't have a game tomorrow. I'll be having breakfast with Caroline and this Brock guy before we catch the flight to Toronto in the early afternoon. A day's rest will do wonders for me.

"Good. Get some rest."

I skip out on grabbing food with the other guys, opting to get room service and playing hermit in my hotel room. After my salmon fettucine arrives, I turn on the television and flip through, trying to find anything to take my mind off everything.

Landing on some Channing Tatum movie, thinking it will be mindless entertainment, doesn't really pan out. It's a story of his wife getting amnesia and not remembering him at all. He attempts to romance her all over again, because if she fell in love with him once, surely, she would do it again.

Does that theory hold water in real life? I don't know, but I can hope that if I have the chance to show Odette the man I am now, maybe there's a chance she'll fall in love with me like she did when I was still a dumbass boy.

Brock is a likeable guy; I can see why Caroline likes him so much. He looks like he's worked manual labor his whole life—broad, strong, big hands that are calloused and nicked. He has a hard time not touching her. I think he's making the effort, maybe for my benefit, but that's stupid. Caroline's comfortable with it, she doesn't show any reaction other than leaning into it every time his hand finds her.

I've asked him about a hundred questions, because at the end of the day, this man will potentially be a part of my daughter's life.

But he hasn't given me a single red flag. Not that I expected him to, Caroline has always had a good sense of people's character. She wouldn't pick an asshole. Not knowingly, anyway.

Brock is also divorced. His marriage lasted six years and he has two sons from it—the youngest is sixteen, oldest is twenty. It sounds like he has a great relationship with them both. He gets along amicably enough with his ex, too.

Seems like Caroline found herself a drama-free boyfriend.

She looks good, too. Relaxed and happy like I haven't seen her in a long time. Our marriage took a toll on us both, one we ignored for way too long.

"We'll be in Seattle in a few weeks," she says. "I miss Tori."

"She misses you, too," I say. "She's also excited to meet Brock."

"I'm excited to meet her, as well. I've never been to Seattle, so that's a bonus."

"It's a great city, I'm sure you'll enjoy it."

"How's Odette?" Caroline asks. "Tori's absolutely in love with her."

"She's a great mentor."

"Gav, you know that's not what I'm asking."

Talking to Caroline about Odette makes my skin crawl. It's ridiculous, really. She's my friend before she's my ex-wife. But it somehow feels like a betrayal to talk to the woman who came between me and Odette. Even if it was completely unintentional.

But then again, Odette and I aren't anything more than friends. Fuck, we're barely even that. Besides, the situation is an anvil on my shoulders, and who better to talk about it with than the only other person that was involved?

"She was there, Caroline. At our wedding."

"Oh, Gav," she gasps, her hand going to her mouth and tears instantly pooling in her eyes. "I can't imagine how hard…"

Brock takes her hand and squeezes it softly.

"I always knew I did her wrong, but her telling me what it was like to watch…I don't know how she could ever forgive me."

"This is my fault," Caroline starts.

"Stop that," I admonish. "It was my decision to take you with me to Boston."

"Because you knew I didn't want to start my life as a mother under my parents' roof," she argues. "You did that for me." Caroline was always strong-headed and independent. She'd been eagerly anticipating getting out of New York and starting a life away from her family. She wanted her own identity. I thought I could give her that by taking her with me. When, really, it only replaced her title as daughter to wife.

Except with me, she got to make decisions for herself, she didn't have to put on any kind of dog and pony show for "appearance's sake".

Our parents wanted to be supportive however they could. My mom had instantly offered to be the primary caretaker so Caroline could work. But I knew we couldn't rely on her with her health issues and Caroline's mom loved her career. Caroline wouldn't have had much of a team had she stayed home.

So, we worked out a deal with our parents. They'd help support us financially until I could start making money and pay them back. We didn't need all that much, not with what my scholarship covered and the savings both Caroline and I had. My expenses were mostly covered, and Caroline was good about figuring out how to minimize expenses with cloth diapers and homemade baby food and whatnot.

We didn't live lavishly those first four years, but we also weren't a total financial drain on our parents. I was able to pay them all back quickly once I was drafted.

"I did that as much for me as I did it for you," I remind her. There was so much I was going to miss out on because of travel for hockey, I didn't want to add to it by not having my kid live with me.

"She must hate us," Caroline says quietly.

"No, I don't think she does. But she carried what we did by herself," I say. "Whereas we had each other for emotional support, and eventually Tori to focus our attention. Ode was alone."

"You were all in a hard situation. No matter what you did, someone was going to suffer for it," Brock says.

"Yeah, that's true," I agree. "I feel like a thief, though. Like I stole a crucial aspect of her life that she's never been able to regrow or find again. And maybe I did. Maybe she wanted children early in life or had dreams of young love that lasted until you die of old age together. But because I broke her heart, she never took the chance on anyone again."

I remember she once told me she didn't want to have children. Her mother had complications with pregnancies before she was able to have Odette and those complications came back afterward. Odette remembered her mom having a miscarriage when she was about six years old and never wanted to go through anything like that.

But she might have changed her mind.

"There's no guarantees in life or love," Brock says somberly.

"There is hope, though. And I think I stole that from her, too."

15

ODETTE

"Odette! You're here," Tori says excitedly when I make it to my seat at the arena. Isla was the one to extend the invitation, but I suspect it was at Gavin's behest. He's been less visible in my life the past two weeks since the birthday party. They've been on the road, so I'm sure that's the main reason. But I think he's taking what I told him that night to heart.

It was a nice surprise to get Isla's text. Holding Gavin's advances at bay like I did, I thought I might miss the opportunity to keep these new friends.

As much as I love the decadent life I had in New York, I equally love the peacefulness of the Pacific Northwest. If I'm going to stay, an established circle of friends helps.

"I was happy for the invite," I tell her, taking a seat next to her. "I've never been to any professional…what do we call it? Game, match?"

"Game," she says with that joyous smile she wears so well. Gavin and Caroline really raised an exceptional daughter. I note it often when I watch her with her classmates. She's eager to help others, incredibly encouraging, and celebrates all their ideas and ambitions with them. In all these weeks,

I've yet to see her even mildly frustrated. Tori is like a field of daisies walking into the workroom every day. "Never? Not football or anything?"

"No, never. I can't count the number of runways and red carpets. But games? Not a single one. I didn't even know what to wear," I whisper the last part to her, conspiratorially.

Tori scans my outfit with a wide smile. I opted for high-waisted sailor pants, a frilly cropped blouse with a small pussy bow, and a pair of vintage t-strap heels. It's about as dressed down as I get in public.

"You might get a little cold, but you'll look fantastic doing it. Which is arguably more important."

"You're my kind of girl, kid," I tell her, and she beams. She may hero worship me, a fact that isn't lost on me, but I'm careful about showing any kind of favoritism. I like Tori, though. I know her better because of her father. Liking her doesn't mean she won't get honest critique from me. "You might have to fill me in on what's happening. I don't know much about hockey."

"I can help, too. I'm real smart about hockey," a young girl approaching with Isla says. "I'm Sadie."

"Nice to meet you, Sadie," I say as she takes the seat in front of me.

"Hey, Odette," Isla greets. "Glad you made it." She takes a seat next to Sadie, and I guess this is the daughter she told me about at the birthday party.

"Whose wag are you?" Sadie asks, and I look to Isla for explanation.

"Wives and girlfriends," she explains the moniker.

"Oh. Well, nobody's. But I grew up with Gavin Vaughn."

"Gav is soooo nice," Sadie says dramatically. "He used to play Go Fish with me all the time. But I don't like to play that much anymore. So, he's teaching me chess, which is kinda like hockey plays."

Tori and Sadie take up the conversation of chess, allowing Isla and I to talk.

"I was going to text you this weekend, but since I have you now, would you be interested in helping plan a girls' night? I have a friend coming to town to film. She doesn't know anyone here and needs friends to occupy her downtime. Otherwise, she'll end up getting herself in trouble and her agent will riot."

"Sure, of course. Who are we talking about?"

"Britton Macy."

"Shut the fuck up," she says in an excited whisper. "You're joking?"

"Not at all," I say with a laugh. "She's a client turned friend who will be here for roughly four months."

"I loved her in *Wuthering Heights*. Like, obsessively loved. Like, she's my hall pass and I'm not even bisexual."

"She has that effect; everyone falls in love with her."

"Fuck," Isla cusses and takes a deep breath. "I'm sure I'll embarrass myself, but yes, anything you need."

"Well, I mostly need to rely on you for the guestlist, since I don't know many people, either."

"You got it. No wag will pass up a chance to meet Britton Macy."

"Great, thank you."

"No, Odette. Thank you."

"Will Cillian be thanking me after all this?"

"No, probably not." She laughs as music starts playing loudly.

"What's happening?" I ask Tori.

"Warmups," she says. "They make it kind of a big production. Hockey has this weird cheesy aspect to it."

"I thought they fought all the time?"

"Oh, they do that, too," she says. "They have two sets of rules. The official ones, and the player ones. They're self-governing, of sorts. You disrespect a player on another team, that team will pay it back, and everyone lets it happen."

I try to watch all the players, but my focus keeps landing on Gavin. He skates around in circles for a few minutes, then takes a few shots at goal, before he moves to one side of the ice to stretch.

What does it say about me that heat sizzles in my stomach when all he's doing is stretching his hips. It's not lewd but my mind goes there; to images of him making similar movements over me. To memories that I thought I'd long buried.

Switching my sight to other players doing similar stretches, the same reaction isn't duplicated. It's only with him. He's the only one. In some ways, he always has been, and in some ways, I've always been mad at him for that.

Yet, it's undeniable. This chemistry between us? It's real, even if it can't be seen.

It also can't be denied that I want him as much as I want him to stay away. Gavin is a constant tug-of-war in my heart. They say "the heart wants what the heart wants". My heart isn't what wants Gavin, though.

It's my body. And maybe the ego he bruised all those years ago. It'd really like a chance to show him what he's missed.

"There will be an intermission now," Tori tells me when the skaters leave the ice. "They'll refresh the ice, then the game will start. I'll get some food. Do you want anything?"

"Can I come with? I'd like the whole experience."

"Yeah, of course. I'll show you all my favorites."

Sadie tags along, too, and they chatter, pointing out all the different amenities the arena holds. Tori says there is a lounge reserved for families of the players, but both girls say they don't like it in there as much as they like to be with the fans.

We go from stand to stand, picking out a variety of items. Sadie tries to talk me into a peanut butter hot dog, but I can't go that far down this rabbit hole. I do indulge, though, something I haven't done since moving to Seattle. We end up with birria tacos, vegetarian nachos, salmon chowder, and I grab a local beer, as well.

I'll pay for it all later, but I want to live in this moment, in case it's the only time. I learned a long time ago to savor things, enjoy it all while it lasts. Life doesn't offer guarantees.

By the time we get back to the seats, the game is about to start. The lights dim and a movie-like production starts to play on the big screens overhead. Each of the Blades is announced with their picture projected. I can't deny Gavin is the best looking, though all in all, the team is very good-looking.

He's right, though, this is obviously a younger man's sport. Some of the men look barely old enough to drink.

The game starts; everything moves so fast, it's impossible for me to keep up. Tori is good at giving me commentary throughout. Every time the whistle blows, she explains why, making sure I understand the concepts of things like offsides and icing.

"Brighton is hot dogging," Tori says.

"That's not going to end well for him," Sadie says.

"What's that mean?"

"It's showboating. Some of the younger hotshots do it, usually an elder player will have a few words for them," Isla explains. And sure enough, Vaughn skates over to the kid, chest to chest. We can't hear what he says, but the younger player tries to talk back. Vaughn just smiles while one of the guy's teammates pulls him away.

"Looks like it's going to be a chippy game," Tori says, then turns to me to explain further. "It's going to be very physical."

I watch with rapt attention, standing to cheer with everyone else when Seattle scores a goal. The arena chants along with the music and it's more fun than I could have anticipated. Looks like I've been missing out by avoiding sports in favor of classy dinner parties and industry events.

"You're enjoying yourself," Isla says during the intermission between the first and second periods.

"Much more than I thought I would," I confirm.

"Hockey is the best," Sadie sings.

"I have to agree with you there, Sadie."

"Really? So, you'll come to more games now?"

"Do you want me to?"

"Yeah, you're pretty and I like your shirt."

"Oh, well, thank you. You're pretty, too."

"I know, my dad says it all the time. *You're as pretty as your mom, Sadie Baby.* That's what he calls me. Even though I'm not a baby, I let him call me that. I'm going to be old and he's still going to be calling me that," she says, rolling her eyes, but she smiles as she does it.

"Your dad is a nice guy."

"Yep," she says. "The whole team is. But Hugo is kinda weird."

"It's a goalie thing," Tori says. "They're all a bit weird."

"I guess you'd have to be," I say.

"For sure," Sadie says.

The second period starts with a bang. The young "hotdogger" from the other team makes a shitty hit on Letty. I only know it's shitty because Tori tells me it is after the arena boos in unison. Letty leaves the ice and immediately walks the tunnel to the locker rooms.

"He hit his bucket pretty hard, they'll go through concussion protocol," Tori says.

"Is that common? Concussions?"

"They've made strides to make the sport safer, but not enough," she says. "That fucker should have been ejected, but they gave him a two-minute minor instead. The league will review it tomorrow and likely have a hearing that could end up in a suspension, but that doesn't prevent anything like this from happening again."

"Will this be one of those self-governing things that you talked about?"

"Mmm, one of our guys will be on that kid's ass as soon as he leaves the box."

We score a goal on this power play thing, but as soon as the guy's penalty minutes are up, he beelines it for the puck. Vaughn gets on the ice at the same time and heads straight for him, dropping his gloves in the process.

"Oh, shit," Sadie says.

"Sadie," Isla warns but not too harshly.

"Sorry, Mom. Oh! Kick his butt, Vaughn!"

They trade blows, the kid getting a few body shots off on Gavin, but nothing in the face. It's the other way around for Vaughn, though, and soon, the kid is on the ice with Gavin atop him. The officials let it go for a minute before interfering and pulling them off each other. Gavin spits at the kid's feet before he skates over to the box. The other guy gets another penalty, too, and the rest of the game, he plays much cleaner.

"It's like gang rules," I say.

"A little bit, yeah," Tori agrees. "Honor goes a long way in this sport."

Honor. It's not a word I would have associated with Gavin before. But that would have been my broken heart talking. It was honorable of him to stick by Caroline and to make sure his daughter had the best he could offer.

The question that always plagued me was why couldn't he have given them what they needed without marrying her. I know the biggest part was financial. Then when I'd heard he'd been drafted and he was making plenty of money, I hoped that maybe the situation would change.

I'd waited for four years, dreaming of him showing up at my doorstep, begging for another chance. But that didn't happen, either. As more years went by, I settled on the fact that it was never going to happen. There would never be a day that Gavin showed up at my door full of regret.

Until now, anyway. But now is too late. Those fantasies of him fighting for me died a long time ago. Now, the only fantasies I have of Gavin Vaughn are of his head between my thighs after a long game of him fighting.

Because holy hell was that the hottest thing I've ever seen.

16

GAVIN

Tori told me she was at the game last night. I didn't know until after, when Tori texted to say she wasn't waiting for me. But that didn't lessen the boost to my ego from just knowing she'd come to watch.

I wish I'd seen her, though.

This feels like progress, like maybe she's not fully opposed to me in her life. She said she could offer me friendship, but the sadness in her voice made me believe that wasn't exactly true.

I've mostly backed off the past couple of weeks while we've been on the road, but we're home now, and I happen to have two days without games.

"Gavin," she answers when I call, hoping to spend time with her.

"Odette," I mimic. "What are you up to?"

"I'm about to be knee-deep in my emotions. Why?"

"I was hoping I could pick you up, take you to lunch. But maybe that's not what you need right now. What's going on?"

"Flare-up. I wouldn't be great company," she says. I hear the anxiety in her voice and maybe even some fear.

"What do you need, Odette?"

"Rest, I think." Her voice breaks some, even though she tries to hide it.

"All right, Ode. I'll check in with you soon."

She hangs up without another word, only ramping up my worry for her. I don't know what a flare-up is, exactly, but it doesn't take long to find the results on Google. Hashimoto flare-up comes up with page after page of symptoms and personal stories from those who suffer.

The most common things being fatigue and cold sensitivity. It's November, which in the PNW means chilly temps, rain, and the occasional windstorm. I bet that mammoth of a house of hers is impossible to keep heated.

The image of her tiny body shivering under a blanket forms in my mind. It's probably not what's happening but I can't seem to shake it now that it's there. I spend another thirty minutes basically doom scrolling before I take action.

Another hour later, I'm at her door knocking.

"Gavin," is all she gets out before tears stop her words.

"Hey, hey, it's gonna be okay, Ode." I step into her, carrying my bag of supplies in one hand and using the other to wrap her up.

"My hair is falling out," she says, her voice rattling as much as her body.

"Ah, fuck, babe. Come here," I say, bending to leverage under her ass and pick her up. "Where's your room?"

"Upstairs," she says, then she darts her eyes to mine. "I'm not going to fuck you."

"Not why I'm here, Odette." I laugh.

"Why are you here," she says, relaxing some in my arms as I take the stairs as quickly and carefully as I can.

"You sounded like you needed some comfort. I brought some over."

"You? Are you the comfort?" she asks skeptically.

"I wouldn't dare to presume such an idea," I answer, feigning aghast.

"Okay, good," she says with a sigh as I walk into her room and place her on her enormous bed.

"Is this a king size?"

"No, bigger."

"Why?"

"Wouldn't you like to know," she snarks, and I'm glad she at least has her moxie.

"Fuck yeah, I would, but again, not why I'm here. Bathroom?"

She points to a door, then rolls herself twice in the comforter on her bed, releasing a pained groan as she does. Her bathroom has an extra-large bathtub, because of course everything in this house is oversized. It takes a few minutes to find the right temperature, but when it starts to fill, I pull the essential oils from the bag and drop some into the water. Then I go to find her closet and rummage around. I'm trying to find a bathing suit because I don't think she'd appreciate me dumping her into a bath naked as much as I would like to. But other than three drawers full of the sexiest, skimpiest lingerie I've ever seen in my life, I have no luck.

Though, like everything here, the closet is massive and full, I could have missed her stash of bikinis.

"Hey, Ode?" I crawl up the bed, moving away the blanket and her mass of hair until I find her face. It's blotchy with tears, reminding me of a time I don't want to remember. "Do you have a bathing suit?"

"Why?"

"I've started a bath," I say.

"I bathe in the nude, weirdo," she mumbles into the blanket.

"I figured you wouldn't want to do that *with* me. And I was going to get in with you so I can massage your shoulders and help you relax."

"That sounds…presumptuous but also like heaven. I really want a hot bath."

"Okay, so we're on the same page. Swimsuit?"

"I swim in the nude, too."

"You're fucking killing me here, Ode," I say, starting to unroll her from her blanket taco. "Nude it is."

"I'm too tired to argue with you, Gavin. Just get me in the bathtub." Her arms wrap around my neck, and I feel fresh wetness as tears fall.

"How long has this been going on?"

"I've only had a couple before, but never as bad as this. I woke up in the middle of the night, freezing cold," she says when I place her on her feet next to the tub. "I think I overdid it yesterday."

"Tori said you enjoyed yourself." I stretch her chin up and look at her neck, not knowing why. I have no idea what a swollen thyroid looks like, but if I don't get familiar with her neck, I won't notice when it is.

"I did, my body didn't." She runs a hand through her long dark hair, too easily finger combing out a clump. "L-look."

"Is that normal?"

"I don't know. I don't know what to do, Gavin. What if it all falls out?"

"That's not going to happen," I say, untying her silk robe and finding nothing underneath. She's suffering, so I suffer in my own way and don't take her in the way I want. I don't touch and explore every inch of her soft skin with my mouth.

Instead, I take her hand and help her into the tub. She exhales a deep sigh when she submerges her shoulders under the water. I go to the counter and take a hairbrush before undressing down to my boxers and climbing in the bath behind her. She doesn't move at all, not even a flinch as she buries her face in her knees.

"My business depends on how I look," she says. "I can't lose my hair."

I pick up a different bottle of oil and dump some into my hands, slowly massaging it into her scalp.

"You're not going to lose all your hair," I say, even as I watch more strands easily fall out. "You have healthy, thick hair. You'll survive losing a little while we figure out how to prevent it. But even if you did lose it all, you'd still be the most beautiful woman I've ever seen. Your hair doesn't change that, or the fact that you're the best at what you do."

"My brain says you're right, but my nerves can't hear that right now. Oh god, that feels amazing." She melts under my fingers, her body falling back into mine. I'd been trying to keep from being skin to skin with her, not wanting to blur boundaries just because she's in crisis. But fucking hell, she's soft and impossibly silky against my hard muscles. My cock reacts all on its own.

"Try and relax," I say, scooting back an inch.

"Your dick is making that a little hard," she says, but can't do it without laughing.

"Your ass is making my dick hard; this is your fault. I'm trying to be a friend here."

"Well, I'm sorry I have such a great ass," she says. "Whose crazy idea was this?"

"Mine. But you didn't argue."

"We could have gotten in the sauna."

"Of course, this place has a sauna," I say.

"Right? I'm not sure it's in functioning condition. This house is crazy, what was I thinking!"

"You'd have to answer that one, Odette." I add more oil to my palm and work her nape, making her moan.

"I haven't done many overly lavish things in life. I lived in the same shoebox apartment for years, it barely had furniture so I could fit all my racks of clothes and shoes. I amassed all this wealth and didn't do anything with it," she says. "My sole focus was styling other people's lives. When I moved here, I needed new distractions. This house is taking the brunt of it."

"You're styling it instead of people."

"That is exactly what my mother said. Lower, please?"

"Sure," I say, working my fingers to her shoulders. "This isn't weird for you?"

"Are you fucking kidding me?" She laughs. "It's the strangest thing I've ever done. But I've also never felt like this. I think I was on the verge of a panic attack when you showed up, so thank you for that. I'm sure I'll be mortified later when my brain starts functioning properly. But it isn't anything you haven't seen before, I guess."

"Yeah, it's pretty weird for me, too."

"Really? Aren't you athletes all man-whores? I figured you'd have a piece of ass in every city you play in. Don't you have a harem of them here at home?"

I don't know why, but I like that she already thinks of Seattle as her home.

"Is that what you think?"

"Are you telling me it isn't true?" She turns her head to see me. "You aren't hooking up with groupies, or whatever they're called, since your divorce?"

"There were a few times. Before—" I hesitate on how much to say. I don't want her to feel pressure, but damn it, she's naked in my arms and doesn't have her armor up. Maybe now is as good a time as any. "Before a gorgeous brunette returned into my life and reminded me of what I've been missing."

"Gavin…" she says.

"Shh." I stop her, my thumb pressing to her lips that have more color now than when I got here. "I told you before, this is not a transactional relationship. You don't owe me yourself just because I want you. If friendship is all you can give, I'll take it gladly. I'll be the best one you've ever had."

Her eyes bounce between mine, weighing what I've said. I imagine she has a hard time trusting anything I say. I can't blame her, but I hope she finds the sincerity she's searching for.

"You really mean that, don't you?" she asks, her breath tickling my thumb that I haven't moved. I like the feel of her lips. I'd like them more on my mouth or my cock, but I'll take what I can get.

"Of course, I do. I still care, Ode. Whatever you need, I'll try my hardest to give." My other hand falls from her shoulder, inadvertently catching some side boob action. I close my eyes for a brief moment, trying to keep my composure. "Sorry."

"It's okay," she says quietly, turning back around, but snuggling deeper into me at the same time. A cup sits at the side of the tub, and I use it to wet her hair, she hums in pleasure as the heat soaks her scalp.

Gently, I wash her hair, and once I get the conditioner worked in, I brush through her long strands.

"See," I say, showing her the brush, nearly clear of hair, when I'm done. "There's not much here." Odette releases a relieved sigh. I get the conditioner rinsed out as the water starts to cool.

She wastes no time hopping out of the tub and giving me the absolute best view of her glorious ass as she does.

"What else do you have in your bag of tricks?" she asks, wrapping a towel around her and setting another one on the tub ledge for me. I stand, enjoying the way her pupils pop to life as she takes in the water streaming down my chest. Then I push my soaked boxers down over my ass and step out of them. They were barely hanging on, anyhow.

"A dry bean soup mix that's Tori's favorite whenever she doesn't feel well. My mom makes it in mason jars and sends it to us every few months. And a heating pad."

"Suddenly, I'm not feeling so cold." She swallows hard when her eyes drag down my chest and lower to my cock that's enjoying her attention. "I don't think you play fair, Vaughn."

"Me?" I laugh. "It was your naked ass rubbing against me the last half hour. Who the hell doesn't have a fucking bathing suit anyway?" I grab the towel and wrap it around my waist before I step out.

"I lied. I wanted to see what you'd do."

"Are you kidding?" I ask, looking up to see her smirk. "You fucking tease."

She apologizes again, but this one is full of silent laughter.

"You hungry, Ode?" I ask, stepping closer to her. So close that she has to tip her chin up to keep eye contact.

"Not for soup." Her chest heaves, the towel holding on for dear life over her ample breasts.

"For what?"

"To feel beautiful," she says, so softly I almost ask her to repeat it.

"I don't want you to hate me tomorrow, Odette," I say, cupping her cheeks. "I don't want you to wake up and think I took advantage of this situation."

"You're so fucking nice, Gavin," she says. "I appreciate it, I do. Everything you've done for me tonight; I can't thank you enough. But right now, I need you to set that aside and give me some of that feral attitude you have on the ice. I need you to fuck me into oblivion."

"And tomorrow?"

"Forget it happened and just be my friend," she says. "You can say no, if it's too much to ask."

17

GAVIN

Forget? Not a chance in hell. Can I say no? Not a fucking chance. If all I get is one chance to be with Odette again, I'll use it to show her how good we could be together. How nobody could make her feel the way I will.

"Are you up for this?"

"You think I won't be able to keep up with you, hotshot?" Odette asks, a brow raising steadily over one amused eye.

"You've had a rough day, pumpkin," I tease. "I wouldn't want you to wear yourself out too quickly." I finger the towel, right at her cleavage, pulling her an inch closer.

"Pumpkin?"

"Hotshot?" I fire back, and she smiles wickedly. "Be sure, Ode. If we do this, you need to be one hundred percent." I won't have her hating me for this, too.

"You need to be one hundred percent, Gavin. You can't fuck me tonight and lay claim on me tomorrow. That's not what this is. It's not what I need."

I've been laying claim to her in one way or another since that first night in front of the shop she worked for at eighteen. I may have placed obstacle after obstacle, but I always saw her as my end game. When I've imagined myself old and retired somewhere with Tori coming over to visit with my grandkids, it's been Odette my fucked-up brain envisioned by my side. So, no, I don't agree with her terms entirely.

But fuck it. I drop my towel and stand there waiting for her to do the same.

"Birth control?"

"I'm covered," she says breathlessly, her eyes, once again, darting between mine. "Clean?"

"Absolutely."

"Then fuck me, Gavin," she purrs and releases the twist holding up her towel. Finally, I get to take her in without shame or fear. She's thin, yet with curves from her full tits and ass. Her skin, flawless and unmarred, is the opposite of mine that's consistently finding new scars. Her nipples harden while I study every inch of her body, from her still wet hair that clings to her shoulders, to the toes she has painted a shade that matches that perfect mouth of hers.

I can't wait any longer.

Palming the back of her skull, I pull her mouth to mine. Dive in. She asked for feral, she'll fucking get it. She matches my intensity, her own hands finding purchase in the curls at my temples, her leg rising against mine as if she's trying to climb me. I help her by pulling her knee up to my hip. She rises on her toes to keep balance as she starts to writhe against me. Hip to hip.

We're so ready, but it's far too soon for my cock to drive in. She wants oblivion, not a quickie.

Abandoning her head, I snake my hand down her side, over the ample curve of her plump ass and slip my fingers into her cunt. She cries into my mouth and tries to rise further, but her height won't allow it. I help with a hand on her ass, easily lifting her up so she can wrap those silky-smooth legs around my waist.

"Get inside me," she cries.

"Fuck my fingers, Ode. I'll get you there," I tell her.

"It won't be enough," she practically whines, and I stifle a laugh while I insert another. She hums and starts working her hips in earnest.

"Do you dream of this, Ode? How long have you been aching for me to make you come?"

"I haven't," she pants.

"Liar." I walk us out of the bathroom and unceremoniously drop her onto the bed. She pouts at the sudden change, since it robbed her of an orgasm. She can play games, but I want those played in truths. "You can come when you tell me the fucking truth."

She narrows her eyes but doesn't recant.

Dropping to my knees on the floor, I pull her body to the end of the bed, placing a leg over each shoulder and her cunt right where I want it. She's beautiful everywhere. Perfect. Odette props herself up on her elbows, allowing a clear view down her body to where I perch at her entrance. Still, she says nothing.

I tease her first with soft air that makes her eyelashes flutter. Then I scent her, just the tip of my nose grazing her folds and clit. That makes her lips part, and her blink lasts a long few seconds. A kiss to her thigh and another a little closer. She twitches, needy and impatient. I feel the tension in her legs as she curls her toes behind my back.

My tongue slowly takes a first taste, not too deep or long. Just enough to have us both anticipating the next.

"I fucking knew," I whisper.

"You knew what?"

"That I remembered the way you taste. The way you smell. Like an iced cinnamon roll."

"I do not," she protests.

"You fucking do. And it's been burned into my senses for decades. I couldn't escape it, ever," I say before going in for another taste. Only this time, I don't stop, I can't. Not when she's this delicious, this ready and willing. Not when her thighs tighten around my head because she is just as hungry for this as I am. Her hips rock, matching the same rhythm as my tongue, my nose bumping her clit with each thrust as she earnestly fucks my face. I pull away slightly to ask, "The truth?"

Her hand finds the top of my head, pushing it back where she wants it as she cries out one single word that sends my own head spinning.

"Forever."

Seconds later, she shatters, and I savor every ounce of it, my fingers tight on her thighs holding her close.

Forever. Just like I'd hoped.

Standing, I flip her over to her stomach.

"On your knees, pumpkin. Ass in the air, arms stretched out in front of you." She obeys, and I collect the last remnants from her pussy, spreading them over my cock so we both shine with it. I'd love to wrap her hair around my fist while I ride her, but she's fragile enough about it and that's not the sort of damage I want to cause her right now.

I want to cause the kind that makes every other man insignificant. Boring and underwhelming. I want to make this an experience she can't get over, so that she'll be willing to come back for more. I want her body to beg her mind and her heart for more of me. Hell yes, I'm laying claim to Odette Quinn. She doesn't have to accept that yet, but she will. I can wait a little longer, it's already been twenty fucking years, after all.

Lining my cock up to her, I push in without warning. My mind screams *mine, mine, mine,* as Odette moans my name. I want to punish her for making me wait so long. But it's me who takes the lesson. Me who learns with every drag against her clenching pussy what I could have had before now if I'd been stronger. Braver. Wiser.

We should have had this before. Her clawing at the sheets of her impossibly large bed, me gripping her ass, spreading it wide so I can see myself enter her.

"Fuck, Gavin. That's…it's so…fuck."

I climb over her, my knees on either side of her ass, still pounding into her as I lean over. Pressing kisses across her shoulder and up her neck to her ear. "Good?"

"Mmhmm."

"Do you want to come again?"

"Need," she gasps. "Need to. Oh, fuck."

Snaking an arm under her breasts to hold her to me, I roll us over so I'm on my back. I pump into her, moving my fingers to play with her clit. She's so sensitive she instinctively tries to squirm away from them before huffing and pushing herself against them to get what she needs. Her arm raises above her head, finding my curls again as she crashes through another orgasm.

"You're a hair puller," I whisper. "I like that."

"Oh god, sorry."

"Don't fucking be, keep doing it," I demand, then reposition us again. I prop her head and shoulders on pillows before I kneel between her legs, taking another taste of her. "It is fucking cinnamon. Taste for yourself."

Wrapping my fingers around her wrists, I stretch our arms above our heads and seal my mouth to hers. She strains to meet me, again trying to match my energy, but she's worn out already. Still, I won't go easy on her just yet.

She wants feral oblivion. I widen her legs with my knees and slam back into her. I swallow her gasps and moans, but I don't stop. I release one of her arms and immediately she's yanking at my hair, pulling my head back so we stare at each other while I fuck her with abandon. Sweat beads at the apple of her cheeks, and I lap it up.

"I've miss…" she starts, biting her lip to keep the rest of the words inside.

I've missed it, too, my head screams while my body threatens to rebel if it doesn't get what it wants soon. My hips push into her, finding the right spot that makes her eyes roll back. Yeah, I've missed this. I've missed this connection; the physical one and the one far less obvious.

I've missed the way she clenches around my cock and the way she pushes her gorgeous tits against me. I've missed the way she stares up at me in awe, like I'm some fucking immortal god.

I've missed how one look from her is enough to make me feel like I could conquer cities, countries, and worlds with just my two bare hands. Most of all, I've missed the affection that I still see there. It's all I need, a spark that I can nurture into an inferno.

Some hope.

With that in my heart, I rear up and fuck her ferally now.

"You're going to come with me and those haunting eyes of yours do not leave mine. Do you understand? They don't fucking leave mine." She nods, her sight a little glazed over but she does as she's told. I thumb her clit, so lightly, barely a touch, and her body levitates off the bed, her lashes shuttering. "Odette."

"Sorry, sorry. Fuck, Gavin, I'm so close."

"Come, Ode," I get the coarse words out as I feel the first stream leave me and enter her. Her body shudders, and she fights to keep her eyes open as I empty into her, and she takes everything I have to offer while she gives me the same. No, there's no way I'm not laying claim to this woman. There's something indelible between us that couldn't be erased by even time. She's completely spent, the only part of her moving is her chest still heaving to regulate breath. "Stay put."

I head back into the bathroom to clean up, and get a warm washcloth and the lotion to combat muscle fatigue. After gently cleaning up Odette, I sit behind her and start rubbing the lotion in at her neck and shoulders.

She hasn't said anything, she's just followed me with her stare, taking in every step I make. Yet, she's not fussing to make me stop. She's not tensing up, instead she's relaxed and languid. I move my thumbs in circles over her collarbone and down her arms, she falls farther back into me, her breathing growing shallower by the minute.

"You're a great dad, aren't you?"

"I'd like to think so, but only Tori can really say. I try to be, anyway."

"She moved back here to be close to you. I think that is probably answer enough."

"I guess," I say. "Though I think partly, she wanted to give her mom the space to create a life that didn't revolve around being a mother. Once she realized what all Caroline gave up."

That does make Odette's muscles firm under my fingers. I'm not implying that Caroline was the only one to give something up, not at all. We all did. We all paid a price. But if Odette wants to go down that road of conversation, she's going to have to say the words. She's already said several times she doesn't want to talk about it.

"Will you tell me about getting drafted?" she asks, and so I do. Leaving out some of the details, like Caroline and Tori being by my side. I focus, instead, on the nervousness I felt, then the joy, then the apprehension because it's very difficult to feel worthy to play on a team of men you grew up idolizing.

I tell her about my first professional practice and my first game in The Show. How I was so worked up I didn't sleep the night before and ran on pure adrenaline. What I don't tell her is that the first game I played in New York City, I nearly looked her up. The urge to track her down was stronger than almost anything I'd ever felt, but I tamped it down, not wanting to disturb any life she'd built for herself. I definitely don't tell her that the urge never left, or that every time I stepped off a plane in New York, I searched the crowds, hoping for a glimpse of her.

She makes comments here and there, or asks questions for more details, and laughs when I recall the way the guys razzed me as a rookie. It's a sleepy laugh, muffled by the pillow she snuggles into.

By the time I've finished telling her about my first season, I've massaged every inch of every limb, and her eyes are barely open.

She hasn't kicked me out, though. So, I snuggle in behind her and pull the comforter up around our shoulders while I listen to our hearts matching tempo. Tomorrow won't be so easy with her, I fear. She'll wake with her shell firmly intact, all the cracks from today repaired. She'll go back to being the strong, independent woman who doesn't rely on anyone for anything.

I'll go back to admiring her for it, but it will be different now. Because I won't forget that when she did need something, it was me she let give it. Not just the sex, she let me comfort her, which means measurably more.

Realistically, I know where this goes. She'll keep me in the friend zone. She'll likely even keep dating the stuffy guy. For now, it's enough. For now, I'll take what she gives.

For now. Not forever.

18

ODETTE

G avin's body is the most ridiculous thing I've ever seen.

I woke up at least a half hour ago, and after a moment of wondering what the fuck I did, I've been studying him the entire time. Every inch, every muscle, every bruise and scar. Most are new, but a couple I remember from before. Like the tiny one at the corner of his mouth. It sits at the edge of his bottom lip, an old injury from a stick to the face. He told me the story once, just as he told me new stories last night.

It was as enjoyable for me this time as it was then. His voice soothes me as much as how he worked my muscles with his massage.

Maybe if I was a better woman, I'd have been scandalized or ashamed to wake up next to him this morning. I wasn't, though. I wanted something last night and I asked honestly for it. There's no shame in that. There's none now, either, as I ogle him while he sleeps. If he feared me doing this, he should have left before I woke.

What does exist is an apprehension that I've given him something he won't so easily back away from. And a fear that I've left a gap for him to crawl through.

The sex was…exactly what I hope for every time I get in bed with a man. Only, Gavin didn't disappoint. He was relentless, never stopping his consistent thrusting, never showing any sign of tiring, even as I barely held on to consciousness.

Everything he did for, and to, me last night was exactly what I needed without knowing it was what I needed. He knew, though. Hell, he even came prepared. Though, I don't think he anticipated it ending in my bed.

I didn't, either, when I opened my door to him. Weakness isn't something I show others. We all have it, in one form or another, but I never wear it proudly. Showing it to Gavin didn't scare me, and that's what I fear the most.

He shifts, and the blanket falls off him, baring his ass for me to see. Two taut globes just willing me to bite them. It's not fair how beautiful his body is. Or how well he uses it. He's incomparable. Preston surely could never fuck me the way Gavin did last night, though he has gotten somewhat braver in bed.

What do I do now?

Do I wake him up, ask him to leave, and break this little fairy tale I've been in? Or do I let it last a little while longer? Take what I want, what I've missed. What was stolen from me. Sooner or later, I'll return to my senses but right now…right now, I'm still feeling reckless and emotional. Right now, I'm ready to show him what he's been missing.

Slinking back down under the covers, I snuggle into his side. He turns on his side, his arm coming around me and pulling me closer. My cheek rests on his pectoral, a firm but not uncomfortable pillow. The bonus is that his nipple is right there for the taking. I dart my tongue out, tasting it before pressing a kiss there. He hums and his cock comes to life against my leg. I press another kiss to his chest, my eyes upturned to his face. He still sleeps, though the pressure of his fingertips deepens. I press another, lower this time, then another still lower. His eyes remain closed, even as his dick wakes up fully. When I've trailed kisses down his chest, over his abdomen and happy trail, I look up again.

"Ode," he moans sleepily. I sigh in relief that it's my name he calls. Then he opens those sky-colored eyes. All his attention on me as I prop just above his hard erection. I raise an eyebrow in question. Does he want this as much as I want to give it? "You have no idea how good you look with your head between my thighs."

"Not as good as I'll look with your cock in my mouth," I say, making the appendage twitch against my waiting lips.

"I'll have to see that for myself before I can decide. Years of faded memories and torrid fantasies don't count," he says. Has he fantasized about me? Would I have wanted him to when he had a wife by his side? Ignoring my wayward thoughts, I drag my tongue up from base to tip, savoring the silkiness of him.

He smells of the oils we bathed in last night, but he tastes salty and manly in a way I haven't had in so long. This isn't something I do. If I'm being honest, I'm usually a selfish lover. I live my life like men in that way, I do what I want, take what I want. And I *want* Gavin's cock so deep down my throat.

"Don't be gentle," I purr before swallowing him.

"Ah, fuck, Ode," he groans, his hips rising. I start a steady bobbing, my tongue curved to cradle what I can of his girth. I may be out of practice but I'm also a huge overachiever. So, I go deeper, and he curses. His hips find a rhythm, one hand in my hair while the other curls around his head so he can look down his body. Gavin's heels push into the bed, allowing him to rise more. I nearly gag, but relax my throat to try to accommodate.

A rush of feminine power washes over me as I work him with my mouth and hand. This beautiful fucking cock is hard because of me. Gavin Vaughn, star hockey player, is losing his mind because of what I'm doing to him.

I'm not the type to get starstruck. I wouldn't have lasted in my career if I were. But the way he's watching me is heady and euphoric in a way that I think most would feel if they were meeting their celebrity idol.

I could become addicted to this. It's fucking terrifying.

But nothing could pull me away right now as the first drops of pre-cum leak from his tip. I pull up and am about to dive down again but he stops me.

"No. Get up here," he says, then pulls me up his body. He sits up and helps lower me on his cock. I gasp at the fullness and he mutters, "That's better."

With his arms wrapped around me and my legs twining around his waist, he pumps in. Eye to eye, noses grazing, he whispers things I'm not sure he'd say if we weren't so impossibly connected right now.

"I missed you. More than you could know, Ode. I didn't understand then. I didn't know what I know now."

"Gavin," I warn, but it comes out as more of a needy whine.

"Just listen. Let me say it, just once. Look at me, Odette," he says, at the same time he doubles the effort with his dick. "I loved you. I never said it, but you should know. I loved you and I have mourned us every single day."

I gasp as the tears form in my eyes along with the rush of blood to my core. A sob escapes as I orgasm, my body not knowing what to do with all the sensation.

Gavin never lets me go. Not even after I've shattered and buried my face in his neck. He pets me in the most soothing way, and I love it.

I love it.

I hate it.

I want to run from it as much as I want to cling for more.

How could he possibly know that I needed to hear that? It's the one thing I've questioned the most, convincing myself that he must not have. That he couldn't have felt the same as I did because how could he walk away from that and pretend like we never knew each other. When what we were was sweet and caring and beautifully in love. I knew it. But I convinced myself it must have all been a lie, it was the only way I survived the idea that he was creating that same sort of love with someone else.

I housed myself in doubt while he found comfort in her. They didn't marry out of romantic love but there must have been affection and love making in all that time.

My skin prickles, a chill taking hold, as if the ceiling has opened up and snowflakes have started to fall on my bare body.

"Shit," Gavin cusses, pulling the blanket around us. "I'm sorry, Ode. That was selfish and I promised I wouldn't be that with you."

"I needed to hear it," I say, trying to keep my words steady. "It just brings up more..."

"I understand," he soothes. "Do you have food in that huge-ass kitchen of yours?"

"Some." Untangling myself from him, I rise from bed and move into my closet to find a wrap. My comfort with being naked around him has vanished and been replaced by muddled thoughts. I can feel him watching me as I go, but I avoid looking at his face. I can't be trusted when I look at him. At least I'm self-aware enough to know that Gavin makes me weak in ways I don't allow myself to be. The past twelve hours or so excluded, of course.

As I tie the wrap securely closed, I also don that invisible armor. Padlocking the steel cage I keep around my heart, I raise my head high and pull my shoulders back, ready to face the consequences of my actions on the other side of the wall.

He's walking out of the bathroom, the sweatpants he came in last night hanging low off his hips. It's easier to face him when he's dressed, but only marginally.

"Let me make you some breakfast and I'll get the soup simmering, then I'll get out of your hair."

"Is it even still there?" I ask sarcastically, raising a hand to my head.

"It's still there. Maybe less indulgence next time you come to one of my games, though," he says, winking, as he walks out of the room.

"Gavin," I stop him. "Thank you. For last night, thank you."

"What are friends for, Ode?"

The best sex of my life. You're in trouble, girl.

Sighing, I follow him downstairs. He rummages through my kitchen, placing items on my counter.

"Avocado toast, okay?"

"That sounds good, I still have some of the bread you made," I answer, pulling out a few pieces and popping them into the toaster.

"Do you have a crockpot?"

"I'm ashamed to admit that it's the only way I know how to cook. I used my oven in New York as storage. I didn't cook anything in it the whole time I lived there."

"Storage?" he asks, laughing. "For what?"

"A bin that had all my winter scarves and gloves, mostly. Stop laughing, storage in New York is hard to come by!"

"Suddenly, this house makes more sense."

"Yes. She's too big for me. I really only use a handful of rooms. But I love her." I pull the crockpot out of the cupboard, and he laughs again.

"How old is this?" He takes it from me, seeing all the spots of worn off paint and the dents from not being handled as lovingly as it could have been. But those aren't from me, it came to me that way.

"Old." I shrug. "It was a thrift shop find shortly after I moved to the City. It's one of my oldest companions."

He gives me a funny look but dumps the contents of the mason jar in it, then fills the jar up with water and adds that, too.

"Should be ready in eight hours."

"It's that easy?"

"Yeah, my mom has it down to a science."

"How is she doing?"

"Good," he says with a wide smile. "She's been regulated for a handful of years now; it was like meeting her for the first time. There's a clarity or awareness in her now that was never there before."

"That's really special, Gavin. I'm glad she's found something that works for her." It always occurred to me that her mental health weighed on him more than he let on.

We make small talk while we eat breakfast. Mostly about my college experiences and my first jobs. It's foreign to me, talking about this to someone who doesn't already know. Usually, the people in my life know more details about the path my career took than I do. I haven't had to sell myself to anyone in so long now. It's probably the same for Gavin.

But we don't know each other's life stories, and I realize he stayed as closed off to me as I did to information about him. For me, it was a decision made out of self-preservation. Was it the same for him?

When we finish eating, he cleans up, telling me to stay put at the table that overlooks the water. I can see his reflection perfectly in the glass and count every time he looks up from dishes and wiping down my counter.

Part of me wants to turn around. Part of me wants to run back to New York. I won't do that, though. No matter how complicated he makes me feel, I won't let his presence make decisions for me. That's not who I am.

Men don't rule me, I don't center myself around them.

No matter how good they are with their dick.

19

ODETTE

"Who are these women we're meeting?" Britton asks as I pull into the parking lot of the bar I've rented out for the night. It's a burlesque club, and it was highly recommended for a girls' night venue.

"You already know Vanessa," I say. Britton has been a friend for long enough that she and my bestie have crossed paths on more than a few occasions. "The rest are mostly wives and girlfriends of Seattle's NHL team."

"How do you know them?"

"Someone I grew up with is on the team."

"Oh? Oh! Look at your face! This is not just a *someone*, this is a *someone* you've done naughty things with." She narrows her perfectly lined eyes at me. "You dirty slut, how dare you keep this information from me?"

"Oh, fuck off." I laugh at her mock outrage. "You went to Saint Barts for an entire month with that Javier guy and didn't tell me until a year later that you weren't there for filming."

"Only because he turned out to be a drug lord. How embarrassing." She sighs with the dramatics only a great actress can deliver. "Besides, I was so young."

"You were thirty-one," I remind her.

"Which is very young when you plan to find your way into immortality before you die. Which I do, thank you very much."

"Well, when you find that Lestat or whoever, send him my way. I swear I saw a frown line this morning."

"Bullshit! You still look the same as when I met you, you're like that *Price is Right* guy, you age backwards," she says, getting out of the car.

"You need an eye exam."

"You need to get laid, you'd frown far less," she snaps. This is always how we've been. While Vanessa is my classy conspirator, Britton is a wild spirit always looking for fun and adventure. "Oooh, you have been getting laid! It's written all over your face. Woman, you telegraph too easily. I need to teach you some tricks."

"Stop looking at me," I grumble, and she laughs louder.

"You and I are going to have a long talk later, my friend."

"Yes, we are. You need to fill me in on what happened with you and that southern hottie who co-starred with you in that last movie."

"Ah, Miles Jameson," she says wistfully. "I think I could have made myself a wife for that man. If only I was the one he wanted."

"Don't I know that feeling all too fucking well," I mumble, opening the door and ushering my friend in ahead of me. Seems we really do have some catching up to do.

The space is romantically lit with dim overhead chandeliers and candles on the tables. Its décor reminiscent of the twenties and thirties with perfectly draped crisp linens and dark wood. A few rope swings and acrobat bars hang from the ceiling so the performers will be seen from the entire room.

Everyone else is already here, because, of course, the Hollywood starlet is always fashionably late, even though I showed up at her hotel twenty minutes earlier than planned. Vanessa greets us with two glasses of pink champagne.

"Hey, thanks, Vanessa," I say, air kissing her.

"Of course! Britt, great to see you, it's been far too long."

"Not since our girls' trip to Dominican Republic, we should do that again soon."

"That was three years ago, and I still haven't recovered. I'm convinced you don't know the meaning of the word relax," Vanessa says.

"I do know," Britton argues. "It means party until five in the morning, nap for five hours, and then start again."

"If five hours is only a nap, I haven't had a night's sleep in eight years," Isla says, stepping up to the three of us. "Hi."

"Hi, thank you for your help with all this," I tell her. "Britton Macy, this is Isla Wylder."

"Wylder? Oh shit, you're married to Cillian. I didn't put it all together when Odette said NHL wives. You, my new friend, are a very lucky lady."

"You know of him?" Isla asks, grinning like she knows exactly how lucky she is.

"My director for this film is a gay Canadian man with an obscene infatuation with your husband."

"How obscene?" Isla asks.

"Simon has worked with the most famous A-listers in the game, but he'd faint on sight if your husband walked up to him. Who can blame him, though, right? You've married a very pretty man."

"As long as he keeps his teeth, anyway," Isla teases. "Come on in and meet the others."

Two hours later, the show is done, and we're all teetering the line between buzzed and on-our-ass drunk. Except Isla, who passes on every alcoholic drink but has a second helping of the dessert being passed around.

"How did you two meet?" Willa asks Britton and me.

"I'll never forget it," Britton starts. "I could have ruined my entire career before it had ever really taken off. I was cast as Claire in *The Brownstone,* fresh on the scene at only twenty-two. The studio had pushed a stylist on me for my red-carpet debut event. I was sent to the event to be introduced and first impressions matter, you know? Except the stylist was trying to dress me like some sexy sixteen-year-old straight out of a Britney Spears video or that movie *Clueless.* Short plaid skirts and thigh-high stockings. I argued and said I refused to be infantilized. The studio was pissed at me for being 'bratty and problematic'. Anyway, I searched for up-and-coming stylists and found a video of Odette."

"I was barely older than she was," I add. "I'd made a few videos with styling tips and put them up on YouTube in the hopes that someone might see them. They were so poorly made and awful, but this was before we had the technology to make cutesy little cuts for TikTok."

"They weren't awful," Britton admonishes. "They were insightful, and you had a style I could relate to. Anyway, I got in touch, hired her to find me an outfit for that red carpet and another for the afterparty. The press ate me up and the studio never said another word."

"What did you dress her in?" one of the other wives asks. I've only just met her tonight and can't recall her name. Madison, maybe? Or Mackenzie. I've had too much champagne to recall.

"I dressed her in something very reminiscent of an iconic Brigitte Bardot red dress from the fifties. Everyone at that time was dressing as scantily clad as they could get away with, looking more like they should be stepping on stage at a rock concert rather than walking the same sidewalks as Marilyn Monroe and Audrey Hepburn," I say. "I wanted Britton to stand out as classic and classy, because she is, so long as her mouth is shut."

"Oh my god," she laughs. "I can't argue it, but how dare you say it in front of a room of strangers."

"You just showed this room of 'strangers' your whole ass a few minutes ago," Vanessa reminds her. One of the performers had offered to teach

Britton some tricks on the overhead bar and she eagerly accepted despite not being dressed quite right for it.

"Also true." She shrugs and drains the remnants of her glass. "What can I say? I'm nursing a heartache."

That's met with a round of sighs, and someone says, 'do tell'.

"Yes, Britton. Spill some tea," I say.

"It's a tale as old as time. Girl falls in love with a boy whose heart was taken by another a long time ago. She's practically a ghost to him now, they haven't spoken in years. But he holds a sense of responsibility and devotion to her that I can't crack through," she says, with a sad smile. "Honestly, it would make the *best* movie."

"Would it have a happy ever after?" Willa asks, sympathetically.

"We'll have to wait and see, I guess. But I have hope."

"He's an idiot if he doesn't see how great you are," someone else adds.

"That's the thing," Britton says, resting her elbows on her knees and placing her face in her hands. "I think he does. The way he looks at me tells me he does. The small things he does for me; be it checking in to make sure I've eaten, or that my stress level isn't too high after a long day. He makes sure I relax and laugh, that it isn't all work all the time. He's protective of me, wary of some of the studio big wigs that stand too close and expect too much attention. And maybe that's who he is with everyone, but it felt special."

I can't help how her words conjure a picture of Gavin in my own mind. He does those sorts of things for me. It's been two weeks since we had sex, but he hasn't pressured me since. In fact, that morning after breakfast, he left as if we hadn't shared anything but a friendly meal, and he's been nothing but *friendly* since. He checks in with a call or a text every couple of days, making sure I feel well, have eaten, gotten sleep.

We've become oddly amicable, and I find myself concerned for him most days, too. Wondering how beat up he is after a game, which I've been watching all from the comfort of my own house. I haven't braved going back to the arena, though he's offered tickets. The worry that it sends the wrong kind of signal lives in the back of my mind like a lead weight chained to my ankle.

Or it's because of the signal it sends to me. I want to be there, to experience the ride with him as much as I can before I lose the chance. Every day, I lie to myself that I don't care about him as something more than just a guy I know. Every day, I pretend that I don't want him back in my bed. Every day, I remind myself of how much it hurt to watch him say I do to Caroline. How I sobbed in my backyard until my parents came home to find me and my father had to carry me inside.

Then I see Tori at school and am reminded of why. The more I grow to know her, the more I don't hate that my heartache was part of the price to raise her, because she's exceptional in so many ways. There's no way to know if she'd be who she is today if Gavin hadn't made the decision he did. Am I so selfish that I can't see that? No, of course not.

When he calls, I often steer the conversation to her, and I've learned how great of a life they gave her. Now that she's not some faceless, nameless kid, I'm thankful for her in ways I couldn't have expected.

But then there is Preston. He takes me out a night or two every week. We go to fancy restaurants that remind me of my life in New York. We have intellectual conversations about art and travel that remind me of my life back in New York. We sometimes have sex, and that, too, reminds me of my life back in New York, and the way I sought men who weren't exactly available.

It's probably why he's attracted to me. Preston is easy; not exciting or challenging, but I know what to expect with him and there's comfort in that.

"Maybe the best way to get over him is to get under a hockey player. Who on the team is single?" Britton asks.

"Blom, if you like hot goalies with a side of strange," Isla says. "He's a sweetheart, though. Then there's Letty, Axel, Vaughn."

"A side of strange sounds mildly intriguing, but who is this Vaughn guy," Britton asks, looking directly at me with a shit-eating grin.

"Gavin, he's the one I grew up with."

"What's the story there?" she asks.

"We graduated high school and went our separate ways," I say, trying to sound very unattached and casual. "Didn't see him again until I moved here and met his daughter at work."

"You teach his daughter?" she asks.

"Mentor," I correct. "I'm not a professor."

"Are you dating?"

"Yes, but not him."

"So, he's a free agent?"

"I didn't say that," I say, taking another long sip of my drink and not looking up to see the various women laughing.

My defenses are lowering with Gavin, I can admit that. He's not as far off the table as I've kept him before, but he's not part of my place setting yet, either. The week between him telling me he was marrying Caroline, and the day of their wedding, shaped the person I am. It's not so easy to set that aside. I live by the rules that hurt girl made for me. They've protected me well, so far.

Willa quickly shut the conversation down by saying there's nothing wrong with a woman going after what she wants if the man is single and willing.

Maybe Gavin isn't willing and that's why he hasn't been back at my door. Or maybe he's who he says he is and I just don't know how to trust him.

And that's exactly why I keep going back to Preston. Because he doesn't cause this mental turmoil. He also doesn't cause the same explosive orgasms or the knot of anticipation in my tummy when I'm about to see him.

"There's some piping hot tea there," Britton whispers to me. "Isn't there?"

"Scorching hot."

20
GAVIN

"When you bringing Quinn back around, Vaughn?" Letty asks when we get off the ice after morning skate. "I miss her."

The coaches kicked our asses today, the price you pay when you lose in spectacular fashion like we did last game. We're usually a cohesive unit, but something was off. I chalk it up to the holidays approaching, life always feels busier from Thanksgiving to New Years, and even though we've all been doing this for so long, it's never easy to not be home with our families.

"I'm trying to get her to come with me tonight," I answer. Willa is hosting a bowling night for the team and families. A way to get together, have some fun, blow off whatever funk we've been under.

I can't see Odette bowling, but she hasn't said no. She hasn't said yes, either. But a win is a win, and I'll consider it that, unless she declines. It's been a good couple of weeks with her; I haven't seen her, but she's answered all my calls and texts.

We've been talking like friends. Little by little, I'm gaining ground. Regaining the trust she once had in me that I shit all over.

She laughs more with me now, though. There's less defensiveness in our conversations and she's starting to tell me of her escapades over the years. Like the first time she met George Clancy, one of the biggest A-list actors of our generation. She immediately disliked him, saying he was the epitome of a nepo-baby. He hated that she didn't swoon for him and pursued her for weeks, until she told him she had an STI so he would leave her alone.

Or how her first summer in the City she'd gotten an internship and couldn't go home but didn't have the money to stay, either. She slept on the floor of a friend's closet-sized apartment in Harlem. It was infested with roaches and had a single shared bathroom for the entire floor. When it got to be too much for her, she'd find some random guy at a bar to take her back to his place so she could sleep in a bed and catch a shower uninterrupted.

I hated that story, but she said it made her more determined and driven, she called it her "blood in the cut" summer. Basically, she was overwhelmed with so much anguish that she learned how to own it and focus it into another direction.

There were also the tales of the first client that she dressed for the Oscars, and the first time she released a limited collection of her own designs, something she's only ever done four times.

Odette always downplays her success by saying anyone could do it if they just keep their head in the game, but that's not true. Not the way she has, anyway. Anyone in the public eye for any length of time gets bad press or has to maneuver through a scandal or two.

Not her.

I searched and couldn't find a single negative comment about her online. Everyone that knows her, loves her. She's an enigma. Stoic, but funny. Posh, but kind. Relatable, yet unattainable…the kind of woman other women want to be and be friends with. The kind of woman men want to befriend, fuck, and wed.

"Great, she can be on my team. Her ass is going to be amazing throwing the ball," Letty says, side-eyeing me.

"Keep running that mouth and you won't make it to tonight," I grumble to his uproarious laughter.

"Lock that shit down already, man. Is your game that dead?"

"Yes," I admit. "I haven't used it in two fucking decades, asshole."

"Want some tips?"

"From you?" I laugh. "Hell, no. I've seen you slapped by more women than I've seen you checked into the plexiglass, my friend."

"Rude," he mumbles.

"Hey, take it as a compliment," Blom tells him. "I always do."

"Of course, you fucking do," I say and he gives me a grin. He doesn't have his bridge in, so his missing canine is the focus. "If Ode does come tonight, she might have Britton Macy with her."

"Fuck yes," a few of the guys say simultaneously.

"Don't be assholes," Cillian warned. "Isla and Willa like both Odette and Britton. Don't run them off."

"Run them off?" Letty asks, appalled. "We want them to be part of the family."

"You haven't even met Britton yet."

"If Odette likes her, so will I," he tells me.

"You're a chucklefuck."

"You know it and you love it about me."

I can't argue. We give each other a lot of shit, but Letty is one of the best of us. He'd do anything for any one of us, no questions asked. I wink at him, and he throws a towel at me. Then I text the woman this whole conversation is centered on.

ME:

Letty misses you.

ODETTE:

He misses looking at my ass.

I smile at how well she knows him after only spending one day with him.

ME:

That's all of us, pumpkin.

ODETTE:

I'll be there. Bringing Britton so they
can obsess over her instead.

ME:

I'll pick you up at six.

I text before tossing my phone in my locker and heading for the showers, trying not to get too big of a head over her saying yes. It's a slow walk with Odette. A marathon, not a sprint. Good thing I have great stamina.

"So, you're Vaughn?" Britton Macy says when she opens the door of Odette's house to greet me. She's shorter than I expected. Otherwise, she looks exactly like what I expected, thin, with long wavy blonde hair. The type of woman you'd think of when you think of California beaches and hanging poolside under the sun.

"I am. Nice to meet you, Ms. Macy."

"Ah hell, call me Britton so I don't feel like I'm at work and you're the new make-up artist intern trying to impress me," she says.

"Last thing I want anyone to be thinking about tonight is work."

"I bet. Your last game was brutal," she says, stepping aside and letting me in. "Odette will be right down; she's finding me a coat. She didn't approve of my choice."

"Occupational hazard, I'd guess."

"Has she tried to dress you yet?" Britton asks.

"No, but I know she's helping some of the wags with dresses for an event we have coming up."

"Sounds like the Odette I know and love. I was worried Seattle would change her *too* much."

"You know, I think that all the things that really make her who she is have never changed," I muse. "She's still strong, vivacious, fun loving, determined. I can't see that ever changing. Or her love for fashion."

Britton stares me down for a few silent moments, the corners of her mouth slowly curling up.

"You'd treat her well, wouldn't you? If she ever gave you another chance."

"Like she always deserved," I say instantly. I'm not surprised Britton knows our history; she's been staying here with Odette since she got to town. I imagine there has been talk about the men in Ode's life. I only wish it excluded the stuffy dude.

"Well, may the odds be ever in your favor, or the force be with you, or whatever. You'll need it."

"I'm up for it," I say. "I'm not giving up without a fight."

"Have you met the other contender? Preston? He's pretty," she says, slyly.

"I have," I confirm. "I'm not worried."

"No?"

"No. She fell in love with me once. I wasn't worthy of it then. But I'm not the same person."

"Neither is she. I've never known her to give a man as much of a chance as she has him."

"Her heart is the same. That hasn't changed."

"Quit talking about me," Odette says, striding into the room looking like she's going anywhere but a bowling alley. She hands a jacket to Britton, something sparkly and multicolored. It looks straight out of a disco movie. "Here. If the paparazzi gets word of you tonight, at least you'll look the part."

"Holy shit, is this what I think it is?"

"Yes, and if you spill beer on it, I'll never speak to you again."

"I'm afraid to even try it on. There are only, like, what? Six of these left in existence."

"Four," Odette says. "Put the coat on. You may not have been born when it was made, but I think it's designed for you nonetheless."

I have no idea what the importance is, but Odette is right, Britton wears it well as she spins around after donning it.

"I need a protective bubble."

"You'll have a whole hockey team, it's sort of the same thing," I say. Odette finally turns her attention to me.

"Hi."

"Hi," I greet back, stepping up and kissing her forehead. "You look great."

"Of course, I do," she says, playfully acting scandalized at the idea that she doesn't always.

"Well, let's go then," Britton says. "I'm ready to meet these men I've been hearing so much about."

"What have you heard, exactly?" I ask, following the women out the door.

"That goalies are a little weird. Lehtinen is a handful but a sweetheart, and it's hot when y'all fight."

"Who told her that last bit?" I ask Odette as I open the car door for her.

"Probably Willa," she lies.

The guys instantly fall at Britton's feet when we get to the small bowling alley that Fane and Willa's partner has rented out for us. Britton expresses her gratitude to them, saying how much she misses going out to normal places without being swarmed by fans and people who hope to catch her doing something worthy of going viral.

She's still being crowded by Oliver, Axel, and Hugo, but she doesn't seem annoyed by it. I think she's enjoying the attention of my teammates as they play against each other on one lane.

Odette and I have been playing with Cillian and Isla, none of us taking it nearly as seriously as the rest of the group. Isla says she won't even play with her sister anymore because she's that good and it's taken all the fun out of it. But Willa's boyfriends seem to be as competitive as she is.

"We haven't seen Tori the past couple of games," Isla says. "How's she doing?"

"Great," I answer. "Loving school and living on her own. She's been busy, though, trying to get caught up on a project before her mom gets to town for Thanksgiving."

"Caroline's coming here?" Isla asks, and Odette's head turns away as if she's watching the other bowlers.

"Yeah, bringing her boyfriend to meet Tori."

"You think she'll like him?" Cillian asks.

"I do. I met him on the last trip to New York and there isn't anything not to like about the guy. He's basically head over heels for Caroline, so that's good."

"Excuse me," Odette says. "I need the restroom."

She walks off, and Cillian winces.

"Did we fuck up?" he asks.

"Nah, just some unresolved issues. I'll go check on her." I leave the couple and wait in the hallway for her.

We can't keep dancing around the situation. Whether she wants to talk about it or not, we need to, if this relationship is going to progress. Even as just friends. I can't pretend like the past didn't happen. That I didn't hurt her or have a wife for decades.

I don't want Odette to relive the past, but she needs to face it. I need her to face it.

She's startled to see me when she exits the restroom, her face still a few shades paler than I'd like it to be. She stops, and I crowd her, placing my hands on the wall behind her, one on either side of her head so I can lean in low and close.

"I'll never do anything to hurt you again, Ode. I promise that with my whole chest. Whatever you need to do to move forward with me in your life, you do it. You want to rage at me? Hit me? I'll take every bit of what you dish out," I say, rubbing my nose against hers when she tries to look down. "What I won't do is continue to play as if the past twenty years didn't happen. I know it's upsetting for you to hear me talk about her. I can't help that any more than I can help how much it kills me to know you're still seeing Preston. Or how it fucking guts me to think that you might still be having sex with him."

She does look away then, a clear confirmation that she is. I take a step back, squatting while I rake my hands through my hair a few times.

This isn't the right place for this conversation. It's not what tonight is supposed to be about for my team.

I blow out a long breath, then stand back up, staring her down.

"I deserve that, I guess," I grit out, pulling my shoulders back and craning my neck until it pops, relieving a miniscule amount of tension.

"It's not about you," she says.

"Isn't it, though?"

"Fuck off, Gavin. As if you and Caroline didn't have sex all this time. As if I owe you anything…we aren't dating. We're barely friends."

"It's more than friendship and you know it," I say. "Is he married?"

She blinks, surprised at my question.

"Separated," she says so quietly.

"Fucking hell, Ode." I clasp her chin, pulling her face to mine. "I'm right here. Right fucking here, offering you everything I have. I'd cut my own heart out and drain myself dry for just a shot at a second chance with you. Can he say the same?"

"I've never had to ask."

"Will he divorce for you?"

"Would you have?" she snaps. She has me there; up against the boards, fucked either way.

21

ODETTE

The rest of the night is strained between Gavin and me. Though, we both put on a good face. I think Cillian, Isla, and Britton are the only ones that really notice the tension.

Regardless of their attention, I don't feel bad about what I asked him. The truth is he didn't ever leave Caroline for me, and when she left him, he didn't come running.

Would it have made a difference if he had showed up at my doorstep, freshly divorced? I can't answer that, but at least I'd have known he thought about me. As it stands now, I still feel like I wasn't a consideration at all until I met Tori.

Bringing up Preston was a low blow. Gavin's been back in my life for a few months. I've had a lifetime of imagining him with other women. I fucking watched him kiss his bride. He doesn't understand the turmoil I've been through.

Or what I go through every day now. Because, fuck, I like him. As a person, as a father, as a great support to his team. He's dedicated, strong, loyal to all of them. Plus, I adore Tori. It would be easy to fall back in love with him.

If only I could forget the rest.

It's not even hard for me to hear about Caroline so much, it was more the fact that he had seen her when he was back in New York. It's not a detail he shared with me. Tori wasn't with him, so was there an obligation to see her? Is that what it would always be like if Gavin and I were together? Would she be a constant figure?

Of course, I don't expect him to forget it all. But I could never be with someone who didn't make me a priority. I'd need to be the top woman in his life, minus his daughter, of course.

I'm not sure I'd ever feel that with Gavin.

I know I'm not with Preston, and again, there's comfort there. A safety net that doesn't allow me to ever fall in love with him. No married man I've ever been with has said they'd leave their wife for me. It's not something I ever wanted anyway.

The men that *have* promised me forever weren't emotionally stable enough to keep it. Gavin may be, but I don't trust it all the same.

"I was thinking of going home with Hugo tonight," Britton says. "But if you need a good girl talk, I can postpone."

"No, Britt. Go and have fun. I'm fine, I promise."

"You sure? That conversation looked intense."

"I'm positive. Besides, I wouldn't want to break Blom's heart, he's been looking at you like a puppy dog in love for two hours straight."

"I know, it's pretty adorable."

"It is," I say, linking my arm with hers as we walk to the doors.

"Looks like they got word of you," Gavin tells Britton. "We're going to go out in a group, women in the middle, guys will surround you."

"Well, fuck. There goes a nice evening." She pouts.

"Don't worry about it, sweetheart, we got this," Hugo says, coming to stand at her side.

"Stay close to me," Gavin says. "Blom is parked right next to my car, we'll load Britton into the passenger side of his rig and you get in the driver's seat of mine and scoot over. Okay?"

I nod and we all start moving through the double doors to a crowd of shouts and camera flashes. Gavin keeps an arm wrapped around me with Letty following close behind. But before we can make it to the vehicles, an overzealous cameraman lunges in, pushing me aside to get a shot at Britton.

Stumbling, the only thing that stops me from hitting the ground is Gavin, who lifts me off my feet and hands me to Letty as if I weigh nothing more than a sack of potatoes.

"Get them to the car," he says to Letty, before he turns around and gets nose to nose with the guy who shoved me. "You want to put hands on someone, asshole, you put hands on me."

"I didn't mean…"

"Bullshit." Gavin spits the words in the man's face. "You knew exactly what you were fucking doing. I'm going to teach you to never fucking touch her again."

"That would be assault! I could sue." The guy tries stepping back, but Gavin stalks him.

"I fucking dare you to," he growls. The man tries to shove Gavin away, but he doesn't stand a chance against the wall of a man. Fists raise and it's the last thing I see before more guys join in the scrum and obscure my vision.

"I don't have his keys, Blom," Letty says.

"Put her in with Britton. I'll stay with them."

The men load us into Hugo's truck and Lehtinen immediately turns around to join the fray.

"I'm sorry, this is all because of me," Britton says, nervously sighing.

"Darling, we live for this shit," Hugo says, standing in the open door of his truck, blocking anyone from us. "They'll have it handled in short order."

"I don't want anyone getting in trouble," she argues.

"Won't happen."

I hope he's right, I think as I strain my head from side to side, trying to catch a glimpse of Gavin.

"Is this a regular sort of thing?" Britton asks.

"We're hockey players, it's not irregular." He shrugs.

"It's kind of hot," she says, and Hugo grins devilishly.

For as mad at him as I am now, Britton isn't wrong. It did unspeakable things to my lady bits when Gavin placed me safely in Letty's arms and faced off with the asshat. At the same time, I'm worried. My fingers tremble some, so I ball them up in my fist and try to shake the wariness of him potentially getting a fist to the face.

It's different watching him on the ice, when I can see every move and know it can't go too far.

Violence like this has never been something I've experienced.

"He's okay, Odette," Hugo says, tuning in to my concern. "He's got the whole team and Damian in there with him. But I think he's pissed off enough to take the lot of those chucklefucks all by himself. Vaughn looked like he wanted to cut that dude's twig and berries right off, drop 'em in a blender, and water his flower bed with it."

"He did," I agree, still watching. Still waiting for him to emerge.

"Seems awful protective of you, darling."

"I'm sure he'd be that way with anyone," I say.

"He'd stick up for anyone, sure. He wouldn't be murderous, though."

Finally, the crowd breaks up. I catch sight of Vaughn as he heads straight toward us, his eyes boring into mine through the windshield.

He looks...fine, actually. He's not even disheveled, his curls in perfect place, just as they were before all of this. Other than the tension he wears in his jaw, he shows no sign of being in any kind of altercation.

Hugo moves aside only when Gavin is within a few steps.

"Are you okay?" he asks me, palming my face and turning it side to side as if he's looking as hard as I am for any injury on him.

"I'm okay, you caught me." He stills at my words, a silent promise crossing his face. It's as if I can hear him promise that he always will.

I look away so I don't risk believing it.

"How about you, Britton? All good?"

"Yeah, Gavin. Thank you."

"It's our pleasure," he tells her. "Come on, Odette. I'll take you home.

"You're trembling," he says, finally breaking the silence as we approach my neighborhood. "You're sure you're not hurt?"

"I'm okay," I say. Physically, I am. Emotionally, not so much. He takes my hand in his and I don't fight it. I was worried, scared for the first time in I don't know how long. Fear isn't something I live with.

Well, that's a lie. But the fear of heartache is different than a fear of surroundings or people in general. One I am mostly able to control, the others are spontaneous and unpredictable.

Gavin parks in front of my house, and as he always does, tells me to stay put so he can come around to open my door and help me out. As soon as I stand, he wraps me in his arms.

"Will you fight with me?"

"What?" I ask, looking up.

"Invite me inside and let's fight this out. You can say all the things you've been holding in. Let me have it, Ode. Let me carry the full burden of what I've done," he says. "Let's see what we can work through, and what we can't."

"I don't..."

"I know you don't want to talk about it. I'm asking if you will, though. Please, Ode? I think there's a lot we still need to say."

It's then I notice a bloom of redness under his jaw.

"Did you get hit?"

"By his camera. It's nothing."

It's not nothing. Gavin put himself in harm's way for me and my friend he only just met tonight. I inhale a long breath, letting out an audible sigh.

"Come in, Gavin."

He follows me inside, through the kitchen, and to the small bar I have set up in my living room. I don't offer anything to him as I pour myself a finger of whiskey. One single swallow to bolster myself for a conversation I once wanted so badly.

"Why were you trembling?"

"I was scared," I say.

"For me?" he asks, but I don't answer. "So, you don't hate me?"

"No, I've told you I don't."

"Did you ever?"

"I tried to," I say. "I tried to hate you both so that I'd hate myself a little less."

"Why did you hate yourself?" he asks, standing closer now, though I haven't turned to look at him. "You didn't do anything wrong. Nothing was your fault. I explained that."

"With words, Gavin," I say, spinning toward him. "Your words were something I thought I could understand. I hated them, but I understood them. What I *saw* was a contradiction to everything you said. I spiraled with thoughts that you had lied to me, that our time together was a sham, a fling. That I was nothing but a good time that you'd both laugh about later. That's why I hated myself. For falling for the ruse and for you."

"It wasn't a lie," he argues. "We were not a lie."

"And neither was your marriage."

"Not in every way, no."

"How was it a lie, Gavin? You lived together, supported each other, raised a child together, slept together. In what ways was it a lie?"

"In the way we loved each other, which wasn't the way a married couple should. In the way that we didn't plan to live out our lives together. 'Til death was a lie." He runs a palm over the stubble on his jaw. He's frustrated, but so am I.

"What am I supposed to do with that? I can't unsee your wedding day. I can't relive those months where it felt like I was drowning in sorrow."

"No more than I can change the decisions I made."

He's right, of course. Neither of us can do anything about the past.

"What would you change, if you could?"

Gavin doesn't answer right away, walking to the wall of windows, lights across the lake shimmering like night stars in the darkness.

"It's hard for me to say. Because now I know what I would have missed out on in Tori's life if we hadn't gone through with the marriage," he starts. "It was hard being away from her so much, but at least when I was playing at home or it was the offseason, I was going home to her every night and witnessing as many of her firsts as I could. Watching her grow into who she is now with a front row seat instead of one that was only placed out for me on off days and holidays. I don't know if we could have made it work any other way, at first. But later, after I was signed and was making money, there were options. Ones I thought about starting from the time Tori was about six years old and started school."

"But you didn't explore those options," I prompt.

"By then, it had been almost seven years. I hadn't heard many updates about you, but I figured you were probably happy and living the life you'd dreamed of. I convinced myself that I was nothing but a mess you'd swept up and tossed out years before. I'd change that, if I could. I'd find you and see if there was some spark of love still alive. If I'd done that then, maybe I'd have saved all three of us from some hurt."

"All three of us," I muse quietly. Caroline is just as much a part of this dysfunction, even though I don't think I've ever had a single conversation with her. I've never been able to convince myself that she suffered much in any of this. She got a loyal husband, a wonderful daughter, and a comfortable life, after all.

"Yes," he says, looking over his shoulder at me. "Another thing I would change is the sex. Your accusation earlier was right, we did have sex. Sometimes, not even often. But enough that it confused the situation and cemented us into a union we never meant to be long-lasting. She should have been free to fall in love with someone else and I should have been free to continue being in love with you."

His words fuck with my mind. I see them together in my head, their bodies entwined while he calls out *my* name. It's an old fantasy, dark and twisted, it's played out in my mind so many times. For so long, I hoped they would fall apart. I don't know what kind of a monster that makes me, wishing a family would fracture and break. Rejection can decimate everything good inside someone, and for a while, I let it.

"Did you ever think of me?" I ask, my voice breaking while I force out the last word.

"Of course, I did," he says, furious now. In a second, he's standing in front of me again, crowding my space with his smell and drilling those eyes into my own. "All the time. I was in love with you. I don't remember a time when I wasn't. I'll never know a time when I'm not."

Without bidding, I pull his face to mine, our mouths colliding. I'm aware how much of a sucker I am for his words. When you've waited so long to hear them, it's hard to swallow down the reaction to them. Our argument hasn't dampened the arousal I felt earlier at his protectiveness, and him saying these things now only reignites it all.

He meets me with the same unhinged intensity. It's not enough, though, I need more to soothe the need, the nerves, the years of wanting. My hands move to his belt, then the button and zipper on his pants. I reach in, feeling him grow harder as he unbuttons my own blouse, yanking my bra down so he can weigh my breasts in his hand. Our mouths never stop.

Not when I push his pants and boxer briefs down over his hips or when his thumbs play at the waistband of my skirt. I've craved this moment since he left my bed last time. I'd never admit that to him, but I have. His body haunts me, his cock the star of my dreams.

He lifts me and moves me to sit on the edge of my kitchen counter. He pauses then, waiting for me to say stop, maybe. I grab the hem of my skirt and pull it up as far as I can, widening my legs…giving him access and answer.

When he reaches between my thighs, he finds me bare, and he sighs, a smile twitching at the part of his mouth that wears the tiny scar. Smiles aren't what I'm after right now, I need release. A brutal ejection of all this residual despair I've held on to.

"Why didn't you come to me as soon as Caroline left?" I ask when his fingers slide in.

"I wanted to. But I didn't want you to think I was rebounding. It felt like fate when you ended up as Tori's mentor." He adds a finger, and my head falls back. "Everything came rushing back when I saw you standing right over there, and nothing else mattered. I know what I lost, Ode. I live with that every day."

His mouth nibbles along my neck, his fingers get replaced by the tip of his cock.

"I don't know how to forgive it all, Gavin."

"I'm only asking you to try," he says, thrusting. "We finally have our chance, Ode, nothing's in our way but us." He punctuates his statement with another thrust, and I grab on to his shoulders. His muscles bunch and stretch under my fingers. He pulls my hips into his over and over, heat racing to my chest the closer he brings me to the edge. "Stop fucking around with the other guy and give us the fair shot we didn't have before."

"What if I can't?" I can have this every day if I can figure out how to trust him and the things he says. "What if I never feel like anything but your backup plan?"

"Ode, no. You're the end game. You're the rest of my life. You're my eternity," he says until I'm coming for him and him for me in a swirl of emotion. My body is elated, my mind a tornado of thoughts that I can't focus.

Or trust.

Gavin holds me while we settle, our breaths synchronizing.

"I don't know how…"

"I do. Let me take the lead," he whispers at my temple. "You're shaking again."

"I'm still scared."

22

ODETTE

Yesterday was the best day I can remember having in a long time. Gavin stayed over after our fight that wasn't much of a fight at all. We're too old for those theatrics, I guess. We're still quite good at cutting each other with words, though. Or maybe that's just me.

Regardless, he spent the day with me by waking me up with breakfast in bed. After, we took a walk around Gasworks Park, since it wasn't raining. He said I should get a dog, something tiny, yappy, and that looks like a hairball. I laughed off the suggestion, but honestly, it's an appealing idea.

I told him I've never had a pet. I've never had a relationship.

He held my hand and said that the last part wasn't true.

I changed the subject to Tori. When he had the chance, he changed it to Preston.

"You and me," he said. "Just you and me."

To which I said, "You'd have to tell me when you're planning on seeing your ex-wife."

And I hated myself for speaking it, for the pettiness it made me feel, and how insecure it made me sound.

"That's the very least I'd need to do," he said without judgment, then he kissed me, and I forgot what I had been so concerned about moments before.

When we got back to my house, he stripped me naked.

"Are you ready to give up your side piece?"

"I thought that was you," I teased, but he didn't find it funny.

"Drop to your knees, pumpkin. Take your punishment for that remark."

"You shoving that cock down my throat is hardly punishment," I'd snarked back. What was punishment is how he edged me for forty-five minutes before he let me come. Gavin has fucked me ruthlessly every time, but something changed in him yesterday. He was possessive and I liked it more than I can admit.

He left before lunch, needing to get to the iceplex. But not before he said he wouldn't be fucking me again until I stopped my "play dates with the stuffy dude". I missed him minutes after he left.

So now, I'm meeting Preston.

A breakup, of sorts. How do you break up with someone you are casually seeing? I typically stop accepting invites. That doesn't seem sufficient enough for this situation. Gavin wants definitive. Though, I've made him no promises other than that I would try. It's all I can do.

Try with Gavin and cut it off with Preston.

As a child, I thought love made you stronger, happier, a better human. It was like that when I fell in love with Gavin. And then it wasn't anymore, and I lost a lot of that little girl. I no longer dreamed of wedding dresses and happily ever after.

Yesterday I felt some of that youthful euphoria again walking through the park. It was the first time I thought that a second chance might not be out of reach. I'm holding on to it with every ounce of strength, even though my instinct is to run as fast as I can to the nearest airport and board the longest flight I can find.

Preston is already seated at a table in the café when I walk in. His face lights up when he sees me approach, which only makes me feel like a bitch. Though, I never made promises to him, either. And really, he's the one who is married.

He stands to greet me, leaning in to press a kiss, but I step back. Confusion dawns on his features.

"Odette? What's wrong?"

"Sit, please. We'll talk."

The server comes by and Preston orders himself a glass of wine, while I opt for tea.

"I had something I wanted to ask you," he says.

"What's that?"

"A French artist, Colette Durand, is doing a pop-up exhibition next week in Paris. I bought flights."

Well, that's…awfully fucking presumptuous of him.

"I can't go with you," I say. "In fact, I can't see you anymore. Not like that."

"Are you friend-zoning me, Odette?" he asks, sitting back in his chair.

"I am," I tell him, then thank the server as she sets my tea in front of me.

"Because of the hockey player?"

"Because we were never going anywhere, Preston. It's been fun, but it's run its course."

"And if I don't agree?" he asks, taking a sip of his wine. He doesn't thank servers. It was something I noticed right off but thought it was more of a distraction thing than rudeness. Over the course of the past couple of months, I've realized it's a personality trait. Preston is somewhat of an elitist. A snob. The more comfortable he was with me, the more he let that show.

"You're entitled to your opinion," I state calmly. "You aren't entitled to me."

"Noted," he says. "The ticket is yours anyhow. You can come as a friend."

"I'm not sure I can squeeze Paris into my schedule next week."

"Well, keep it in mind. Just in case something frees up," he says, and I get the feeling he's not taking me seriously. As if he thinks I'll be inviting him back to my bed in a matter of days.

Here I was thinking I didn't take rejection well.

"No, not the Armani," I say, opening the door to Gavin. I wave him in while I try to finish up the conversation. "Stacia, no. Trust me, you want the Wun. I promise you, it is not too much, it's perfect."

"Fallon said the same," she says.

"Trust him, too. He's got a better eye than I do."

"That's bullshit, but fine. I'll wear the Wun."

"Perfect, you'll look gorgeous in it."

"Thank you, Odette."

"Anything for you, darling," I say before ending the call.

"Stacia Carmichael?" Gavin asks.

"Mmhmm," I confirm as he wraps me in a hug.

"The hottest thing in pop music Stacia Carmichael?"

"How much do you know about pop music?" I ask, wrinkling my nose at him.

"As much as Tori tells me, she's a big fan. I took her to a Stacia concert when she was twelve."

"She puts on a great show, I bet you had a good time."

"I did, actually," he says, lifting me off my feet and walking us into the living room. "Did you take care of that thing?"

"By thing, do you mean Preston?"

"Is that stuffy dude's name?"

"You know it is," I say, raising an eyebrow. He sits on my sofa, arranging me on his lap. I love that he's so much bigger than me, that he's strong enough to manhandle me to his heart's delight. It's nice to relinquish some control for once.

"What did you tell him?"

"That it was over."

"And what did he say?"

"He asked me to go to Paris with him next week."

"I'm sorry, what?"

"He bought me a ticket already."

"Presumptuous of him," he says, circling my waist, his calloused fingertips grazing the skin between my trouser waistband and the slightly cropped shirt I'm wearing. It sends a shiver up my spine, and he grins at my reaction.

"That's what I thought," I say. "How was practice?"

"Good, we're ready for tomorrow," he says into my neck, nuzzling it. "Caroline and Brock fly in next Monday. I don't expect to see them. It's just a heads-up."

"You know I wouldn't expect you to never see her, right?"

She's Tori's mother and has been Gavin's friend his whole life. Only, with how new this situation is, I'm not sure how I'll react to seeing her and Gavin engage with each other.

"I know, it's more that you don't want to be blindsided or left out of the loop," he says, his thumbs rubbing circles on my skin. "I understand."

"Okay, then," I say and pull my shirt over my head.

"Holy fuck, woman," he growls, taking in my barely there strappy black bra. "We doing this, Ode? You and me, we trying for real? I need to hear you say it."

"If you can be patient with me. I don't know how to do this and when I give it too much thought, anxiety still blooms in my chest."

The apprehension that's been settled deep down inside for so long is only slightly diminished. Something Vaughn said the other night struck me, though. He knows what he's been missing. I've been missing out, too, on him. The only man I've ever wanted. He's been offering me what I used to dream about, and I've been too fearful to take it. I don't live any other part of my life under fear, I'm not going to let it take over this part, either.

"This chest?" he asks, placing a hand over my heart.

"That's the one," I answer. He looks at his own hand, almost sadly, but not fully. A little hopeful, too. "It's worried this is too good to be real, and that at any moment the other shoe will drop."

"I'll protect it with my life, Ode." He presses a kiss to it. "I don't want you to go to Paris with him."

"No? I really love Paris. It has the best vintage shops," I say, leaning into his palm that's now massaging my breast.

"I'll take you for your birthday," he mumbles between the kisses he trails over my skin. "Buy you all the beautiful old stuff you want."

"My birthday, huh?"

"Mmhmm, I'll be retired so we can spend as much time there as you want."

"You remember my birthday?"

"Of course, I remember. You made me take you skinny dipping because you said it was a childhood rite of passage that you never accomplished."

It was the most fun we'd ever had, and we almost got caught by the elderly couple that lived on the small lake we dove into.

"We had a lot of fun that summer."

"We can have it again," he says. "I vote we start now. Once I can figure out how to get you out of this contraption, anyway."

"You want to have fun with me, Gavin?"

"I want a life with you, but that includes fun. The dirtiest fucking kind you can imagine, Ode."

"Oh yeah?"

"Yeah. I've been holding back. I'm not going to do that anymore."

"Holding back? Why?" And how? Holy shit, the man can already fuck me like a piston with no end in sight.

"There is a long list of things I want to do with and to you, Ode. I just wanted you to be all in, first."

"What kinds of things?" I ask, pushing his head back so I can lick up the column of his neck.

"I want to fuck you on every surface in this house, which is going to take a while since it's so big."

"Too big," I moan.

"I want to tie you up to your headboard, tease you endlessly while you can't touch me back," he says, then strains up to kiss me. "Then I'll let you do the same to me."

"That could be fun."

"First thing I want to do is eat that plump fucking ass of yours, though."

I burst out in laughter. "I did not expect you to say that."

"It's been on my mind for a minute," he says, winking.

"What else has been on your mind for a minute, Gavin?"

"That I don't want to fuck this up."

"Then try not to, and I'll try, too," I say as he finally finds the clasp of my bra and pulls it off me. "Britton is gone again tonight. She and Hugo are having a lot of fun, too, I think."

"So, we can fuck right here?"

"If you get naked." His tongue finds my nipple, and I lose thought for a split second. "I like the new flowers."

Gavin is still sending them regularly; I'm starting to think he's never going to stop. The latest bouquet is a huge spray of baby's breath. Delicate and feminine, nestled between hardy greens, it's unlike anything I've seen before.

"I'm glad," he says, switching breasts. "Let's get naked."

Gavin strips me of my clothes before he takes off his own. Bare, we stand in the middle of my living room eye to eye. The world stops around us. An invisible bubble forms, protecting us from the outside, silent and still.

It feels right. Like the first time I dressed Britton. Instinct told me it was the choice that would change my career. This feels life-changing, too. As if I'm not making the wrong decision by giving us a second chance.

"You are devastatingly fucking beautiful, Odette Quinn."

"I could say the same about you," I tell him, raking my sight over his ridges. He's so incredibly built. No fat anywhere in sight, just muscle layered on muscle, down to thick lines that seem almost like directions to his cock, which is already hard and proud.

"Why did you change your mind?"

"Do you want me to change it back?" I tease.

"No, you brat," he says, reaching around to give my ass a swat. "Call me curious."

"It's what I always wanted," I say after a moment. I'm not quite as composed as I thought I was, and tears well as I spill some truth. "I've done stupid things, Gavin. I let men fuck me the way I imagined you were fucking her. I fuck men imagining they're you, that it's one last time before they walk away to their pretty wives."

"Ode." He pulls me into his chest, cradling my head in his strong hand.

"I made up so many make-believes about you that I couldn't trust reality anymore. But it's what I've always wanted, so I'm trying to be brave enough to listen to my heart telling me it's real."

"It's real. I'm sorry things weren't different, I'm sorry about so much. But you and me? We're real."

23

GAVIN

Once, at a teammate's wedding reception, Isla told me that she gave Cillian a second chance because if she didn't, she was certain of misery, whereas getting back with him held a chance of happiness, despite the risk of it all falling apart again.

It seemed horrifically fucking sad, at the time. I understand it now, because I think that's what Odette feels. She has so little faith in me. Why should she have it? I've only been able to offer her words, which mean fuckall.

My only option is to show her that I'm loyal to her, which takes time. At least she's giving me that now. I'll use it to earn back every damn piece of her heart that I crushed before. Her behavior with men? That's my fault. Solely.

I broke something real inside her and I own it. I have to.

I'm not sure what prompted the change in her the other night, but I'm grateful for the opportunity to show her it can be different this time. That *I* can be different.

"You're it for me, Ode." She softens but I can still see the tinge of fear. It breaks me. The only chink in her armor is because of me. I could crumble under the thought. Except Odette doesn't deserve that, she deserves a man that can be strong in the one place she can't be. One that will help prop her up, love her without condition, and fight for her every motherfucking day.

And that's exactly what I'm going to be. Even if it takes me the rest of my life to prove it to her.

"I like the sound of that," she whispers as if she's afraid to send the words out into the world.

"I'll tell you every day," I say before leaning down to kiss her. Starting at her lips, then her cheeks, her jaw, her neck, I traverse her body. Teasing her senses, feeling every twitch of anticipation as I travel down until I'm on my knees, ready to worship her like the goddess she is. "Rest your foot on my shoulder. I'm going to devour this cunt like it's my last meal."

"Well, I hope it isn't that…Oh fuck…" Her words stop as soon as I shove my tongue in her as far as it will go. "Gavin, fuck, that's…fuck."

I grin as my fingers glide over the globes of her ass. Spending her whole adult life in the fuck-me heels has given her the most amazing lower body; firm and toned but not hard. She's still soft, womanly, fucking mind-blowing.

Wedging my index finger inside her, I slide it up, playing with the pucker of her ass. She hums the most pleasurable sound I've heard. I apply a little more pressure, bit by bit, until I'm in and she's pulling my hair like it's the only thing keeping her standing while I work her clit with my mouth.

Her hips start to keep pace with me but, before long, she's grinding faster. Fucking my face as she tries to find her first release. A moment later, she does, her heel sliding down my back and her fingers tightening.

I love that she pulls my hair, that I'm the one she's anchoring herself to while she falls to pieces. In this instance, she trusts me completely. I want this feeling always.

When the ecstasy of the moment has washed over her, I lower her leg and stand. I'm painfully hard, stroking my dick to help ease some of the need. It doesn't do shit.

"Will your windows hold if I fuck you up against them?"

"I think there's only one way to find out," she says, her eyes gleaming.

"You're not afraid someone might see?"

"Let them." She slowly backs up until her back is against the large windows that overlook her yard and the lake beyond. Her eyes follow my palm. "You going to put that inside me, Gavin, or just play with it yourself?"

Prowling toward her, I lift her up, and she immediately wraps those legs around my hips, letting me ease her down onto my cock. Her warmth sends a shiver down my spine.

"This is my favorite place."

"My living room?"

"Inside you, Ode. It feels like home after a long road trip. Like I'm finally able to sleep in my own bed after endless shitty hotel beds. I never want to leave."

"Don't then. Don't ever leave me again," she says, a tear spilling out of one eye.

"Never, pumpkin."

Then I fuck her. Staring at those brilliant eyes the same color as the barely lit lake behind her, the sun quickly setting. I fuck her to the soundtrack she makes with moans and sighs. I fuck her until she comes all over my cock, and then I fuck her some more. We have so much time to make up for.

When she starts to get a chill from her back against the cold window, I move her to a blanket in front of her fireplace and let her ride me until she comes again, her face upturned and her dark waves trailing down her back. I'll never forget how she looks, her tits bouncing, one arm braced behind her on my thigh, the other playing with her own pussy as she calls my name.

Then I cover her spent body with mine, taking over all the work, rolling my hips into hers, our hands entwined on either side of her flushed face. She's so wet but there's enough friction to send us both into a frenzy when I steadily build pace and intensity. I watch for every clue, making sure she never has a second where she isn't as worked up as me.

Odette pulls my face to hers by my hair, crashing her lips to mine as we both lose control, her cunt clenching around me like a vise, holding me in as I fill her up.

Emotion the likes I've never felt rush through me. It's a combination of elation and utter regret. Like I've just won the Stanley Cup but somehow lost it, too. I finally have the only woman I've ever been truly in love with, and I regret all the things we never had, never shared. She's in my arms, heaving with me and yet, I miss her.

We roll to our sides, her head buried under my chin, my leg hitching over her hip where I can cocoon her in my arms, keep her warm. Make her stay.

"Did you ever want children?"

"Maybe when I was little and everyone talked to us about growing up and finding a husband so you could raise a family," she says. "But no. I don't think it's what I'm here for, if that makes sense. That's not my purpose."

"Are you sure?" I ask when she looks up through her lashes at me. I brush her hair off of her face, tucking it behind her ear.

"I'm sure. Why? Do you want more?"

"It's not anything that ever crossed my mind."

"Until now?"

"I wouldn't deny you anything, Ode. Whatever else you want in life, I want to help you get."

"That's sweet of you," she says, pressing a kiss to the underside of my chin. "But I think we can check that one off the list."

"What is on your list?"

"I'm not so sure, anymore. I expected to move here, do this for a few years, then have a huge desire to go back to New York, or maybe Los Angeles. I love it more than I thought I would, though. Maybe mentoring fashion students is my purpose. Or maybe it will lead to something else exciting and new," she says. "What about you? What are your plans after this season?"

I've been thinking about that a lot. When I made the decision to retire initially, I was terrified. Worried that I would become some irrelevant man with nothing to do every day. Nobody to take care of, nobody to talk to, I'd end up lonely and grumpy, yelling at the clouds all day or some shit.

Then I thought about what I love most about hockey. Winning is great, but it's really being part of a team that is what I'm going to miss the most. It's something I can still have in a different way.

"The way you talk about your students has inspired me. I'd like to coach. Not in The Show or anything. Maybe peewee hockey, start with the youngest group, where it isn't so serious and doesn't require a rigorous travel schedule. You know?" She nods in understanding. "Maybe dote on my girlfriend. Perfect my gluten-free baked goods and learn how to cook more vegetarian meals for her."

"She sounds like a lucky lady."

"Nah, I'm the lucky one."

"Maybe we both are," she says, snuggling back into my chest, where she falls silent and eventually into sleep, a soft smile on her face.

***

"You guys played amazing last night," Tori says before she shoves a heaping fork of omelet in her mouth. I haven't seen her in a few days, so I asked if she'd come over for a late breakfast and to hang out with her old man. She's not an early riser, which works out well for me when I have to be at the arena for an early morning skate.

She probably only rolled out of bed an hour ago, whereas I've been up for hours now. I'll catch a nap later, though, before heading to the arena for tonight's matchup.

Tori's right, we played great last night. Cohesive and like a team of guys that love each other. We do, sometimes it just doesn't translate to the ice. But we have a winning record and I have high hopes of keeping it.

"Glad you could make it to another game. I always love it when you're in the stands."

"I know you do. I might not get to another one for a while, though."

"You're a busy kid, I get it."

"You're busier these days," she says, side-eyeing me as I take a seat next to her at the breakfast bar.

"You could say that," I say, shrugging as if there is nothing to talk about.

"Dad! Oh my god, spill. What's going on with you and Odette?"

"What do you think about her? Now that you know her and not just *of* her?" I ask.

"She's fucking fantastic. Like, literally. She's inspiring and inspires all of us to be better but stay authentically us. Do you know what I mean? I guess you probably do. It's a lot like Coach Cole. He wants you to improve your skill but not lose your style," she starts rambling, her hands moving a mile a minute. "We all totally love her. If she really likes something we're working on, she'll say she'd wear it. We live for that, like those people on that baking show hoping for a handshake, you know? She's told me that twice already. I marked those days on my calendar, I'm keeping count. And I don't think she has favorites, she sees the strengths we all have so we aren't competitive with each other, just ourselves. I think we all want to make her really proud. Which is kinda funny because she's not a professor who is grading us or anything. But we want her high opinion more than any of our teachers. She's like a best friend and is always honest and encouraging. I can't say enough nice stuff about her."

"Jesus, inhale some air, kid."

"Sorry! I could talk about her for a while. I'm not trying to hero worship her or anything, she's just really great, is all." She takes a bite of the cranberry orange scone. "Dad, holy shit. This is good."

"I'm getting better."

"For her," she states. "You're getting better for Odette."

"I mean, I have always been somewhat of a perfectionist, you know?"

"Yeah, but this is more than that," she says, propping her chin on her fist and studying me. "Do you love her?"

"Is it weird if I tell you I don't think I ever stopped? I don't know how that's possible, but I think I never stopped."

"Not weird," she says, her voice watery. I throw my arm over her shoulders and bring her in for a hug. "Not weird, Dad. Romantic as fuck."

"Where did you get such a foul mouth?" I ask, kissing the top of her head. She smells the same as she always has, like the day we brought her home from the hospital.

"All my real-life role models are hockey players," she says. "Sometimes I spit, too."

"You do fucking not." I laugh.

"No, it's not that bad," she says. "I don't want to influence your choices by how much I adore her, but I think you two would be good together. In a profound way because you're both similar in so many ways. I can see how you'd both quietly support each other."

"Quietly?" I ask.

"Yeah, you know, not making her desires about you. No one taking over the other's dreams and making decisions because you think you can do it better. Letting the other person be the loudest person in their own decision making."

"This doesn't make you sad? Because of the divorce and everything."

"It does, but maybe not the way you'd expect. I've talked to Mom about your marriage, since you told me why you got married. I understand.

So, I guess it makes me sad for all three of you. None of you really got a fair chance."

"I don't think I tell you enough how glad I am you moved back here," I say. She's a smart kid.

When we announced the divorce, she was understandably distraught. Then she got mad and directed most of that at me, probably because I was the one gone for so much of her life. It fucking sucked having the one person you love most in the world run away from you.

When I put it in that perspective, I get exactly how Odette felt.

"I don't think I tell you enough that I'm sorry for how I acted," she says. She hasn't ever apologized. I'd never expect her to, anyway. "I acted like a brat."

"You were processing a lot of feelings," I tell her.

"That doesn't mean I should have used you as my punching bag."

"You're wiser than your years, Victoria Vaughn. But I'll be your punching bag anytime you need one. Sometimes we just need a place to focus our frustrations."

"I appreciate that more than I can say," she says. "Now. Are you dating Odette or not?"

"You're a nosy little shit."

"You're an avoidant butthead," she says, causing me to laugh.

"We're *trying*."

"Trying what?"

"Trying to see if we can have a relationship. Trying to see if she can trust me again."

"Is that like dating without definitions or something?"

"It's like I hurt her and I'm working on making it up to her," I say. "As far as definitions go, I did throw out the word girlfriend and she didn't take off running."

"Ah, that's a good start." She smiles and pats me on the back.

"I thought so."

"You're a good man, Dad. Loyal and strong, I'm sure she sees that. She's brilliant."

"You're brilliant," I mimic.

"No, you're brilliant."

"No, *you* are brilliant," I repeat, wrinkling my nose.

"You're a dork," she says, laughing. "I love you, Dad."

"Love you, too, kid."

24

ODETTE

"Good afternoon, everyone," I greet as I walk into the workroom. There are eight students here now, making it a busy day. But it's the Monday before the long weekend for Thanksgiving, I used to get as much done before school breaks, too. Nothing ruins a vacation like stressing over work you didn't get done.

They all ring out their own greetings while I casually walk the room, looking over what each is working on. A couple of them are still trying to perfect their newly acquired patterning skills, but they're getting there. It's one thing to have an eye for fashion, it's another to be able to execute it yourself with patterns and sewing techniques.

Most of us learned to sew with the basics of hemming up a pair of pants that you loved but were two inches too long. Or a maxi dress that you wanted to turn into a mini. Those are easy enough, but darting, buttonholes, sleeves, zippers, pleats…that shit takes some learning.

Drake, who exclusively made menswear before starting school, is draping a dress on his form. I stop and watch for a few minutes as he adjusts, then steps back, then adjusts again.

"That print is gorgeous," I tell him.

"I thought so, too," he says. "I found it in the dollar bin at this fabric shop near my mom's house in Boise. I've been holding on to it for inspiration to strike."

"Looks like it has."

"It's for Tori," he says, his cheeks flushing slightly.

"Is it a secret?"

"For now."

"It's safe with me," I say, stepping closer. "The dress form doesn't have the same curves as her. I'd suggest bringing the waistline up."

Drake cocks his head, then makes a few adjustments to his pins before he smiles and nods.

"Thank you. Something felt off, this falls much better."

"Anytime. You've got this, she'll look fantastic in it."

I move to Celine, who sits on her table, scraps of different fabrics strewn around her while she sketches on her pad.

"How's it going today?"

"I'm frustrated," she says, sighing.

"What's up?" I ask, hopping up to sit next to her.

"Another student suggested my designs aren't commercial enough and I'll never make money."

Oof.

"What makes you design the way you do? What do you want people to think of your designs?"

"I want women to slip on one of my dresses and feel like they're wearing a piece of art," she says after a moment.

"They will. Because you are an artist. Typically, I'd say money isn't always good for art, and sometimes it's even the death of art. However, fashion is different. Jean Paul Gaultier has a net worth of about three hundred million. All by creating wearable art. I wouldn't call his design history commercial."

"No," she agrees.

"It's said that Cecil B. DeMille was asked how you make an epic film. He said, start with an apocalypse and build up from there. I don't know if he really said that, but I believe in the concept for all art. And you, my darling, are a brilliant artist. Don't let commercialism get in your way, make your own success. Be loud and unashamed."

"Start with an apocalypse," she muses. "I like that. Thank you, Odette."

"It's what I'm here for," I tell her. "And you're here for a reason, too. Don't ever forget it."

For how much I questioned taking this position in the beginning, I'm happy I did. I'm more than a mentor to these students; I'm a consultant, and advisor, a therapist, of sorts.

I love being every one of those roles. So much so that I haven't missed styling at all.

Tori comes in after a time and gets busy at a worktable. I watch from my office to see if she looks like she might need help. Occasionally, she'll look up and send me a smile that borders on bashful. Instead of trying to puzzle out what it means by myself, I walk out to talk to her.

"What are you up to today?"

"Not too much, just finishing off this jacket," she says, making a cut to the fabric she's working on. "I wanted to say something, though."

"I'm all ears."

"I'm really happy for you and my dad. I don't want it to make things weird, even though I realize I probably just did."

"You didn't make it weird. I'm glad you said something, I wasn't sure how much you knew."

"He was tight-lipped about it. I think it's that sport superstition thing where if they say it, it won't happen. He likes you a lot."

"That's mutual."

"I'm glad. Truly," she says. "Will you be at the game tonight?"

"We're trying to work out how to get Britton there without causing a scene."

"Oh my god," she says under her breath. "Dad said you two were friends, but it would be amazing to meet her."

"Hopefully, we'll see you there." I pat her hand before moving back to my office, hiding my emotion as I go. Her acceptance of me means so much because she means so much to Gavin. Honestly, she's beginning to mean a lot to me, too.

That might be the big downside of this job, I can easily see myself getting attached to these kids.

"Maybe we should have gotten a suite," I say for the fourth time.

"No," Britton protests. "I told you I don't want to see the game that way. I'm sure it will be fine with the wags."

"The wags will be fine, I'm not sure about the crowds sitting around them, though."

"It will be fine," she reassures. "Vanessa is meeting us there?"

"Yes, she's only been to one game before."

"You say that as if you're a seasoned vet. How many games have you been to?"

"Just the one, asshole." I laugh.

"The first of many, I'll assume by how much time you and Mr. Vaughn have been spending together the past week."

"We'll see."

"I'm proud of you, Odette. It's not easy to give second chances."

"It's terrifying, Britt."

"It's brave. And love is worth the risk."

I hope she's right. There's still a feeling of impending doom that has settled at the bottom of my heart. It's a constant, quiet chant. The end is nigh, the end is nigh. I can't shake the fucking thing and it worries me that I'll self-sabotage.

It's human nature to avoid painful situations, to avoid danger. Maybe it's human nature to see the dream ahead and tell yourself you'll never reach it. Being cognizant is the struggle. I'm trying very hard to stay in the moment, keep to reality, and take what Gavin tells me as truth.

"Logically, I know you're right."

"Old habits are hard to break, though, yeah?"

"Most definitely."

At the arena, Vanessa's waiting for us at the entrance closest to where the families sit.

"Can we get inside now, it's as cold as my mother-in-law's heart out here," Vanessa says in way of greeting.

"Yep, we're ready," I tell her, pulling the tickets up on my phone.

"Shouldn't you both be wearing jerseys emblazoned with your men's names or something?"

"Hugo is not my man," Britton says. "We're just having fun while I'm in town."

"When I can figure out how to make it stylish, I'll consider it. Until then, I'll stick to my own wardrobe, thank you very much," I add. "Come on, drinks and food, first."

"Didn't that throw you into a flare-up last time," Vanessa warns.

"I'm going to be much pickier tonight. But Britt wants the full experience." We walk into the arena and immediately people pause mid-step, making double takes at Britton. She pretends she doesn't see or hear. If someone comes up to her, she's always very pleasant, but once it starts, it's hard to stop the crowds of people.

It makes it hard for her to experience mundane things, like a dinner out at a burger joint, or popping into a Target to grab a box of tampons. She's not the type of person to rely on an assistant to manage every little detail of her life. Britton lives for these moments, when she can go somewhere with a crowd of people and just…live.

Getting food is easy enough, there aren't interruptions from fans. Nobody seems to notice her except the young gal ringing up our veggie burgers, whose smile grows the size of her face when she notices who is paying her. The kid looks like she might cry from excitement. Britton winks at her and throws a fifty-dollar bill in the tip bucket, a silent thank you for not drawing attention.

We get to the seats early, most of the others aren't here yet, but Tori shows up shortly after. She takes a seat next to mine, her fingers nervously tapping on her knee.

"Britt, this is Gavin's daughter, Tori," I introduce.

"Hi," Tori says loudly. "Shit, sorry. Hi."

"You're stunning," Britton says to her, causing Tori to blink in astonishment. Having a famous Hollywood starlet tell you that is probably jarring, even though it's not a lie. "It's great to meet you."

"You, too. I mean, it's nice to meet you, too. But you're also so pretty."

"I like you already," Britton says.

Isla, her daughter, and Willa arrive next, and conversation turns to our meals. Sadie is a vegetarian and applauds our food choices. I ask her about her favorite meals and favorite restaurants. She rattles off all sorts of information and suggestions. Making note of many of them, especially one vegan restaurant that specializes in breakfast.

Soon enough, warmups start, and Britton's sight is glued to the ice.

"I could get used to this," she says, causing Willa to laugh.

"It's not a bad view," she agrees, homing in on Zander Fane, one of her two boyfriends.

"Where's Damian tonight?" I ask.

"He was in New Orleans for the weekend, but his plane should have landed in SeaTac a few minutes ago. He'll come straight here."

"Can we make big neighs the next time I stay over?" Sadie asks her aunt.

"Beignets? Yes! Those turned out delicious last time you helped."

"Yeah. Plus, Uncle Damian lets me put so much sugar on mine. He's the best."

"I might have to have a talk with Uncle Damian," Isla says.

"No, I don't think you need to do that," Sadie says emphatically, shaking her head, making all of us laugh. "I'm his favorite niece. He always says so."

"You're his only niece," Isla says.

"For now, but I'll still be his favorite after you give me lots of sisters and brothers."

"Who says I'm giving you lots?"

"Daddy."

"With the number of nights I babysit, I'd say Cillian is right," Willa adds.

"Shut it," Isla says to her sister, looking a little ashamed. The lights dim, saving Isla from any more teasing about her apparently active sex life.

The first period moves fast but neither team scores. Britton gets animated every time Blom makes a save, which is a lot. He's a beast in the net tonight. Or that's what Tori tells me. I've been trying to watch more games at home, but it's hard to learn it all without someone explaining it to you.

At first intermission, I excuse myself to use the restroom. My phone vibrates in my handbag, and I see that I missed a call from Fallon. Reception is spotty in the arena, but if I walk outside to make a call, I can't get back in. I type out a text message instead.

ME:

> I'm at a hockey game. Is it urgent, or can I call in the morning?

After grabbing another beer for Britton, I make my way back down toward our seats. Many women are standing, giving hugs to a woman whose back is to me.

"Why didn't you sit up here with us?" one asks her. "We've missed you."

"Oh, we have seats down by the benches tonight," the newcomer says. She turns just enough that I can see her profile.

Caroline.

She's missed. This is her world. Her family. My mind reels as panic sets in.

I glance at Britton and Vanessa, who notice me and give me wary looks. My hands shake, a little, at first, then violently. I look down to see that my phone is vibrating.

FALLON:

Josephine thinks it's an emergency,
but that's just theatrics. Call me in
the morning. NOT TOO EARLY!

I stare at the message, unmoving, unsure of what to do, when more messages come through.

VANESSA:

This is your spot, Odette. Not hers. Not
anymore. Remember who you are.

BRITTON:

What Vanessa said.

Remember who you are.

Who am I?

I'm motherfucking Odette Quinn. Stylist to the most A-listers of all A-listers. I've dressed wives of presidents and prime ministers. I've had dinner with literal princesses on private yachts in the French Riviera. I've been to the Oscars, the Grammys, the Emmys. I've hobnobbed with the most rich and most famous and never felt like I was less than any of them.

I'm a woman who doesn't take shit, who doesn't cower. Who doesn't run away from a fire that she can put out herself.

I'm not the girl in her mother's flower bed crying over a broken heart. Not anymore.

Setting my shoulders back and my head high, I take the few steps down to my seat with the wives and girlfriends. Where I fucking belong.

"Mom," Tori says to Caroline, getting her attention. "Odette is back."

"Oh, sorry," Caroline says, turning to me. "I just came up to say hi. It's good seeing you, Odette."

Is it? Or is it as strange for her as it is for me?

"It's nice to see you, too, Caroline." Not a lie, not the truth, either. I haven't seen her since she wed the boy I loved. But that's not who we are anymore. Now she's the woman that raised an exceptional young woman I've come to care for. It's a fine line that I stand on with Caroline.

"I'll see you for breakfast, sweetheart," she says to her daughter before waving and walking off.

Had I expected her appearance tonight, my reaction may not have been so visceral that I needed my friends to bolster my backbone. But I didn't expect, there was no time to fasten my armor tightly. Did Gavin know she'd be here?

Did he hope that we wouldn't run into each other?

"Sorry," Tori says quietly. "She didn't mean to make anything uncomfortable."

"It's fine, you're here, her friends are here. Of course, she'd want to come say hello."

"You're the wag now, though," she says. "Dad wants *you* here with the team family."

I cling to her words. Gavin wants me. If he'd known Caroline would be here, he would have told me. My insecurities need to take a back seat to what I know.

The game starts back up and my nerves settle as I watch Gavin skate around, handling the puck like he was born to do. I rarely pull my eyes away from him, even when he's nowhere near the puck. If he's on the bench, I watch the bench. I watch him as he watches the play in front of him.

The second period passes without me really seeing the game. Just him.

When the third period starts, I try to stay engaged in the game that is now tied two to two. All the women around me, as well as Damian, who arrived late in the first period, are feeling the intensity, knowing how much our players want this win.

Quickly, we score another goal. Cillian slapped the puck into the opposing net, assisted by Zander. The arena erupts in noise, the enthusiasm so contagious even my prim friend Vanessa is on her feet, hands raised in the air with both Britton and I smiling at how she's living in the moment.

With only a few minutes left in the game, Gavin scores a goal, making it much harder for the other team to catch up. Not impossible, Sadie is quick to say, but difficult.

My phone starts buzzing in my handbag again.

FALLON:

I'm so sorry. But yes, emergency.
Call when you can.

What absolute shit timing.

Josephine Marcus is about as diva as they come. A singer with a voice to rival the likes of Whitney Houston and Celine Dion. The attitude of a demon spawn. Why I have not dumped her from my client list by now, I still question. She's an awful person, but she pays a premium for us to put up with her.

She's a great reminder of why I wanted to step back from my business. I don't miss the late night or early morning calls because a client is fretting over what to wear to a party that might result in a single photograph of them hitting the press.

I still want to make people feel beautiful in what they wear, but my perspective has changed.

As the last second ticks off, a player on the other team slams into Gavin, knocking him flat on his back, his head bouncing off the ice.

25

ODETTE

Tori gasps and grabs my arm. Half of the arena gasped with her; the other half is too distracted by the win to have seen the hit.

"Get up, Dad," she chants, and I wrap my arm around her as we both stare down on the ice. He's not moving. Neither am I, but Tori trembles in my arms. "Come on, Dad. Get up."

The crowd starts to quiet as everyone notices Gavin hasn't gotten up yet. My heart beats wildly. Britton rubs my arm. There's a scuffle on the ice, our guys attacking whoever hit Gavin, but I can't pay attention to that right now.

Finally, after what feels like several long minutes but is really only seconds, Gavin's chest heaves. He tries to get up, but the trainers are there to stop him. Conversations are happening that we can't hear. Gavin shakes his head a few times and I'm relieved at the movement.

"He's going to be okay," Isla says, turning around to assess Tori, who only nods but doesn't say anything.

After a few more minutes, Gavin stands with the help of Cillian and Letty.

"Oh, thank fuck," Tori says, breaking down in tears now that the initial shock has passed. "Can I see him, Isla?"

"I'll see what I can do," she answers. "You two make your way down to the family room. I'll see who I can get in touch with and find out what's going on."

"Thank you, Isla," I say.

"Of course," she says before asking her sister to take Sadie home with her. Meanwhile, I give my keys to Britton and tell her to take my car home. Isla says she'll meet us downstairs, and Tori takes the lead since I have no idea where to go.

It's a long walk to the other side of the stadium, through the throngs of people trying to leave. I hold Tori's hand tightly, not wanting to lose her but also to comfort her, as she's still visibly shaken.

I am, too. But breaking down won't do either of us any good. It's terrifying to watch someone you love quit moving.

Someone I love. Another truth. One I've been too scared to admit. Seeing him lying there makes me not want to fight against it so hard. Because we've missed so much time already. What if we don't have much left?

For months, I've thought maybe it wasn't worth the risk. When really, it's the only thing that is. I could spend the rest of my life without him with the assurance of being lonely and heartsick. Or I can take a leap of faith and maybe finally find the happiness I've so desperately missed.

Sounds like an easy decision when your trauma finally takes a back seat in your life.

We come to a bank of elevators with security standing in front of them.

"Hey, Tori. Hope your dad is okay," one of them says to her, pushing the button.

"Thanks, Sam. I'm sure he is, he's tough."

"He sure is," Sam says, holding his arm over the doors that have opened and letting us in.

We exit the elevator into a long hallway that's eerily quiet compared to the bustling thoroughfare above. It's like a whole other world down here. But as we get farther, we start to hear chatter from members of the press loitering in the hallways. Before we reach them, Tori opens a door on the left that leads into a room filled with sofas, armchairs, and tables. A small table is set up just inside the door and laden with snacks.

A baby cries softly from the corner as several toddlers run in circles around their mothers. I recognize many of the faces, but not all. Isla once told me a lot of the wives with smaller children choose to come down here for the games, where the little ones can run free instead of sitting mostly still in the stands.

Tori takes the first available seat, pulling her knees up to her chin. She holds her phone tight and stares at the blank screen. Probably hoping her dad will text her that he's fine.

"Do you want some water? Or coffee, maybe?"

"No, thank you, Odette. Can you just sit with me?"

"Of course," I say, taking the seat next to her on the sofa and once again wrapping an arm around her.

"I've seen a lot of guys get injured. But never my dad. It used to scare me a lot when I was little. I'd have nightmares about a blade cutting him. I never told him that, I didn't want him to quit for me or anything."

"You kept the fear to yourself," I say. "Something I can understand."

"I'll miss watching him play, but I'm also happy he's retiring. It makes me feel like an asshole to say that."

"You are nothing like an asshole, Victoria," I reassure. "Nothing at all."

A man walks toward us. "Tori," he says when he's close enough.

"Brock? Why are you here? Where's my mom?"

"She's…" he starts to say when Isla walks through the door.

"Hey, Johnnie is going to take you back to where Gavin is. Both of you, go on back," she says, pointing to a door on the far side of the room.

"Thanks, Isla," I say.

As soon as we're through the door, a man wearing a Blades shirt meets us.

"Come with me," he says. "I'll take you to him."

Tori bursts through the door into the room Johnnie takes us to, rushing to her dad, who sits with his back to the door as Caroline stands in front of him, her hands cupping his cheeks.

"I love you," she tells him.

"Dad," Tori cries when she rounds the table he's sitting on. He wraps her in his arms, whispering things into her hair, and Caroline wraps her arms around the both of them.

I stay where I am, just here, holding the door, wondering where I belong in this situation. Tori is the priority, of course.

But how is Caroline here already? And why? And what the fuck did she just say?

And what the fuck am I supposed to do? Interrupt? Wait on the sidelines?

The panic from earlier resurfaces, but now it's mixed with the fear I felt when he was lying on the ice, and the small relief of him getting to his feet, and the love that I finally feel. Tears spill from my eyes. I don't wipe them away. I don't move.

Because Caroline is in my spot. But it's also hers. And I don't know what to fucking do as my heart tells me to run and my head screams don't be so stupid.

This is my only nightmare in life. Falling in love and having it taken from me again. Why is she here? Why is she the first in the room with him? Why does she think she has that right?

Why did he let her? It should be me checking him over. It should be me touching him.

"Ode."

The logical answer is that he wants her here. Her. Not me. She's more important. Like she always was. They were best friends. Are they still? Probably. Why wouldn't they be? They know everything about each other, they've had a lifetime together.

I'm just…what? The distraction? The backup plan? The placeholder until his wife returns?

Someone brushes by me. I don't see who because my eyes are to the ground and blurry from the tears.

"Ode. Pumpkin, come here," Gavin says louder. I blink up and see him, Tori still in his arms but Caroline is gone. "Will you come here? Please."

Unsteadily, I take the steps until I'm standing in front of him, scanning every inch of his face to make sure he's okay. He's pale, but there aren't any marks, no blood.

"Are you okay?"

"I'm fine. I just got the wind knocked out of me. I think they're going to run me through concussion protocols, just to be sure," he says, reaching to pull my face close to his. "Are you okay?"

"It's terrifying," I say, not explaining that I mean not just the hit he took. I don't say much else, as Tori and I take seats in the chairs against the wall while we wait to see when they'll let him go home. Tori looks ready to fall asleep, obviously wrung out from the stress.

"Tori, go home, get some sleep. I'll call you in the morning."

"Are you sure? I could go home with you. What if someone needs to wake you up every half hour or something?"

"I'm sure, kiddo. I told you, I'm fine."

"Okay," she says, getting up to give him another hug. "I love you, Dad."

"I love you, too. We'll talk tomorrow."

She waves at me, which I return with a soft smile before she leaves.

"Ode," he says, snagging my attention back to him. But just then, Coach Cole walks in with two other people.

"How are you feeling, buddy?" Coach asks him.

"I keep telling everyone I'm fine," Gavin says. "Wish someone would start believing me."

One of the other men shines a light in Gavin's eyes. The room is small, and I feel in the way. Or like an interloper, somewhere I'm not supposed to be. Yet I don't want to leave Gavin, either.

A lot of medical terms are thrown around, but at the end of it all, the general consensus is that because he lost consciousness, he needs to be on concussion protocol with another assessment in about twenty-four hours, then another in forty-eight. He'll miss tomorrow's game. The tension in his jaw tells me he's pissed about that, but he doesn't make a fuss.

Everyone leaves. As soon as the door shuts behind them, Gavin's shoulders slump.

"It's for the best, Gavin."

"I know," he says. "Doesn't mean I don't fucking hate it. You go home, too; I'll clean up and head over when I'm done."

"Britton is there tonight."

"I don't fucking much care."

"Okay." He grabs my hand as I start to walk past, stopping me. Neither of us says anything else, it's more a silent communication. I imagine he's trying to explain why Caroline was here, while I'm trying to convey I'm ignoring it because I'm just thankful he's okay.

I'm trying to ignore how much it hurt because I don't want to cause him more stress.

I did that same thing once before.

"I'll see you soon," he finally says, and I leave with a simple nod.

I have to call an Uber to get home, but it gives me the opportunity to call Fallon, who rants about Josephine and her dramatics. She has an event the day after tomorrow and refuses to wear anything he's offered.

By the time I get home, I'm vacillating between flying to Los Angeles first thing in the morning to handle her, or just firing her. Neither option is very appealing.

My step falters at my front door. A new bouquet was delivered. Large, beautiful, full of bright tiny yellow flowers. The same my mother used to plant. So similar to the wedding arrangements etched in my memory.

I take a long, deep inhale. So slowly, so calmly, I push the bouquet off the table inch by inch, watching the edge of the vase as it begins its unbalanced dance onto the marble floor below. The sound of glass breaking is somehow cathartic.

Or I've completely lost my fucking mind. Who can say?

"Odette," Britton calls from the top of the stairs.

"Don't come down in bare feet," I say. "I broke the vase."

"Is Gavin okay?" she asks, peering over the banister at the mess I made.

"I think so. They're keeping a watch on him for a few days to be sure."

I view the pieces of glass, the dim reflection of the hanging entryway light twinkling on a few of them. Is that what my heart looked like from the inside when Gavin broke up with me? Of course not, heartbreak is a metaphor. It's not real.

The pain is. The lasting effect. Obviously.

"Are you okay?"

"No, darling." A laugh bursts out of me, and I feel like I'm verging on hysteria. "Caroline was with him. When we finally got to see him, she was already there."

"Bitch. Why?"

"I don't know. We didn't really have a chance to talk about that."

"But you will, yeah?"

"He's coming here when he's done at the arena," I say. "I may have to fly to L.A. tomorrow, should only be gone a night."

"Okay," she says, cycing me like she doesn't trust my mental state, either. "Why?"

"Josephine wants to wear *that brand*."

"The brand we don't speak of? Gross," Britton says, dramatically acting like she's going to gag.

I have rules when you contract with me. The first one is that I choose the brands I style a client in. If a brand or designer doesn't align with my morals, I won't use them.

There is a major label that was run by a man with many children. Several sons, one daughter, all of whom worked in the company. When the man died, he left control to his sons, completely cutting out his daughter because he didn't want a woman to run his brand.

I refuse to dress women in clothing that doesn't support women.

One up-and-coming starlet hated that about me and wouldn't sign on with me because of it. That was fine by me, but she made a big stink about it. Page Six picked up the story. It's a well-known fact about me now, one Josephine is aware of.

"I may have to drop her; she's causing Fallon to pull his hair out."

"His hair is far too pretty for that."

"Right?"

"And, Gavin?"

"I don't know, Britt. It felt so…"

"Familiar?"

"Yes."

"Give him a chance to explain. If it doesn't sound legit, call me down. I'll stab him in the heart for you."

"Love you, Britton."

"Love you to prison and back, Odette," she says, making her way back upstairs.

Bypassing the glass, I walk into my living room. Pulling the throw blanket off my sofa, I wrap it around myself and lie to watch the moonlight on the water. It's calming and I need that right now.

I need rationality, understanding, patience. I need a motherfucking explanation.

What I get is Caroline's words lulling me to sleep. *I love you. I love you. I love you.*

Gavin got in late. I remember waking up when he carried me to bed last night, but I was back asleep before I hit the pillow. I woke up this morning to his body curled around mine, my face buried in the bare skin of his chest. For a few minutes, I lie still, listening to his soft snore, barely audible. Just loud enough to know he's alive.

The hit from last night flashes in my memory, sending a fearful shiver down my back. I'm so thankful he's okay.

I love you. I love you. I love you.

Fuck.

My mind is my worst enemy. My biggest nemesis.

Or, hell, maybe it's Caroline.

"How are you feeling?" I ask, nudging my nose under his chin to wake him up.

"Normal," he says, looking up at me. "I don't think I'm concussed."

"Thank fuck," I say, relieved to hear it. "I need to shower."

Snaking out from under his arm, I head straight to the bathroom. I've got three hours until my flight and I still don't know what I'm going to do with Josephine. But I've only got today to deal with it, I won't miss more work than I must. Which means, I'll probably have to fire her, because I can't trust that she won't pull shit like this again.

By the time I've rinsed the conditioner out of my hair and am stepping out of the shower, I've convinced myself it's the best option.

Gavin sits on the edge of the bed when I walk back into the room.

"You're sure you're okay?" I ask again, pulling my carry-on suitcase out of the closet.

"Yeah," he says. "What are you doing?"

"Fallon has an emergency. I need to go to L.A. for the night." I step back into the closet to get dressed. Gavin comes to stand in the doorway, watching me warily.

"Just one night?"

"Yes. I need to fire a client and I'd rather do that in person."

"Odette," he says, staying my hand after I fasten my bra on. "Are you running?"

"I'm running late, if that's what you mean." I pull a dress off a hanger and pull it over my head.

"That's not what I'm fucking asking."

"Then what are you fucking asking, Gavin?"

"Is this impromptu trip because of Caroline?"

"Not everything in my life is about you and your ex-wife," I say, my back turned to him so he can't see how affected I am. "I have a career. A life of my own."

"I didn't ask her to be there, Ode. I didn't even know she was at the game."

"Why was she with you?" I collect the few items I'll need for an overnight and brush past him to place them in my suitcase.

"She was worried."

"So was I. So was your daughter."

"Can you stop for half a minute and look at me please," he pleads, not continuing until I look at him. "I did not ask her to be there. She just showed up. I told her to leave, to go find Tori. Thank you, by the way, for taking care of her. I'm sure she was terrified."

"She was," I say, trying to find a lie on his face, but I don't.

"I'm glad you were there for her."

"She loves you," I say. "Caroline. She said she loves you."

"We've had love for each other since we were kids," he says after a sigh. Maybe he'd hoped I hadn't heard what she said. "It's not like how I love you."

My heart sinks and soars, not knowing which of his words it should cling to. This isn't how I want him to tell me he loves me. On the back of professing love for another woman, in the middle of an argument, as a balm for my pain.

None of this is right.

"I don't know where I fit, Gavin. Last night, I felt like a placeholder, only there until she arrives. I'm either in the starring role, or I'm nothing at all," I say.

"You are that, Odette. I don't know what to do to make you see that. I want you to think about whether I've done anything to show you differently. Have my actions since trying to win you back given you any reason to believe that I'm not absolutely, irrevocably committed to just you?"

"I…I don't—" I start but can't finish. I do know. I know it's my insecurity rather than his actions.

"Take your trip, handle your business. I'll be here when you get home, waiting. Missing *you*."

26

ODETTE

Josephine Marcus is the most exhausting woman I've ever known. She's gone now, though. She begged me not to end our working relationship in the end, but it was too late. The comments she made about Fallon were unforgiveable and I'd never put an employee, let alone a partner, through such mistreatment.

She called me a cunt when I said I wouldn't change my mind. I told her I embraced that because cunts are warm and have depth, two things she sadly lacks.

That sent her out the door and Fallon into a fit of laughter. Then we celebrated over a bottle of rose´ before I crashed in his spare room and caught an early flight back to Seattle this morning.

Mostly, the celebrities I've worked with have been pleasant enough. You get a diva attitude here and there, but usually, they're congenial enough because they want what I offer.

Fallon and I will be weeding out the problematic ones and thoroughly vetting any new clients, so as to avoid situations like this in the future.

I text Gavin that I landed safely but I don't go straight home. Instead, I go to the school. I missed yesterday, I don't want to miss today, too.

Gavin asked me to let him know of my flight status while I was gone, and I've done that. Though we haven't talked about much else, besides how he feels. He consistently assures me that he's fine. There's been some guilt on my part. It started as a small voice telling me I shouldn't have left him.

Tori took time off school to stay with him. I made sure he was in good hands before I ran. Because that is what I did. Firing Josephine could have been a phone call.

Gavin was right to accuse me yesterday morning. We're at some kind of crossroads, I think.

He wants me to finally place my trust in him.

I want him to set some boundaries with Caroline. Even though I haven't asked him to. Their relationship isn't normal and none of us know how to navigate it. Yet, I think he is the one that needs to take the reins there. If he won't, if he can't, I don't know how I can ever feel like I'm the woman he loves.

When I get into my office, I check for any voicemails and emails that need to be returned. I've called in a ton of favors for the end of the year designer spotlight we have planned. I want all the best stylists and buyers to get these kids the most exposure I can. They're hard workers and so damned creative, they deserve every bit of attention the industry has to offer.

One email, however, is not industry related.

> Can we meet for coffee? I'd like to apologize, if you'll let me.
> Regards,
> Caroline

My initial response is to ignore it. Then it's to tell her no. Then I realize that it's not my gut that needs to answer her, it's my heart. Building a life with Gavin will be impossible if Caroline and I aren't amicable, at least.

We're not enemies. I don't hate her. I don't even know her, honestly.

I can meet this afternoon. Par La Main at four.

She thanks me as if I've done some magnanimous thing instead of just accepting an olive branch.

The rest of the afternoon passes quickly, the only student coming into the workroom is Benji and I spend time with him as he explains his vision for his future brand. He speaks without doubts, confident that everything he's dreaming of will come to fruition.

I keep his attitude close to my heart when I walk into Par La Main to meet Caroline. She's already waiting for me at a small table in the back corner, a French press pot and two mugs in front of her.

"Hi," I say as I approach. "Thank you for this, I was up too early today."

"I figured. Tori said you were on an early flight," she says, pouring me a cup. "Thank you for meeting me."

"Does Gavin know we're here?"

"Only if you told him. He's upset with me, rightfully so. I fucked up the other night," she says, then pauses. "It's not the first time. I fucked up with you when I found out I was pregnant, too."

"Is that why you asked me here? Because Gavin is upset?"

"No. I've wanted this opportunity for a long time. After my behavior the other night, I thought it was best to just ask for it." She takes a sip of her coffee before she continues, "Let me start there. My boyfriend wanted to see a game; he'd never watched hockey until we started dating. I didn't tell Gavin or Tori I'd purchased tickets, but Tori texted to tell me you were at the game with her, and I thought I'd use the opportunity to meet you again. It was stupid and I made a worse decision when Gav got hurt. I was operating on old habits, not new situations. I took care of him for so long, I forgot that it's not my place anymore."

"You love him."

"He's family, Odette. He's been family since before we knew the meaning and he's the father of my daughter. I'll always love him, but not how you're meant to love a spouse or a partner. That isn't something we've ever shared between us."

"He's said the same," I say. "How is that possible?"

"How did we spend so much time married? Necessity, at first. I'm sure he's explained why we got married," she says, and waits for my acknowledgment. I nod. "It may have seemed like we'd have a support system back home, but that wasn't really the case. Neither of our mothers would have been very helpful. They could offer some financial help, but I would have been on my own in most ways. Plus, the toll it would have taken on Gavin being away from the baby. It wasn't an easy decision, but I think I underestimated the long-term impacts. For both of us, and for you. I was selfish enough at eighteen to pretend that you wouldn't be hurt by it all. That you'd move to Manhattan and live a wonderful life and forget all about us. I believed that because it was easier for me to believe it. It let me live without the guilt that I'd come in between two people in love. After a while, we became complacent. We moved through every day completing all the tasks we had to, flashing smiles for friends and family. Putting on a believable show that crumbled to nothing every night when we were alone. Then one day, I met a man. Only then did I realize just how fucked up our life was."

"Even then you didn't end it," I prompt.

"It's hard, you know? Regretting our marriage but also not, because it gave Tori the childhood she had. I don't know how to reconcile it, Odette. I imagine it's the same for Gav. What I do know is that I'm glad you have each other now. That I don't want to get in the way of that, and that I'm sorry for what we put you through. What *I* have put you through."

"Reconciling was hard for me, too, until I met Tori. I adore your daughter, who I know wouldn't be the same person if she wasn't raised the way she was," I say. "I understand the reasons you got married. I don't harbor any hate there."

"She loves you, if you didn't know already. She thinks the world of you." She takes another sip of her coffee. "We both hope it works out for you and Gav. If it does, I don't want things to be strained between us. Do you think that's possible?"

"It comes down to this, Caroline. I won't ever step on your toes as Tori's mom, or Gavin's friend," I say. "But when you needed him the most, I walked away without drama. I respected what you both needed even though it fucking broke me to do it. Now, we have a second chance and I need you to give me the same level of respect. I'm not asking you to disappear from his life, not like I had to do. You'll never have to live a day without his friendship and support, you'll never have to know the loss of that. But I am saying that you no longer get to step into the roles that are now mine. He's not yours to comfort and care for after a game, he's not yours to touch, or say you love him. Not anymore."

Caroline wipes a tear away. She'll never understand what it was like for me, and I hope she never experiences heartbreak like that. But maybe she at least sees that it wasn't easy for me. That it still isn't easy for me.

***

After I meet with Caroline, I go to Gavin's. He called to say that Tori left after he took his final cognitive test and passed with flying colors. He's officially off concussion protocol and cleared to skate in the morning.

There are still things we need to figure out, of course. While my conversation with Caroline was productive, it's not her that I need to know is committed to seeing Gavin and I work. We both need to be. So far, I've been too scared to. And he, well, he hasn't taken the control I need to feel safe.

It's not flowers and baked goods that I need from him. Though, I appreciate both. It's certainty that I want, the knowledge that I only come behind Tori. That when he needs to be taken care of, it's me he wants to do it. That I'm more than just the woman he likes to fuck.

Gavin meets me at the door when I get to his house.

"Hello, Mr. No Concussion."

"Hi, Ms. Boss Bitch." He pulls me in for a hug, pressing a kiss to the crown of my head. "Did you get it handled?"

"Of course." He picks me up off my feet, carrying me inside and kicking the door shut behind him. Not stopping until we're in the kitchen and he's setting me on the counter so we're eye to eye.

"Do you want to tell me about the flowers?"

"I don't like yellow flowers."

"I'll make note of it if you explain." He tips my chin up with a finger when I try to avert my gaze.

"There were yellow flowers at your wedding."

"I don't remember that," he says. "I remember being depressed and worried that I was making the wrong decision. I remember wishing it was you standing in front of me. Pretending it was you because that's the only way I could get through the day. I remember missing the fuck out of you. And I remember feeling guilty as hell for those thoughts. All of that I remember like it was yesterday, but if you'd asked if there were flowers there, I would have said no."

"I remembered that detail for you, I guess."

"I'm sad you do. I hate that you've lived with that, and I'd take it away if there was any way I could," he says. "I'm sorry you came home after a hard night to them. I handled some business yesterday, too."

"What business?"

"I called Caroline. I told her that the only woman who has that kind of access to me is you. Nothing like that will happen again, Ode. I promise, and I'm sorry I didn't set some parameters before something like that happened. That, like so many other things, is my fault. I'll own them, and I'll learn from them. Okay?"

"I'm sorry I've been so…fragile."

"You're not fragile, Ode. You're cautious in one area of your life. Only one. Otherwise, you're as strong as any hockey player I know. You're passionate and you care, and you don't let people get walked over or taken advantage of. How could you ever see yourself as fragile?"

"Because yellow flowers send me over the edge."

"Give me all your triggers and I'll steer us clear of them."

"All of them?"

"Every single one, Ode."

"I hate the color navy blue."

"Okay," he says, grinning.

"I can't eat cilantro. I have that gene that makes it taste like soap."

"Fuck, that might be a deal killer."

"Asshole," I grumble, and he laughs. "I prefer rainy locations to sunny ones. The sun is the devil and I'll wilt under it."

"I'm definitely breaking up with you over that," he teases.

"Can we break up before we're even together?"

"You wound me, Odette Quinn," he says, gripping his chest. "It's a wound I earned a long time ago, though, isn't it?"

"I don't want to cause any more wounds, Gavin. I can't *take* any more, either."

"I know, Ode. I said I'd protect you with my life and I meant it. Okay? I mean it." He brings his face close to mine. Seeing me, seeing through me. "I love you, Odette. I think I've been in love with you since our first date. Since the first time you gave me the time of day. I'll be in love with you until I'm in my grave."

"Gavin…"

"Shh." He silences me with a quick kiss. "Don't say anything. Not until you're ready. I haven't had enough time to prove myself to you yet. But I swear I will. I'm still only asking you to try to keep giving me that time."

If he's by my side, I can give him all the time this life has left for us.

"Okay."

"Yeah? You mean it?"

"I mean it," I reassure. "But can you try not to take any more hits like that on the ice? I've never been more frightened."

"I'll try," he says, pressing kisses to my forehead.

"Can I call you my boyfriend? I've never had one before."

"Yes, Ode," he says, then fuses his mouth with mine. His tongue pushes past my lips. Again, he lifts me with ease. This time, hauling me into the primary bathroom. When I'm back on my feet, he steps away to run water into his large garden tub.

"We're taking a bath?"

"Yes, and I'm taking that ass."

"Oh, are you?" I ask when he turns back to me.

"Do you have a problem with that?" His hand finds the chignon at the back of my head and pulls. "Girlfriend."

"No," I say, pulling my dress over my head, then unclasping my bra and letting it drop. When we're both bare and the tub is full, he helps me in.

"Stay put," he barks as he hurries back into his bedroom. He returns with a bottle of lube that he places on the edge.

"You just happen to keep lube handy?"

"Listen, my hand was getting quite the workout until recently."

"That's hot," I purr.

"Yeah? You wanna watch?"

"Yes, please," I say, resting my chin in my palms. Gavin is already hard. "But you won't need the bottle if you stick that cock in my mouth first."

"Fucking hell, woman." He steps into the tub with me. "You're first, though. If your mouth touches me right now, I'm going to explode."

I smile, scooting up on the ledge and arching my back so my rear pops out of the water.

"Go ahead, boyfriend." Gavin wastes no time in burying his face, and tongue, in. "Oh, fuck."

His fingers expertly play at my pussy as his tongue works my ass into a frenzy. It's not an area I've let men venture. The sensation is almost new, exciting, and holy shit…so good. Especially when his fingers graze my clit, my own grasping to the tub to keep from moving too much or coming too soon.

I can't stop myself when he pushes his tongue in and hums with pleasure, sending a vibration straight to my core. I gasp and grind against his fingers as the orgasm rocks through me. It's so easy for him to make me come.

If I had any ego with sex, I'd be disappointed in myself with how quickly I crumble under his ministrations. But I don't, and I'm not fighting it. It only means more orgasms to come because he doesn't tire easily.

I flop over onto my back, stretching my arms out to the sides and moving my legs as far apart as the tub allows so Gavin can nestle between them.

He kisses me, hard and a little sour. I don't mind it, since he doesn't, either. I like that he wants every part of my body, it makes me feel powerful and alive. Wanted and desired.

"Fuck me until you're close, Gavin. Then finish in my mouth," I say against his lips.

"It's like you're in my head with me," he says as he thrusts in so hard my head falls back. His palm is there, holding me up. Holding me close. He's relentless, water sloshing over the sides and onto the floor, all while he tethers me to his body. I wind my limbs around him, holding on and sighing with each slide of his hard cock inside me.

I love this. Our connection, our union. Hearts throbbing skin to skin. Bodies slapping without a care other than more, more, more.

I love him. But I keep it to myself. It's not the time for the words. I think he knows anyway. I think he feels this as strongly as I do. There's no way he couldn't.

Pressing kisses to his neck, I lay the words there. Silent and invisible but marked forever. A promise to grow stronger for him, to learn to give him my whole heart without fear, to build a life together. To love him until death.

It's our turn. It's our time.

I pull at his curls and nip at his jaw as his rhythm shifts. He's close now.

"My mouth, Gavin. I want to taste you."

"Fuck," he groans, but then he's standing and holding my head where he wants me with one hand. The other stroking his cock. So tantalizing my eyes blur from anticipation. "Open."

When my lips part enough, he shoves it in and holds it deep. I moan around him, gripping his thighs, the muscles tensing under my fingers.

In and out, he starts a slow glide. I lap at him. Waiting and wanting, tasting the pre-cum. Then he's coming, and I'm swallowing him down like it's the only sustenance I'll ever need, while he keeps thrusting until he's totally satiated and so am I.

After he's cleaned us up and dried us off, he wraps a blanket around me and props me back up on his kitchen counter while he cooks me dinner in the nude. It's a nice view, nicer than my lake at home.

"I had coffee with Caroline today," I say. He pauses the knife chopping the onion.

"Why did you do that?"

"She asked." I shrug. "She wanted to apologize."

"That's good, she owed you that. How did it go?"

"Okay, I think. We found some common ground, anyway."

"I'm glad," he says, stepping over to press a kiss to my lips.

"But you should know that if you ever let her touch you again, you'll be missing more teeth than Letty."

"Noted," he says with a huge grin.

27

GAVIN

"She's pretty fucking amazing, isn't she? Or am I biased because I'm her dad?"

"No, she's amazing," Britton agrees.

It's the spotlight that Odette arranged for all the students. Those graduating this year had a full runway show. Undergraduates were given space to set up something like a pop-up boutique to highlight what they've been working on. Tori's little booth has been bustling all day. Instead of just setting up previous designs for people to inspect, she's brought a sewing machine and a bunch of fabric so they can watch her process. Odette's busy playing hostess, so I'm glad Britton came to keep me company.

She's become family the past few months. Even though she moved out of Odette's house shortly after Thanksgiving, she's still been around for filming. Tori's even calling her Auntie Britton now. Britt loves it, since she doesn't have much of a family of her own.

Caroline and Brock are here, too. Other than a casual greeting before the event started, I haven't seen them.

The relationship between me and my ex-wife has grown more distant and much healthier. We're all happier for it, including Brock, who was silently struggling with the relationship Caroline and I had after the divorce. We're in a good place now, though, and I still have all my teeth.

I donated all my navy-blue suits and let Odette fill my closet with new ones. The press loved that; I'm officially the best-dressed player in the league. Our team's social media manager even created a second Instagram page just for "Vaughn's Fits".

It's become a competition, of sorts, for the other guys, constantly trying to outdo me. They never can, but the fans love that they try. It's also been a good segue to talk about Odette and her business, and Tori's aspiring one. A way for me to support them in another way.

That's something that is becoming increasingly important to me now that my NHL career is coming to a close. It's not over yet, we've made it to the playoffs. I have one last run at the Stanley Cup.

With the school year coming to an end, Ode has offered to dress all the guys for our playoff games. And she's designed the wags' playoff jackets.

The team has fully embraced her as part of the family. It's nice, since I already consider her mine.

She still hasn't said she loves me. Not in words, anyway. I've been patient, because I know how she feels. I know she loves me as much as I love her. We only became official just before Thanksgiving, it's April now, that's not that long. It's not as if she's been making me wait for decades.

Every day she shows me how much she loves me by being invested in my life. Throwing herself into hockey so that she understands what's happening with my days and keep up with conversations regarding my career. She hired a masseuse to teach her how to best ease my muscles, not caring that the team has hired professionals for that. Her sauna has been repaired and she added a home gym so I wouldn't have to leave for workouts when I stay over.

Which is a lot. I'll be moving into her crazy cult house permanently after playoffs. The place has grown on me, and I understand now why she bought it. Plus, you can't beat the view, especially when it's the backdrop to her naked body as I fuck her up against the windows.

Odette is always looking for ways to make my life easier, when really, all I need is her to be with me at the end of every day.

I appreciate her efforts, though, and repay her in kind. She's only had a couple more flare-ups, and I stayed by her side while she battled through the exhaustion of them. For the most part, she's handling her disease in stride, and I support every new thing she tries to mitigate the symptoms that crop up. I even went with her to her last endocrinologist appointment so I could ask all my questions. I want to make her life as easy as she makes mine.

I still bake for her and together we're learning how to cook more meals.

It's been eye-opening. Caroline and I never had, in the nearly nineteen years we were married, what Odette and I have. I always wanted to take care of my ex-wife, but it was more like a job, an obligation, rather than a bone-deep need. It's embedded in me to do whatever I can to care for Odette.

"Your daughter is a hit," George says, walking up to Britton and me. Vanessa's husband and I have also become friends. He isn't around much, but when he is home, we try to have dinner with them. I have great respect for him because he understands my girlfriend and has never judged her. She didn't have many close friends, and I think that's why. The way she lived her life before moving to Seattle was what people expect of men, not women.

George is one of the few men who didn't think her a home-wrecking whore.

"Tell me about it," I say. "I've been trying to congratulate her for a solid thirty minutes, but I can't squeeze through the crowd."

"If it makes you feel any better, I heard a buyer from a major store talking about wanting the top on her front dress form."

"Shit, she'd die," I say, pride warming my chest.

I'm moving Tori into my house when I move to Odette's. It will give her room to spread out and work in comfort, as opposed to the small apartment she's been in this year.

It also gives her more room to entertain her boyfriend, Drake. I don't love that aspect, but Odette assures me he's a good kid.

Nobody is good enough for my daughter, though.

"She deserves that and more," Britton says. "I haven't seen a single thing she's made that I wouldn't wear in a heartbeat."

The support she has from all these new people in her life chokes me up, so I don't say anything. Instead, I pat Britton's shoulder as a way to say thank you.

"Embrace that emotion, hockey star," George says. "I'm going to go find my wife and see how much longer before I can drag her off to a bottle of wine and bed."

"It was good seeing you, George."

"You, too, Gavin. Britton, always a pleasure."

"Likewise. Take care of that wife tonight, she's been missing you."

"You know I will."

Britton leaves shortly after, and I finally get a second to see my kid and tell her how proud I am of her. Then I go find my girlfriend. Ode's been working endless hours the past two weeks, preparing for this.

I find her in a back corner, talking to a couple of people I don't know. She's got that smile plastered on her face, the one that says she's not really having a great time, but she doesn't want to let it show.

She's tired. Knowing her, she hasn't eaten anything today because she put everything and everyone else before herself. I wait for her to finish the conversation before I move behind her and wrap my arm around her stomach.

"You need me to find you a snack?"

"No, we're going to start clearing everyone out now. Then I'm going home and straight to that zucchini bread you made. I've been craving it for hours," she says. "Victoria Vaughn was much talked about today."

"So I've heard. Thank you for everything you've done for her," I say, pressing a kiss to her jaw.

"She's done everything on her own," Odette says. "I only put people in front of her."

"You've bolstered her confidence, too, Ode. You've done that for every student here."

"I've tried. I'm just so fucking proud of them all."

"They know that, and they love you for it," I tell her. "I'm going to head home; I'll have food ready for you when you get there."

"You're the best boyfriend a gal could ask for," she says, sinking into me.

"I try. Come home soon, Ode."

Odette wakes me by curling up in my lap. I must have fallen asleep on the couch waiting for her to get home.

"Hey," I mumble.

"Sorry it took me so long; I ended up helping negotiate a deal."

"I don't know what that means," I say, inhaling her scent.

"A very big store wants to buy six items they saw today. Four from the runway show, two from the spotlight students. Vanessa and I made sure the deal was lucrative for the kids."

"That's fucking amazing."

"It is. Tori's thrilled," she says, peering up to me with a sly smile.

"Shut up? Really?"

"Really. They also want the dress she was wearing, the one Drake made for her."

"Holy shit, that's so fucking cool. I should call her."

"She said to call her in the morning. They're all celebrating tonight."

"Yeah, okay," I say, though I grab my phone from under the cushion where I stashed it and send a quick text.

"She told me she loves me tonight," Odette says, emotion thick in her throat.

"Ah, babe. Of course, she does."

"It's different hearing it," she says. And don't I know that all too well.

"Sure, it is, but you had to know how she feels about you."

"I did, but…" She pauses. "It made me realize that I've been a bitch."

"What? To who?"

"To you," she says, adjusting until her face hovers inches in front of mine. "You know how I feel, but I should have said it."

"Then say it, Ode." I press a small kiss to the corner of her lips.

"I love you, Gavin. I love you so much that I feel like I'm walking on clouds all day. I love you so much that my favorite place to be is curled up in your arms, it's where I want to be when I take my last breath," she says, staring into my eyes. "I'm sorry I didn't say it sooner."

"You said it when you were ready. You don't have to apologize for that."

"You're too nice to me."

"I can be not nice to you in bed later, if that will make you feel better."

"Yes, please," she says, nodding. I laugh.

"I love you, too, Odette."

"I know you do. You show me every day."

I'll keep showing her every day. It's my favorite thing to do.

"There's something for you on the kitchen counter."

"A present?"

"Go see."

I follow as she gets up and prances her way into the kitchen.

"Ooh, that smells good. Lentil soup?"

"Yes, but that's not your gift." I nod to the paper sitting on the counter and she snatches it up. "I owe you a trip."

"Paris for my birthday?"

"Yeah, I even found a place with a private rooftop pool."

"Skinny dipping in Paris for my birthday," she clarifies, setting the paper down and jumping into my arms.

"I was feeling nostalgic."

"I like that, but I'm more interested in making new memories with you, Gavin."

"We'll make plenty of those, Ode," I say before sealing the promise with a deep kiss.

ODETTE

There's something special about Paris in the summer. There's something extraordinary about Paris in the summer with someone you love.

It means even more when the someone you love just came off his final Stanley Cup run and won by scoring the final goal.

Playoffs were the most anxiety-inducing experience I ever had. I loved every minute of it, and I traveled with the wags to all the games. I refused to miss any of it. And I made sure all the guys looked and felt like fire every time they stepped into an arena. A small thing, but I felt like I contributed in a small way to the camaraderie and morale, which Gavin says is important.

He may have been blowing smoke up my ass, but regardless, I loved doing it and the guys seemed appreciative. When you look fabulous, you feel fucking fabulous. That must help walking into a game.

Gavin retired as a player after that last game. He'd still been considering coaching at a league level, but the Blades made him an offer he couldn't refuse, and he's taken a position in Player Development.

At first, he thought it might be more demanding than what he wanted. Then he realized how much he'd miss being with the team, with players. He's been a part of a hockey team since he was four years old, that's not easy to give up, and being a coach of little kids isn't quite the same thing.

I'm happy he made the decision he did, even though I would have supported anything he decided. The world of hockey has grown on me this past year, I don't want to give it up quite yet, either. Though I won't miss the stress of potential injury.

Truthfully, I'd probably support Gavin if he committed murder, I'm so fucking head over heels for the man.

It's his kindness that does me in. He never gets angry, even when I'm being a bear from stress or in the middle of some client crisis. There are hundreds of small things that I never had before, like when we walk down a sidewalk, and he makes sure he's on the outside. I laughed the first time, because really, if an out-of-control car came up on the sidewalk, we'd likely both get hit. But it's sweet, nonetheless. He's always thoughtful like that. There's never a time when he isn't gentle with me. Well, except during sex.

A lot like he is when he's on the ice, he gets virile and vigorous. Unsatiable in obtaining whatever his end goal is, whether it's getting the puck in the net, or bringing me to my third orgasm before he finds his own pleasure.

Isla once told me she thinks hockey players are competitive with themselves when there is nobody else to play against, and I can see that with Gavin. He's always improving a skill or trying to outdo some accomplishment he's already made.

There, we're very similar. We want to be the best at whatever we set our mind to. I've strived to be the best girlfriend I can be.

Now, I want more.

We've never discussed marriage. Maybe he worries that it will bring back visions of his wedding with Caroline. Or maybe he's not interested in matrimony again. Part of me doesn't care about marriage. Well, not the kind sanctioned by a state and taxed by the Feds. I don't need a piece of paper to know we belong together.

But those dreams I had as a child? The ones that had me sketching wedding dresses on paper napkins when I was bored? Those have resurfaced.

I want to wear a pretty dress and profess my undying love to Gavin. It's more than want. It's a need, something more like fate, even. I've always thought we made our own way in life, never believing in any kind of divine intervention. But Gavin and I were meant to be together. So, what do I know?

We've spent the day shopping in the city. As promised, he bought me whatever I wanted from all my favorite vintage stores. I'll have to buy more luggage to get it all home, but there were too many amazing finds to pass up.

Now we're at a small restaurant next to the luxurious flat he rented for us. The one with the rooftop pool that overlooks the Eiffel Tower in the distance.

It's my birthday and I'm going to ask Gavin to marry me. It's the only present I want; he's already given me all I could ever think of asking for. And more. All that's left is the title of wife.

And stepmom, which I want just as much.

Nerves have danced around my tummy all day, growing fiercer as the day goes on. He'll say yes, I'm sure of it. So why am I so worried about it?

The server brings the bill and the bottle of champagne I ordered to-go. I told Gavin I wanted to drink it in the pool later. We've eaten enough to keep us full for days; red onion compote, artichokes in pepper, a cheese plate, mussels, followed by the most delectable lemon tart that melted as soon as it touched my tongue

It's truly been the perfect day.

I grab the bill before he can, and he sends me a scathing glare.

"You can't pay. It's your birthday."

"You haven't let me pay for anything this entire trip."

"Right. Because it's your birthday trip," he argues.

"Well, I'm calling this your Stanley Cup celebratory dinner. And I'm buying."

"You're stubborn."

"So are you," I say, then hand the server my credit card.

"We both turn forty next year. We should take a trip for that, too," he says on the walk next door to our flat. "Maybe the Scottish Highlands."

"I could do a couple of weeks with green hills and cows," I say, smiling at the fact that he didn't offer up a tropical location.

Once in the flat, I go to the double doors that lead out to the rooftop deck, swinging them open wide. I place the bottle on the edge of the pool and unfasten the buttons on the front of my dress, letting it drop to the ground.

There's nothing underneath. I was prepared for how this night would end. Or I hope so, anyway.

I dive in, letting the water slide against my skin, the perfect temperature. Like a soothing bath, a balm to my tickling nerves. I come up for air, and Gavin dives in behind me as I prop my arms up on the ledge, floating.

Seconds later, his strong form is covering mine, his arms on either side of my own, and his chin resting atop my head.

"Happy birthday, Ode."

"Thank you," I whisper. "I couldn't have asked for a better day. You spoiled me."

"I had some years to make up for."

I twirl around in the water to face him.

"No, you don't. We're past all that." I wrap my arms around his neck, my legs around his hips, feeling how hard he is already. I take what I want, lowering down onto his cock, not wasting any time. We've had a day full of foreplay, of teasing, and secret smiles. "Fuck, the feel of you inside me never gets old."

"Let's hope not," he says, backing out slightly, only to thrust back in hard. "Lean back, baby."

Gavin places a palm on my back, lowering me until I'm floating on the water, my hair spreading around me and my breasts bobbing. He takes up a slow pace, rolling his hips deep but not fast enough to cause waves around me while I stare up at the stars in the sky. One shoots across my vision, and it brings tears to my eyes as I take it as a sign.

Gavin will say yes. Of course, he will. We're destined, even the stars say so.

His hands roam my body, over my belly, up through my cleavage, wrapping around the back of my neck. He supports me as he pulls my body onto his over and over.

"Gavin," I moan as the pressure inside me builds. "Pull me up, kiss me."

When I'm once again wrapped around him, he picks up the intensity, his lips devouring mine while I bounce wildly on his cock.

"I love you," I say between gasps for air. "Gavin, I want…" My words are swallowed by the engulfing pleasure. It's always so much with him, it's not just my body and his. It's more. It's our souls, our hearts reminding each of us that this is where we belong.

He groans in my ear as my orgasm pulls him into his own. It's my favorite sound in the world.

Gavin holds me in his arms long after we're both languid and spent, his hand rubbing circles along my spine.

"I want to get married," I say.

"What?" he asks, snapping his face to mine.

"Marry me, Gavin? I don't want to wait any longer. I want to be your wife. I want you to call me your wife. I want to call you my husband."

"I should have fucking known," he says, laughing robustly as he walks us back to the other side of the pool. He lifts me to sit on the edge. "Grab the bottle, Ode."

"Are you going to answer me?"

"After you grab that bottle," he says with a nod to the bottle beside me.

I reach for it and pause. Next to the bottle, Gavin placed two champagne flutes and a small pewter-colored box.

"Gavin."

"Open it up," he says. "It's my turn to ask you."

My fingers tremble as I open it to see a brilliant marquise-cut diamond surrounded by caliber-cut rubies in a gorgeous art deco style.

"It's beautiful, Gavin."

"Modern vintage, like the woman I hope will wear it when she says yes to marrying me."

"How long have you been planning this?" I ask as he takes the ring from me and slides it onto my finger. It fits perfectly.

"Since I was eighteen."

BONUS SCENE

"**T**his all feels too familiar," Willa says, bending over the bathroom counter. She closely examines each of the white sticks, waiting for the telltale pink line to appear.

"It's not the same this time around," I say.

"Not nearly," she agrees. "Thank fuck."

"Seriously. I never want to do this again without him."

"You won't have to," Willa says, looking up from the four pregnancy tests to give me a soft smile. "He's going to die when he finds out."

"If I'm even pregnant," I say. We'll know soon enough; it's already been a few minutes since I dipped each stick in a cup of urine. One test would have been sufficient, but I want to be sure.

"You know you are."

"I don't *know*, I suspect."

"You're late and you're never late. Plus, your big-ass boobs are all tender and shit. I can't even hug you without you wincing."

We noticed that yesterday, and though I had already suspected I might be pregnant because my period should have started weeks ago, the tender breasts made it all more real. So of course, she showed up at my door this morning with pregnancy tests.

Just like last time.

Only, not at all like last time. Because this time Cillian and I are secure in our relationship, and I know how he'll react to the news. My husband wants more babies. He wants a brood of them. And he wants a chance to experience all the things he missed before.

Not only those formative first years of life, but pregnancy, too. Though he has his concerns about that. I wasn't exactly in a healthy space when I was pregnant with Sadie, or just afterwards. Cillian worries that I'll have postpartum depression again. It's a legitimate concern, one I've had myself.

But we don't let fear rule over our decisions. Not anymore.

Besides, I'm stronger now and our circumstances are different. Not to mention I have an excellent therapist.

"What are you going to name it?"

"It's a little too early for that," I laugh at my sister.

"Maybe," she muses. "But some women have names picked out before they've ever even met a man."

"Well, that's probably something Cillian will want a say in this time."

"He'd let you choose, but I get what you mean. He's going to be very hands on."

"When is he not?"

"Hands on is not the same thing as handsy. But, yeah, he's that, too. That's how we've ended up holed up in the bathroom with pee strips, after all."

She's not wrong. Willa constantly teases us that we fuck like bunnies. Who could blame me? My husband is very fucking good looking. Not to mention, extremely capable in bed. Sex with Cillian is anything but a hardship.

I was on birth control when we got back together, and even after we were married and had decided we wanted more children, I stayed up on it. I'd just started a career with the Seattle Blades and wanted some time to excel there before I brought an infant into the picture. As much as I love being a mother, I have other ambitions, as well. I don't want to compromise. I want it all.

Someday, I want to help run the organization. The NHL isn't ready for a female General Manager, but maybe I could be the first. I'm at least going to shoot for it and see how far I can get. Cillian knows I want it, he encourages me to strive for it. My dad does, too. Knowing that they believe I'm not only capable but would be great at it, makes me want it even more.

Cill makes me feel like I can do anything. Or, that we can as long as we're together.

And that's why I stopped taking birth control about seven months ago. Because I know I can have a family and a career. I don't have to give one up for the other. Not as long as he's by my side. Which is something else I don't worry about anymore. Cillian isn't going anywhere.

"Can I film when you tell him," Willa whispers excitedly, her face inches from the plastic strips. "Because you are having another baby."

"Shut up?"

"You shut up," she teases. "These are all positive."

"Oh my god."

"So? Yes, I can film?"

"Yes," I say, my voice breaking a bit. Willa's head whips around to me, her eyes narrowing in concern.

"Fear or excitement?"

"Excitement," I promise, and her features relax. "I'm ready for this."

"Hell yeah, you are."

An hour later, Cillian is due home from morning skate. Willa is perched on the overstuffed chair in the corner of our small living room, Sadie on her lap ready to push start on her aunt's phone when her dad walks through the door. She doesn't know why we want to record this, but she thinks it's a fun game all the same.

I'm nervously bouncing from foot to foot, pacing a small circle on the rug. Both Willa and Sadie find endless entertainment in the fact that I can't contain my energy.

"Settle down, Mommy," Sadie says for the eighth time, making Willa laugh. It's a *Shoresy* reference, a hockey show my young daughter shouldn't be allowed to watch. But she basically lives it, so what difference does it make, really?

Oh, hell. We're horrible parents. Should we even be allowed to bring another child into the world?

I bring the back of my hand up to my forehead, fretting at the thought, when Cillian walks in. Dropping his duffle bag just inside, he moves to me instantly.

"What's wrong?" He searches my face before glancing to Willa and Sadie. "You okay, Sadie?"

"I'm awesome," she says, throwing her hands up in the air and dramatically draping herself over the arm of the chair.

"Isla?" His hands cup my cheeks, stilling me. "What's up?"

"Are we bad parents?"

"What," he asks, confusion showing on his brow. "Fuck no, we're the best."

"We let Sadie watch *Shoresy*."

"We're just setting the tone, Mommy," Sadie says, and I can't help but smile as Cillian and Willa laugh.

"Sadie is fine," he says. "Where is this coming from?"

He's right. Sadie is fine. She's sweet, kind, so smart, and funny, too. More than all that, she's loved, and she knows it. She can do and be whatever she wants, and she knows that, too. Our daughter will grow up with all the support a kid deserves. It won't be any different for this next one. Or any others that follow.

I reach up and take one of Cillian's hands in mine, tangling our fingers together as I lower it to rest on my tummy. This time he'll get to watch it grow with me. He'll be here when the fluttering starts and see when a tiny foot starts pressing on the walls of my body.

All the things I dreamed of him doing when I was pregnant before, or when Sadie was so tiny…he'll do this time around. And she'll be right beside him. She's going to be the best big sister. I can see it already, how she'll want to teach them everything she knows and protect them from any harm. Just like her daddy.

"Super-sperm," I whisper, and watch as it dawns on him.

"Isla." Tears spring to his eyes and his voice wavers with emotion. "Is this real?"

I nod and he drops to his knees, his forehead coming to rest where our hands just were. I weave my fingers into his hair, it probably needs a trim, but I like it when it grows out. A few of his tears fall, landing like raindrops on my bare toes.

My big, strong husband, silently having a moment of rare vulnerability. This man was born to be a father. I used to think his purpose in life was hockey, but I know better now. This is the role he excels at most. Father and husband. Family.

Cillian never wavers. He's the pillar holding us all up, just like my dad was for my mother and Willa, and me.

"What's happening," Sadie quietly asks.

"Your mom is going to grow another baby inside her," Willa tells her. "Just like she grew you."

"Like the tomatoes in the pot outside?"

"Something like that," Willa says, stifling a laugh.

"You ready to be a big sister, Sadie Baby," Cillian asks, his words muffled because his face is still buried in my shirt. He stretches one arm out, beckoning her closer.

"Oh, my goodness, yes!" She climbs off Willa and rushes to stand next to her father. Her face turned up to me, a smile on it matching my own. "Is it inside you right now?"

"Yeah, baby. It's very tiny but it's going to grow so fast," I answer, and Cillian makes a soft sound.

"Can it hear us?"

"I don't know," Cillian says. "But I think we should talk to it every day, just in case it can."

Sadie bends her knees, putting her face next to Cill's. Cheek to cheek.

"Hi, baby," she whispers. "I'm your big sister and this is your daddy. He's the best hockey player ever, but I'll teach you all about that when you're bigger like me."

I look up to the ceiling, my hands resting on the heads of the two most important people in my life and take a breath. Just live in the moment, take it all in, imprint it to memory. Willa is still recording, her own cheeks lined with silent tears, but I want to remember this on my own, too. Regardless of how many times I'll be able to revisit the video.

We didn't have the easiest of beginnings, this little family of mine. But the love we share overshadows all the past pain, and here we are, growing again. I didn't think my heart could feel any fuller, but at this moment, it's taking up my whole chest as Sadie continues to whisper about all the people she can't wait to introduce to the baby.

Cillian finally stands back up, looking me in the eyes as he rubs his nose against mine.

"I fucking love you, Isla Wylder."

"I fucking love you, too, Superstar." He seals his mouth to mine before I even have his silly nickname out. It's a deep kiss, but not heated as much as it is appreciative, maybe. Like he's thanking me for something we both play a part in. That's just him, though. He always gives me more credit than I deserve.

"I'm going to be really obnoxious. You know that, right?"

"I'm aware." I smile.

"You're not allowed to do anything. No vacuuming, no cleaning at all. Especially Saint's litter box, that's a thing, right? Maybe a driver, too. Are seatbelts safe for pregnant bellies? Fuck, I don't know how any of this works. I'll hire a nutritionist, or a chef. Both?"

"Cillian," I warn.

"Maybe I should move the bed downstairs, so you don't have to go up and down all the time. Hell, we should probably start looking for a new house. A big-ass rambler, because I'm going to keep you pregnant all the time now. Then we wouldn't have to worry about stairs at all."

"You're ridiculous."

"We're definitely going to need a bigger bed. So all the kids can snuggle in with us for morning cartoons."

"That's my favorite," Sadie says. "You're going to love Scooby Doo, baby. It's kinda scary sometimes but I'll hold your hand."

"You're okay," he asks, another brush of his nose against mine.

"I'm perfect," I promise.

"Thank you."

"For what?"

"For giving me a second chance," he says, his voice cracking again.

"Thank you for giving me one, too, Cillian."

MORE FROM ALISON RHYMES

Subscribe to Alison's Newsletter for Early News and Bonus Scenes

RAINFALL

I met the love of my life at ten years old.

At sixteen, I gave him my heart.

Three years later he was drafted to the NHL and moved across the country.

Five years after, he's back. And he's meeting his daughter for the first time.

I still hate him.

Even if my heart says that's a lie.

At ten years old, she changed my life.

At sixteen, I told her I loved her.

Three years after, I left and broke her heart.

Five years later, I'm coming back home to the surprise of my life.

I hate her for it.

Even though my brain says this is all my fault.

FLURRY

Willa

I've been in love with him for years, despite knowing he could never be mine.

Now his charming new boyfriend is determined to include me in all their plans.

Zander

I've been infatuated with him for years, despite us being in different states.

Now we're living in the same city with the only woman who's come close to holding my heart.

Damian

I've been intrigued by her for years, despite us never knowing each other.

Now I just need to convince the two people I care most about that three is better than two.

Flurry is an MMF Hockey Romance

BROKEN PLAY

They have ties that bind.

June grew up in the shadow of her brother and his best friend, Drew McKenna. She stood back while Drew dated his way through high school and college, watching and waiting. Waiting for him to realize he loved her as much as she loved him.

When he did, it was the happiest she'd ever been. Until she found him with another woman only five years after their marriage.

Leaving her husband was a simple decision, but there was no easy way to cut him out of her family.

When June receives a fresh start to her career, she also finds what could be a new lease on love. Reality hits Drew with a vengeance.

He wants her back.

She wants to make him suffer.

BRUTAL PLAY

Mistress.

Whore.

Lorelai has been called every name in the book. Except for the ones she's always dreamed of.

My love.

Mine.

Noah Anders is the only man to have ever owned her heart. But it's her soul he wants.

Theirs is a battle of wills, tempers, ego, friendship, and loyalty.

He wants retribution.

She just wants to survive.

BITTER PLAY

Reed Turner has loved his sister's best friend, Leighton, for damn near a decade. He's given her space to grow in her career and her life. Now he's ready to claim the woman he's always believed was his. It's too bad another man in her life keeps getting in the way.

Leighton Ward has never been in love. Now, just as so many things are changing in her life, she finds two men vying for her heart. Both hold strong ties to her future and making the wrong decision comes with heavy consequences.

He knows what he wants.
She's as confused as ever.

DECONSTRUCTING DELILAH

A modern-day retelling of Samson and Delilah…

As the son of a preacher, Pope Blackwell believed he learned the difference between good and evil early in life. After all, it was beaten into him regularly. Now as an adult, he's traded in his life of abuse for one where he holds all the power.

When a young woman strolls into his life full of more bravery than she should possess, he becomes consumed by her fire.

Delilah believed escaping her family's abusive ways would be the hardest challenge of her life. Then she met Pope Blackwell.

One sinner and one saint. A world of differences between them.

Faith. Experience. Age.

His obsession only grows as she challenges him until he's ready to topple any pillar that stands in her way, and she'll fight every demon to be by his side.